THE LAST GUARDIAN

GUARDIANS OF HAVEN SERIES

JOAN HAZEL

Credits:

Senior Editor: *Danielle Raver*

Cover: *Nicole Antonia Carro*

Author Website: www.jhazelauthor.com

DEDICATION

For my wonderful husband, Ricky, who believed in me even when I was unable to believe in myself. And to Lori, Jill and Rebecca. Thanks for being my editor, sounding board and cheering section. I can only imagine how tired you guys got of hearing about "the boys"

PROLOGUE

With the sun at her back, the Goddess of Fire cast a long lean shadow on the marble floor. She found humor in how the straight silhouette belied her truly curvaceous form. Respectfully, she removed her bow and quiver, and laid them next to the doorway.

It was a well known fact among the Gods, that The Sisters of All Life and Knowledge did not bestow favor upon those who entered their home carrying weapons. Even if you were a Goddess, you dared not defy their wishes.

Early that morning the Sisters had summoned her. Only they had the audacity and power to demand one come to them, but they truly held her fate within the palm of their hands. To be called by the trio of women could be either a blessing or a curse. In many cases, it was both.

With apprehension, Freyja approached the center of the great hall where sat a large vat filled with crystal clear water. None of the women paid any heed to the Goddess as she approached. Instead, they stared transfixed into the great well where they watched and manipulated the universe and all that dwelt within, both mortal and immortal.

With eyes lowered, Freyja bowed before the triumvirate. "You sent for me?" she asked, trying to hide her irritation.

"We did," the three answered as one. No matter how many times she heard the Sisters speak, Freyja would never become accustomed to the odd melding of sounds that made up their voice.

The Goddess waited. There was no use in asking why they had sent for her. They would answer in their own time since they cared little for her impatience.

"Rise my child." Only the sound of one voice filled the air, and Freyja was grateful for that small kindness.

"We have been watching you," said the sister to her left. She was the youngest of the three and known merely as Lightness. It was she who created and breathed life into each creature that moved in both the earthly and amaranthine realms.

Her words ignited a small spark of fear in the pit of the Goddess' stomach, which irritated her all the more. She was the Goddess of Fire. Her breath alone could command the winds. Yet here she stood, immobilized by the petite woman before her.

Dressed all in red, the middle sister raised her head, appearing to notice Freyja for the first time. Violet upon violet, the colors swirled with the woman's eyes. She was Mother and the decider of all things.

"Do not fear," said Lightness as she gracefully took a seat upon the well. Her calm demeanor did little to quell the odd emotions that rose within Freyja's breast.

"We have decided," began Mother, "that you are to be rewarded for service well done."

"Service well done," the others repeated in unison.

Stooped slightly, the final sister was dressed in black from head to foot. The gilded hilt of a dagger could be seen, hanging in a sheath about her plump waist. She was the sister the Goddess knew best, for she had done this sister's bidding since the dawn of time. This sister was Darkness, the taker of life.

The cold black stare of Darkness pierced into the Goddess. She did not believe it to be possible, but a chill ran through her body. "Give me your hand, child," Darkness said.

Without hesitation, Freyja put forth her hand. Darkness drew her dagger. She pricked the palm of the Goddess' hand

and placed it above The Well of Creation coaxing from the wound three drops of blood that fell into the water below.

The Goddess watched as the wound on her hand sealed itself leaving no trace of a scar. Confused, Freyja gazed about at the faces of the three sisters. "I thought I was to be rewarded," she said.

"And you shall," answered Mother, who dipped her finger into the well and churned the water, mixing the two liquids into a powerful potion.

Lightness then blew across the well the sweetest of breaths, causing clouds to form upon the Earth and rain down the potion from the heavens. The power of the mixture was so great, it transformed those touched by it to be as the Goddess. Born that day, were the three nations of humans who could shift their form.

The first nation, like the Goddess who bore them, took the form of the great cats. The second went to the protectors of mankind, the canines. Finally, the third drop went to the great beasts of the wilderness known as bears, which were chosen for their power and strength.

As she stared deep into the Well of Creation, Freyja saw her children and wept in fear for their safety, for who would protect them now they walked between two worlds?

So, moved by Freya's tears, Darkness consulted with her sisters. Once in agreement, they took two tears from the Goddess' cheek and mixed them also within the waters. Again, Lightness blew upon the water sending forth from the Well two droplets   if   of   rain.

The droplets fell from the heavens, landing upon the head of a young girl. "Anointed by your tears, this child and her kind shall make safe your children," said the Sisters in one voice. "So it shall be."

Still fearing for her children's well-being, Freyja called forth the rocks and the seas, creating for her children a place of safety, but still she needed more. Her mind made up, Freyja sent forth her most trusted of servants to walk upon the Earth as her emissary. Charged with the task of being the eyes and ears of the Goddess, forever he shall stand as their protector.

CHAPTER ONE

The lyrics from Led Zeppelin's Immigrant Song played on a continual loop inside Ægir Thorolfur's head. It was an odd lullaby, but it comforted him as he thought of his homeland and his ancestors. Consciousness ebbed and flowed, causing him to lose count of how many times he had started the lyrics over.

Using their common telepathic link, Saint Wolfe spoke gently to his friend. *Ghost.* Saint called Ægir by his nickname. *Could you please refrain from singing that song?*

Sorry Saint, Ghost gasped. *It helps me not think about the pain.* The faint sound of Ghost's voice echoed in the minds of his pack–mates.

It was at times like this having the telepathic abilities of a shape-shifter, or shifter as they preferred to be called, was a curse. Normally a shifter had control over when and who heard their thoughts, but the intense pain that racked Ghost's body stifled his ability to block thoughts. So, without his wanting, the ramblings inside his head ran free for all his pack-mates to hear.

Mika Elkhart fidgeted in his seat. He leaned over the shoulder of his commander. "How much longer until we are at Haven?" he yelled over the whirring of the helicopter blades.

"We are at least forty-five minutes out," Fergus Wolfe, their commander and pack leader shouted back. Had the group been anywhere other than in mid—air, either of the remaining three members of Delta Pack could have created a wormhole and been at Ghost's side.

Mika leaned back, concentrating on his wounded comrade. Little more than a year separated him and Ghost in age, yet he had always felt older. The anguish in Ghost's voice tore at him and he cursed the fact it was Ghost, not he, that had been left behind to watch over Charles Stone, the last surviving member of a race known as the Guardians.

The four men known collectively as Delta Pack were more than mere guns for hire. Their primary objective as set forth by the Theriontrope Foundation, was to keep the Guardians safe from harm.

For as long as Mika could remember, there were always death threats against the Guardians and Theriontrope Foundation. The threats would always appear when rumors and speculation of "were-wolves and their handlers" surfaced.

Denial of a shifter's existence was easy in the early years since there were no such things as newspapers, television or the internet. But along with advances in technology came advances in media and greater exposure. With greater exposure came more threats.

I am sorry my brothers. Ghost sent the thought out to his adoptive brothers. *I have failed.*

Mika dropped his head in sorrow. He and the others could tell from Ghost's incoherent ramblings, he had lost too much blood, rendering him incapable of returning to human form. That single act would start the healing process. But Ghost was badly wounded and it was evident to all that whoever attacked him had done their research.

The movies had gotten a few things right over the years when depicting the abilities and weaknesses of shape-shifters. Silver couldn't be used to kill a shifter, which was a good thing for Mika since he was rather fond of his silver and turquoise jewelry. However, if the mineral were to be taken into a shifter's body either by ingestion or insertion, the result would be a very nasty chemical burn.

Garlic had no effect. In fact, all four members of Delta Pack were very fond of garlic and any food that was prepared with it. Wolfsbane, on the other hand, was lethal. For some the mere scent of the flower was enough to burn their lungs.

Ghost had spoken of the burning sensation inside his chest which could mean only one thing—the arrow that pierced his side must have been made from a compound containing silver. He also told them, he couldn't be positive, but he thought he smelled the subtle aroma of Wolfsbane. The shaft of the arrow must have been laced with the deadly poison.

By either incredible accuracy or dumb luck, the archer found his mark. One shot to the chest was all that was needed. The arrow pierced deep into the walls of Ghost's heart.

The single puncture would not kill Ghost, but the silver would stop him from returning to his human form, allowing the Wolfsbane to creep into his blood stream. From there the poison would journey throughout his body, tainting his internal organs and eventually stopping his heart. Not only would death visit Ghost this night, but it would be painful.

You will not die. The commanding voice of Fergus Wolfe jolted everyone's thoughts.

Ghost snorted. *This is one thing I am sure even you don't have the power to control, big brother.*

Try to slow your heart rate, Saint jumped in. *It will slow the poison in your system. Dr. Grey is on his way.*

Stay with us Ghost. Fergus added, then severed his link to the younger shifter. "Mika stay with him," Fergus directed. "Try to keep him alert."

Following his leader's orders, Mika relaxed back and closed his eyes, concentrating on Ghost. There was little he or the others could do except keep Ghost talking until Dr. Grey and the medics arrived.

As he connected to Ghost's mind, Mika found jumbled thoughts of Iceland and snow, and it was then he began to fear the loss of the man he had learned to call his brother. Mika felt helpless. Surely Wakatanka, the Great Spirit, would not allow his brother to die. They had been through too many battles and fights for something like this to claim his friend's life.

Mika had not always considered Ghost to be a brother. It was a title Ghost had to earn. Mika was less than a year older than Ghost, and in the beginning, it was only natural he should feel the painful sting of childish jealousy.

Ghost was brought from Iceland to Haven when he was ten

years old. Until then, he had spent his entire young life in the company of his pack. Because of this he spoke only Icelandic. Yet due to his fair-hair and blue-eyes, he easily slipped into his new life.

But Mika was born of the Lakota tribe and, to the eighteenth-century world, he was labeled a savage and treated as such. In the mind of a young boy, it wasn't fair that he should be condemned for the color of his skin when one such as Ghost, who was more of an outsider than he, could be so easily accepted.

How foolish those thoughts seemed. Nowadays he could go anywhere and do anything. No one cared that he was Indian, or Native American as people liked to refer to his ethnicity.

And as a child, Mika also thought it wasn't fair that Ghost seemed to take up most of Fergus' time. Where it had been only Mika who Fergus took bow-hunting or tracking, Ghost began to tag along. Often Mika would complain to Fergus that the "pale one", as he called Ghost, was too small and clumsy, and would only get in the way.

Sensing Mika's frustration at having added a new member to the pack, Fergus took him aside and explained that unlike him, Ghost had not been trained to take care of himself. He told Mika that the land Ghost came from was cold and harsh, so the people in his life shouldn't be. But mostly Fergus told him Ghost needed a big brother to watch over him the way both Fergus and Saint had done to Mika.

It still took time, but Mika learned to be both a big brother and friend to Ghost and now...Now there was little he could do to save his dying friend. Ghost's wounds were fatal, and if Dr. Grey did not get there soon, he would surely die.

With complete calm Mika called out to him. *Ghost?*

What? Ghost answered wearily.

You never told us what happened with that waitress you were seeing?

Wai...tress? Even Ghost's thoughts came in ragged gasps.

You know the one from Mad Mooney's, Mika prodded.

I heard she was quite the cougar, Saint added.

Literally or figuratively, Mika brought back. Maybe if he could get Ghost to talk about his favorite subjects, women and himself, he would remain conscious long enough for the medics to arrive. But it was of no use.

Ghost faded in and out of consciousness as the voices of his brothers filtered into his clouded mind. He was vaguely aware of Mika and Saint's teasing as they discussed his most recent conquest. He knew what his friends were doing and he loved them for it.

Love…That was a word seldom, if ever, found in Ghost's vocabulary, but he did love this new family—if you consider 120 years as new. Each "brother" possessed qualities Ghost admired.

Silent and stoic, Fergus was an unstoppable force. He was a crusader. No questions, no complaints, just do it. Why else would he have taken on the task to mentor an abandoned and confused shifter such as Ghost through "those awkward teenage years"?

Then there was Saint. Too intelligent for his own good, Saint was prone to burst out some fact that had been seared forever into his eidetic memory. Ghost was sure had Saint known Einstein or Tesla he would have given either of them a run for their money. Then again, Saint was 250 years old and it was quite possible that he had known both men.

Lastly, he thought of Mika—the calm within the eye of the hurricane. Connected to the Great Spirit and Earth, Mika was both telepathic and, like Saint, a bit psychic. "Listen and Wakatanka will give you the answers," Mika would tell him. "But you must open both your mind-spirit and your heart-spirit. That is the only way."

This was Ghost's family, two wolves and a coyote; all three great men. He needed to tell them how he felt. He needed to let them know before died.

Guys…I need…to tell…he coughed.

Later Ghost.

You must conserve your energy.

Hold on brother. The voices of his three adopted brothers melded into one. No longer could he tell one from the other.

You must… He tried again, ignoring their attempts to stop him. *All…these years…* No matter how hard Ghost tried, even telepathically his voice came out ragged as his focus became difficult.

Eyes closed, he drifted again to thoughts of his mother and the beauty of his homeland carved from ice and stone. If he listened closely, Ghost could almost hear her voice calling his name, a gentle whisper riding the winds across the fjords.

"Ægir Thorolfur," a feminine voice cut through the fog in his head.

Ægir, that name too had been long from his thoughts. *Mamma?* he forced out. Only she would have called him by his real name. Not Ghost, the nickname given to him by his pack.

"Ægir Thorolfur?" Came the voice again this time closer and louder. It could have been in the same room, or miles away. There was no way for him to tell.

So tired…Mamma…

"I know," she replied.

Feminine, Ghost thought, just a bit raspy and sexy. Okay, sexy was not a term one normally used for their mother.

Sexy? In confusion, Mika glanced to Saint. *Ghost, who are you talking about?*

Hmm… Ghost roused.

"Horfðu á mig sæti," She spoke in his native tongue. "Look at me, Beauty." She sang to him, allowing all to hear.

Ghost opened his eyes and lifted his head. Slowly the luminescent form of a woman came into view. Gold light surrounded her, her face hidden in shadows.

Finally…the Valkyries…have come for me, Ghost forced out. Valhalla…I'm coming…

Do not start that song again, Saint pleaded.

Goddess I'm ready…

Goddess? Saint asked.

*Freyja…*Ghost sighed.

Did you say Freyja? Saint questioned.

Já…

He's hallucinating. Saint said.

A laugh, warm, gentle and feminine, filled the air. "Not Freyja," she said. "But I thank you for the compliment." The apparition's voice whispered, again allowing the others to hear her.

"Do you trust me Ægir?" She asked.

Yes. Defying his suspicious nature, the wolf offered up his broken body to her keeping.

The woman knelt beside him, paying little heed to the puddle of blood that surrounded her. She spoke in words unfamiliar to any of the Pack, yet all understood their power to sooth and heal.

Ghost felt energy, warm and tingling, permeate every cell of his body replacing the cold residing there. Calmness filled him and his muscles relaxed. As the healing force began its journey through his blood stream, Ghost became aware of how hard he had worked to remain conscious and block the Wolfsbane from annihilating his system.

He felt, more than heard, her explain that the arrow was ready to be removed. Asking his forgiveness in advance for the pain she was about to inflict, the woman's hand closed about the shaft of the arrow and with one quick jerk, pulled it free of his body.

Intense heat seared the spot where her hands covered the wound and shot like a laser into his heart. Words, ancient and beautiful, resonated within the core of his being mending the tears they found there. Her song wrapped both his body and soul, cradling them in a loving embrace.

Ghost lay silent underneath her gentle hands. If this was what his transition to Valhalla was to be, then he was ready.

"Þetta er búið," she whispered into his ear.

It is done, he repeated in English.

"You will live to fight another day, my beauty," she said, rubbing her forehead against his. A slight breeze moved across his face, ruffling the fur that lay there. Then it was gone.

Slowly, Ghost opened his eyes. Once again, he lay alone in the grand entrance of Haven. All traces of his mysterious healer—gone.

CHAPTER TWO

CJ Carson woke from a fitful dream. She tried to ignore the knot of snakes that writhed and roiled in her stomach, but found the task impossible. There was no denying the telltale ringing in her right ear or the burning acid that filled the back of her throat. Not to mention the piercing nauseating pain that streaked across the top of her head giving her complete understanding of the term "head splitting."

Stupid migraine, she thought as she rolled onto her side and tried to will the pain away. Maybe if I just lay here it will go away.

Pulling the pillow over her head, she lay perfectly still, trying to think of nothing, yet her mind continually found its way back to her dream and the image of the massive white wolf.

Though his broken body was racked by pain, the great wolf remained the image of beauty and grace. It still made her sad to think of him lying there in a puddle of his own blood with an arrow protruding from his side.

There was something regal about him. His crystal blue eyes, were unlike any she had seen before, and they sparkled with a knowledge and understanding more human than animal. He called her Freyja and she had to laugh. She had been called many things in her life, but never had she been compared to a Nordic Goddess. In truth, she kind of liked it.

Even as a child, CJ always had strange dreams, some cloudy, some vivid. There were a myriad of places, people and animals. Often, she knew or sensed an animal's thoughts and feelings. It was a gift she credited to her imaginary friend, Minky.

14

Minky was a large brown dog that appeared one day while she played in the backyard of her home. He would lie for hours under the shrubs and watch her. Funny thing was, she still carried on complete conversations with him. It was natural for her to hear his voice in her mind and she probably always would.

Instinctively, she placed a hand over her mouth as the first involuntary spasm rushed through her body. CJ forgot her dreams as she was snapped back to reality. "Oh no," she groaned. Her only thought was to make it from her bed to the bathroom without incident.

Barely clearing the bathroom door, CJ hunched over the toilet as the first convulsions began. Wave after wave they came, until there was nothing left except the horrific pain of heaving. Her energy depleted, CJ reached for a damp washcloth and slid to the floor, coming to rest against the bathtub.

Placing her forehead against the cold porcelain of the bathtub, CJ squinted her eyes and tried to concentrate on the clock that hung on the wall across from her. "Two a.m.," she moaned and repositioned her body. She wanted no thoughts in her mind as she fought to will the pain and nausea away. Not again. CJ lurched forward and prayed for someone, anyone to take it all away.

When the last spasm subsided, CJ resumed her former position. The porcelain was a balm against her burning skin. Again, she closed her eyes, placing a towel under her head for a pillow and a cool damp washcloth over her eyes. The minutes passed slowly as the hypnotic tick, tick, tick of the wall clock accidentally set the pattern for breathing.

CJ hated migraines. No, hate was not a strong enough word. She loathed migraines and blamed her mother for their presence in her life. It was her mother who forced CJ into hypnosis at the age of fifteen. After that, the migraines began. They seemed to always come after she had "one of those crazy dreams" as her mom would call them. Of course, in CJ's world simply dealing with her mother could be a headache.

Once, she had asked her doctor if it was possible for dreams to trigger migraines and nausea. The doctor assured her it was impossible for a dream to trigger such an intense physical response. But CJ knew from experience that dreams could have a profound effect on a person. Have a bad dream, have a bad day. Have a good dream, have a good day. Have a sexual dream about someone who was a friend or acquaintance, and the next time you see that person, you can't help but see them a bit differently.

Pinching the bridge of her nose, CJ pushed the thoughts of her mother as far away as possible. Gypsy Lynn Carson was the last thing CJ wanted to think of as she lay there on the bathroom floor. Again, she focused on her breathing and tamping down any last bits of nausea. The thought did cross her mind to get up and take something for the pain, but at the moment moving seemed impossible.

From off in the distance, CJ heard singing. Soft and low, the dark baritone voice drifted across her tormented mind, washing waves of serenity throughout her body. She smiled in the recognition of Minky's voice.

CJ knew it was crazy to still believe in him at her age, but he had been there since she was a child. He knew more about her than anyone else ever could. Of course, she knew he was made-up, but that didn't matter. All that mattered was he was there whenever she needed him, which was more than she could say for anyone else, including her mother.

Minky's plaintive lullaby comforted CJ, soothing her. The rhythm of his words rocked her, calming the intense pain in her head as her thoughts became cloudy. Within minutes, she drifted off to sleep.

The next thing CJ saw was the morning light as it crept through the cracks in the window blind, brightening the once dark room. What time is it? She wondered. CJ pulled the dried washcloth from her face and opened her eyes. Pain shot through her neck as she twisted toward the clock.

"Great. Seven a.m." she sighed aloud. Her body protested as she forced herself to rise. Sleeping against the bathtub was not on her list of top things to do, but then again, neither was throwing up all night.

CJ stared at her reflection in the mirror as she splashed chilly water on her face. It was not the lack of sleep or the fact she felt like hell that caused the furrow in her brow. The crease was caused by one thing–her worry over the wolf in her dream. His humanness haunted her.

"This is stupid Charlie Jean," she shook her toothbrush at the reflection. "You have got to get that dream out of your head," she scolded before she resumed brushing her teeth.

"You treat real animals at your clinic every day, not dream wolves." She continued to ramble as she scrubbed harder than normal. But no matter how hard she tried to push it away, the image of the beautiful white wolf returned. *I just wonder if he lived.*

Yes, came the answer to her unspoken question. The wolf lives.

How can you be so sure? She asked her imaginary friend using the same path her thoughts had always taken when conversing with him.

There are many things that I know Wicahpi.

CJ loved the sound of his voice. Its deep baritone was soothing and calming, and no matter how crazy the thoughts inside her head were, his voice remained tranquil and serene. Nothing ever seemed to shake his resolve.

"You know, if my mother knew I still spoke with you she would think I was crazy," CJ said aloud as she glanced about her bathroom. She heard his laughter inside her head, darkly accented and extremely sexy, just the way she wanted her husband to sound.

CJ found that thought odd. She didn't remember thinking his voice was sexy before, but then again, it was her imagination so it could be as sexy as she wanted it to be.

You find my voice sexy? Minky teased.

CJ's face flamed red at his question. *You heard that?*

Minky's dark laughter filled her mind. Of course, he had heard her. He always heard most everything she thought.

You are not crazy, he said, mercifully changing the subject. *You never were and you never will be.*

Thank you for singing to me last night. She told him in her own attempt to change the subject. She didn't feel like discussing her sanity and she definitely didn't want to discuss whether or not she found any part of him sexy.

It helped you then? He asked, his voice filled with relief.

Yes. Thank you. No matter how hard she tried, CJ couldn't help feeling a bit sorry for herself. One day, maybe, she would find a man. Not simply a voice inside her head, but a real man to be with her when the headaches hit. It would be nice to have someone to stroke her hair or cradle her in his arms. If he happened to sound like the voice inside her head, that would be fine too.

I made you a promise once, Little Star, her imagination said. *Do you not remember?*

CJ stopped what she was doing. She did remember, but she could never find the nerve to test that promise. The proposition was too scary. She could tell, or at least she thought she could tell, that he was waiting on her to see if today would be the day she allowed him to fulfill his commitment.

Yes. She finally answered. *I remember your promise.*

18

Whenever you are ready, Little Star. I am here, the voice reassured her.

CJ said nothing else, allowing her silence to be her answer. She could feel the moment he had receded from her mind, closing the door on their conversation. Unsure of her feelings, she reached for him with her thoughts, searching into the deepest corners of her mind, but he was gone. Their link broken. Once again she had hurt him.

Sadness crept into her heart, as a tear slid down her face. She couldn't explain the utter pain of loss she felt as his leaving.

Damn. It was bad enough she talked to herself on almost a daily basis, but she had hurt her imagination's feelings and had no idea why it should upset her so. "Get a grip Carson," she demanded swiping at the falling tears. "Gypsy Lynn was right, I really do need therapy."

CHAPTER THREE

Deep within the foothills of the Montana countryside, a fire raged. Its flames spiked upward sending the ashes of Charles Stone toward the waiting arms of the Gods.

At first light, Fergus and the others took Charles' body to the edge of the lake where a wooden raft affixed with a funeral pyre awaited its passenger. No one asked where the pyre had come from. It just appeared as they always did when a Guardian of Haven died.

Fergus laid his longtime friend upon the pyre and set it ablaze before he pushed it into the center of the lake. There Charles' charred remains would forever rest at the bottom of the lake along with those of his ancestors.

On the banks of the lake, three men and a lone white wolf stood as silent sentries and watched as the flames rose higher and higher. What was there to say? Nothing would bring the man back, and for the first time since the beginning of its existence, Haven no longer had a guardian.

The large wolf lifted his muzzle skyward and began his long plaintive cry to the Goddess for his friend's safe passage to the other side.

"Well put, Ghost," Saint commented when the last decibel of Ghost's song faded into nothingness upon the wind.

It had been Ghost's choice to remain as a wolf. No matter what the physician had told the others, Ghost felt himself too weak to shift. It took energy to transform from wolf to man. Considerably more energy than he felt he could muster.

It was almost three in the morning before Fergus and the others had reached Haven. Ghost had already been taken to the medical floor of Haven where he was being cared for by Dr. Michael Grey, director and chief of the Theriontrope Foundation.

Dr. Grey had alerted the remaining members of Delta Pack that all tests confirmed the mysterious healer's pronouncement: Ghost would indeed live to fight another day. As far as Dr. Grey could tell, no trace of the Wolfsbane remained in Ghost's blood stream and the x-rays showed no puncture or abnormality to his heart or the surrounding tissues. Not even the hint of a scar remained.

Miracle or no, healthy or not, the energy to shift did not exist within him. And although the physician said there was no damage to his heart, Ghost was sure a hole remained there.

"He will be weak until his blood has had time to replenish," Dr. G., as Ghost called him, told Fergus. "Other than that, he is healthy." According to the doctor, Ghost's recovery was nothing short of a miracle.

He had known protecting Charles was of the utmost importance. He only stepped away for a moment. After much badgering on Ghost's part, Charles had agreed to watch *The 13th Warrior* with him for the umpteenth time. Ghost went upstairs to his bedroom to retrieve the movie; Charles oversaw making popcorn.

With movie in hand, Ghost started down the upstairs hallway when he heard the doorbell ring. He thought it odd since at such a late hour the front gate should have been shut and locked. Normally a visitor would ring the main house on the intercom system before being let onto the property. However, there had been a couple of occasions when a shifter in distress had breached protocol in their confusion. Maybe this was one of those times.

Charles moved to the video monitor that showed the front door. It was one of the many security precautions Mika had insisted on. "Ghost," Charles whispered his name. "The monitor isn't working."

"What about the intercom?" Ghost whispered back.

"Give me a moment. I'll check." The next sound Ghost heard was Charles as he spoke into the intercom. Even with Ghost's acute hearing, he was unable to make out what was said. The answer came back inaudible.

Although the answer was too garbled to understand, something in the stranger's tone sent Ghost's wolf senses into red alert. The hair on the back of his neck stood at attention, as a low rumble of warning escaped his throat.

He heard Charles as he opened the heavy wooden door. Lifting his head, the shifter inhaled deeply. The scent wafting from the foyer was that of not one, but two humans. Three if you counted Charles. Ghost took in their scent again. Yes, human.

One of the men asked for asylum. Something Ghost found extremely strange for a human to do, but as guardian, once asylum was asked for, Charles was bound by Haven's laws to oblige. At least, that was the rule for shifters. Haven had been Ghost's home for more than a century. He was unaware of any rules dealing with humans, especially since very few knew of its existence.

When Charles requested proof of identity from the two men, Ghost knew something was wrong. Pressing his back against the wall, he tried to remain well out of sight.

Hushed tones soon escalated into shouts, followed by the sounds of scuffling.

"Ghost!" Charles cried out.

Without a second thought, Ghost shifted into his animal form, a great Arctic wolf. With teeth bared and ears flat, he ran the length of the hallway and launched himself off the landing toward the intruder nearest Charles.

"Get the wolf!" Ghost heard the command.

He was inches from his target when slicing pain pierced him in the side. Losing balance and direction, the wolf plummeted toward the floor. His body ricocheted off the large mahogany table in the center of the entrance way, sending an oversized bouquet of flowers one direction and his body the other.

Impact with the table knocked the breath from Ghost's body, immobilizing him and he gasped for air while the world spun around him.

The intruders shoved Charles into the study across from where Ghost lay. Through the open door, he could make out the form of the three men. The taller of the two men held Charles' arms behind his back while the other continued the questioning.

Try as he might, Ghost was unable to make out what they were saying. But it became apparent that they were sure Charles either had what they wanted or knew where to find it.

Ghost saw Charles shake his head in denial. Snippets of the conversation wafted into the hall. Repeatedly the man asked about "the other" and Ghost was sure he heard the word "pendant." At least that was what he thought the man said.

In retrospect Ghost realized there were in fact only two things he knew for sure. One: That Charles Stone, the last true Guardian of Haven, was dead. Two: That Fergus Wolfe blamed him.

He had seen the way Fergus' autumn colored eyes glowed with accusations and contempt. It was he who entrusted Ghost to protect and defend Charles while the others had been called away.

Grief and guilt tore at the man residing beneath the white wolf's exterior. Ghost refused to make eye contact with anyone.

Instead, he stared straight into the bright orange and blue flames as they greedily consumed both flesh and wood.

When he could no longer tolerate the sight before him, Ghost padded back to the all terrain vehicle that had brought him and the others deep into the interior lands of Haven. Jumping onto the back of the vehicle, he lay down, placed his chin upon his paws and waited.

The muscles in Fergus' jaw clinched and relaxed as he fought the urge to rear his head back and continue the song where Ghost had left off. Instead he watched with narrowed eyes as Ghost walked away and boarded the ATV.

Ghost's silence ate at Fergus. Normally an open book, Ghost had closed off his thoughts to the rest of the pack. No matter how hard Fergus tried, not even he could penetrate the mental wall Ghost had erected.

Anything? Fergus sent the question to his brother.

Saint met Fergus' gaze. *Nothing,* he answered shaking his head. Fergus nodded in understanding and closed the link between them. He needed time to think.

Just as Fergus and Saint were the last of their species, so was Charles Stone the last of his kind. He was a Guardian—chosen protector of the shape-shifters. Genetically guardians were human though they possessed inordinately long life spans, but unlike shape-shifter's they were not considered immortal. A fact made all too evident with Charles' death.

Charles had been born to watch over Haven and shape-shifters, just as his father before him and his father before that.

Fergus and Saint had known four generations of the Elphinstone family. It was Charles' great grandparents, Seamus and Eleanor, which had taken both him and Saint in when their parents had died. The couple raised the orphaned brothers alongside their own children and treated them as equals.

All guardians, it seemed, possessed some paranormal abilities. They could be either telepathic, empathic or healers. Some were a combination of two of the three. Only Breathag, matriarch of the Elphinstone clan had been all three.

She was also the last female Guardian in six generations. Since her death, it seemed the Guardian's abilities manifested within the males, but not every male possessed those abilities or became a Guardian. Charles' brother Foster had been such.

Again, Fergus let out a deep sigh. This was the day he had long feared. For three generations, Fergus watched as Guardians came into this world. Today he watched the last one leave.

"Come Fergus," Saint spoke softly as he placed a hand upon his brother's shoulder. "There is much to discuss."

CHAPTER FOUR

"Tsk.Tsk. Tsk. Such a pity the Guardian had to die," oozed the pale man with a faint Nordic accent. His white blonde hair and crystal blue eyes were a stark contrast to his dark blue jacket.

"We didn't want to do it, honest," said the smaller of the two men who stood before him. "He wouldn't give up the goods."

"Of course, he would not 'give up the goods', replied the man known as Ivan Thoreau. He raised a delicate well-manicured hand and waved casually as if brushing the sentence from the air. Onyx cuff links caught his attention and he adjusted the fabric of the French cuffs of his pale blue dress shirt.

"However, I am more interested in the wolf. Was he dead when you left?" The man leaned forward. His crystal gaze hungered greedily with anticipation of the answer. The smaller of the two men shifted beneath his stare.

"It was just as you said, Mr. Thoreau," the other added. "I shot him...first chance and he went down. Hard." Sympathy filled the larger man's voice.

"What? Arty," Mr. Thoreau mocked the man who had shot the wolf. "Do not tell me you felt any pity for the beast?"

"Well, yeah. A little..." Arty said. "He was only doing his job, right? I mean...that is what he was there for."

"Believe me when I tell you Arty, that animal would rip your throat out if given a chance. Do not pity him." Mr. Thoreau rose and came to stand beside the others. "Think hard. You are positive the wolf was dead?"

"There is no way he could survive," Arty answered. "I did as you taught me. Straight into his chest."

"Very well," Thoreau said. He placed an arm around both men, steering them toward the large brass doors of his office. "And you are sure that the man called him Ghost?"

"Yea, I'm sure about that part," answered the smaller man called Wyatt. "He yelled Ghost, an' then this big white dog jumped off the stairs."

Ivan sighed. "Not a dog. A wolf."

"Okay, wolf." Wyatt shrugged.

"So the wolf was mortally wounded?" the Boss asked as he opened the door.

"There is no way that he could live," Arty said.

"You would be surprised by what he can pull off," Mr. Thoreau said under his breath. "Nevertheless, we must move forward with our plans."

"What's next?" asked Wyatt.

"All in suitable time, Wyatt. All in suitable time." Mr. Thoreau, not so gently, pushed Arty and Wyatt through the doorway.

"Whatever you say, boss," Wyatt said. "We'll be waitin'."

"Thank you, gentlemen, and please see Miranda for your compensation."

Mr. Thoreau shut the doors firmly behind the two men. He removed his slippers and padded, bare-footed, across the floor to stare out the expanse of windows that afforded him the view of the city skyline.

Could it be that Ghost was finally dead? Thoreau was almost giddy with excitement at the prospect. Of course, the shifter known as Ghost had to be dead. Ivan had designed and built the arrow Arty had used. He had also placed a little spell on the arrow for good measure. The feeblest among them could have shot that arrow and it would have hit its target.

There was no way for Arty to miss, and since Charles was the last healer Haven or Theriontrope had, there was no one to come to the wolf's aid. The combination of silver nitrate mixed with Wolfsbane would surely kill him.

Ivan also knew there was no way Theriontrope Control could have made it in time. One member of Delta Pack gone and three remained. A cruel smirk curved his perfect cupid's bow lips.

Once all the members of Delta Pack were gone, there would be no more Theriontrope Foundation. No longer would he be forced to hide in the shadows. His top priority had been to see to the death of the Ghost Thorolfur. It had been his driving force for many years. "Þetta er búið Bróðir minn." He whispered into the silence of his office. "It is done, my brother."

Ivan placed a slender hand upon his heart as a pang of guilt struck him, but only momentarily. Guilt was one luxury he refused to afford. Again, he swiped it away with the aerial brush tapered fingers.

Oh well. He shrugged. It was a burden to do what he did, but someone had to build a new empire as the old one was being tumbled.

Was the wolf truly dead? Could it have been that easy?

Closing his eyes, Ivan Thoreau concentrated on the shape-shifter known as Ghost. Sending his thoughts through the miles that divided them, searching for any trace of the man or wolf. Nothing.

He wanted to breathe a sigh of relief, yet some indescribable thing niggled in the back of his mind. The thought smoldered there, a fire unable to be dampened. He needed answers and there was one person who could put his mind at ease.

CHAPTER FIVE

Haven sat cold and silent in the early morning light. There was something reverent about the old house. A proper lady draped in shadow and shroud mourning the loss of a loved one. All four shifters could feel the house's sorrow as they entered the kitchen through the backdoor. Even the appliances seemed to hum in hushed tones.

Diana Carter, the housekeeper, wiped her plump hands on the apron tied tightly about her waist. She went to each man and hugged him in turn, as she whispered words meant to comfort. She even hugged Ghost, which they all knew was hard for her.

Diana was a staunch supporter of shape-shifters. She had worked for the Theriontrope Foundation and Haven since she was a young woman. But for some reason seeing "the boys" in their animal form always unnerved her. She never spoke of her discomfort but they all knew how she felt, and out of respect for her, they tried their best not to flaunt their differences around her.

"Doctor Grey called to say he should be here within the hour," Diana said as she rose from hugging Ghost. "There is breakfast in the warmer and coffee on the counter." She stroked the soft fur between Ghost's ears absentmindedly. "I have work to do," she whimpered. Stifling a sob, she practically ran from the room.

Ghost could feel the stares of the others as he hung his head. The distance between he and the others seemed to grow into a gaping chasm. He wanted to say something. Anything. But no matter how hard he tried, Ghost couldn't find the right words to fit. Defeated, he left the room. Saint started after him, but was stopped by a firm hand on his arm.

"Let him go," Mika said. "He must deal with this in his own way."

"I just thought—he has said little since our return." Saint's concern was evident in his tone. "He has even shut his thoughts from Fergus. That is quite unlike him."

"His soul as well as his body must heal." Mika said. "Both will take time. You know this to be true."

"Ghost cannot afford the luxury of time and neither can we." Fergus growled from across the room where he stood with his back to the others.

"His wounds are deep, my brother." Mika walked to Fergus' side. "Ghost has lost much this day."

"Have we not all lost this day?" Fergus snapped. "Is he the only one who feels sorrow?" The sound of Fergus' voice was punctuated by the crack of wood splintering beneath his fingertips.

"I did not mean…" Mika reached his hand toward Fergus' back, but stopped short when he noticed the rise of Fergus' shoulders. The taller man's back bowed as the room shook with the reverberations of a deep growl. Quickly Mika withdrew his hand. There was a time and a place to push Fergus, and Mika could tell this was not it.

As with all packs, there is an Alpha. For Delta Pack, that job fell to oldest among them, Fergus Wolfe. Never had there been a reason for the others to doubt or challenge Fergus' role as pack leader. He had practically raised the three other members and had been a fixture in their lives for as long as any of them could remember.

When Saint was an infant, Fergus fled with him into the night, seeking refuge with the Theriontrope Foundation. With both their parents gone, it had fallen to Fergus to protect and

31

raise his brother even though, in the world of a shape-shifter, he was little more than a child himself.

When Ghost's mother sought sanctuary for her son, Fergus had been the one to travel the frozen lands and bring him to a place of safety. And it was Fergus who, during the turmoil of the Indian Wars, had a Lakota infant thrust into his arms. Taking the infant back to Haven he, along with Saint, raised the child as their own brother.

Seldom did Fergus force his dominance. Each man willingly gave him their loyalty for what he had given to them. But in those rare moments when he did, the others obeyed. Fergus may have been their brother and friend, but first and foremost Fergus was the Alpha of Delta Pack.

Saint stepped forward to speak. "Fergus, I do not think Mika..."

Fergus released his grip on the cabinet. "Do not presume to tell me what others do or do not think."

Saint removed his coat, hanging it by the kitchen door. "I make no presumptions. I was merely trying to suggest that Ghost was not the only one of us who is in mourning." He took the tea kettle from the counter. "We all lost a good friend. Do not forget we have all known Charles since he was a child. Ghost is..."

"Ghost is pouting like a selfish little brat." Fergus spun quickly to face the others. "He had one job. One." Fergus held up his index finger to make the point. "Protect Charles from harm and he failed."

"And almost lost his life in the process," retorted Saint his calm tone masking his frustration. "We could have watched the cremation of two friends today instead of one. Or did you forget that detail?" Saint cocked his head to one side as he questioned his brother.

Fergus tilted his face toward the ceiling and took a deep full breath that expanded both his chest and the black t-shirt that covered it to their limits. He counted to ten in an attempt to calm his temper. Under most circumstances, Fergus maintained complete composure and objectivity. But the death of Charles weighed heavily upon him. It was a senseless murder carried out by humans. That fact alone was enough to make Fergus ill-at-ease.

Very few humans, save for those within the Theriontrope network knew of Haven. No, there was something more at work here and Fergus had a nagging suspicion as to what it was. Earlier he felt the psychic net cast in search of Ghost. Quickly, he latched onto the probe, trying to trace it back to its origins. But before the link was complete, it was gone. Yet in his heart Fergus knew the answer and soon the day would come when he could protect his protégé no longer.

With a heavy sigh, Fergus leveled his gaze on Saint. His brother's forest fern eyes stared back at him. If it had not been for the difference in eye color, Fergus would have thought he gazed into a mirror. Even though the two were separated by at least 20 years in age, the family resemblance was remarkable. Especially, given the fact that shifters almost stop aging physically when they reach their thirties.

"Of course, I did not forget," Fergus groused as he raked his hands through his shoulder length auburn hair. He often found it odd that the same ginger colored hair he disliked so much on himself fit perfectly on Saint.

Most all of their mother's clan had had red hair—a mantel of their heritage.

"Come and sit," Saint motioned toward the island surrounded by stools that was the focal point of the large kitchen.

"All these years and Diana still forgets we do not drink coffee," Mika stated as he retrieved a bottle of water from the refrigerator.

"No, but Charles did," Saint explained as he went to the sink and prepared a kettle of water for morning tea. "I am sure she prepared it without thinking."

"Charles also liked Twinkies," Mika added with slight disgust.

"I still do not understand your dislike of Twinkies." Saint said. "I find them quite delightful."

"Too many chemicals. Do you know what is in those things?" Mika grunted as he threw his leg over the stool and joined Fergus at the bar.

Though still in a foul mood, Fergus couldn't help in seizing upon the opportunity to goad Saint into one of his impromptu lessons, and Twinkies seemed like the perfect topic. Besides, picking on Saint might help to get his mind off Charles' death.

"Chemicals?" Fergus questioned sarcastically. "There are chemicals in Twinkies?" Sarcasm was not an oddity for Fergus, but it was rare. Very few got to see his sense of humor and even less understood it.

"Actually," Saint began as he busied himself making tea. "There are thirty-nine ingredients in Twinkies. Including calcium sulfate, which comes from a gypsum mine in Oklahoma. Then there is Yellow dye number—" Saint paused in his Twinkie lesson when he noticed the bemused expression his brother's face. "What?"

"Nothing," Fergus shook his head as he took the mug of tea offered him and cut his eyes toward Mika who sat stone faced.

"I was merely explaining the make-up of Twinkies," Saint defended. "You seemed confused about them."

Fergus paid close attention to the cream patterns in his tea. "Is there any random fact that does not get stuck in that oversized brain of yours?"

"Of course. There is much I do not know."

"Like what?"

"What kind of a question is that?" Saint snorted as he poured cream into his cup.

"A very good one." Fergus watched the confusion that played across his brother's eyes and waited for an answer.

If I knew that I did not know something, then in fact I would have to have some knowledge of that subject to know that I had no knowledge of the subject." Saint titled his head again as he shifted his gaze from one man to the other. "In essence, that is a circular question," he added matter-of-factly.

Fergus pursed his lips and nodded before he took a sip of hot liquid. "Saint, you make the best tea ever. I never get it right."

"That's because you let the water get too hot. The optimal temperature for this particular blend is between eighty-five to ninety-five degrees Fahrenheit.

"Both Fergus and Mika couldn't help but laugh at Saint. It was not uncommon for Saint to rattle off obscure fact after obscure fact. Fergus was sure it had to be a disease.

"Can I join in the joke?" The slight man asked as he walked into the room.

"Doctor Grey." Saint greeted him. "Could you please examine these two? I think they have taken leave of their senses."

"There is nothing wrong with us." Fergus said trying to quell his laughter. "It's you," he said and pointed to Saint.

Dr. Grey walked across the room and helped himself to the coffee.

"Me? I am in perfect health, thank you," Saint argued.

"Umm humm," Fergus grunted as he took another sip of tea.

"Seriously, what's so funny?" Dr. Grey asked. "After the past 24 hours, I could use a chuckle."

"Saint was only sharing his knowledge on tea making with us," Mika said.

"That and the chemical make-up of Twinkies." Fergus added.

"We all recognize Saint's exceptional capacity for knowledge as well as a photographic memory," Dr. Grey aided Saints defense.

"Thank you," Saint added indignantly.

"It can't be helped that he is a know-it-all." Dr. Grey added with a smirk.

"Can I help it if I have a capacity for knowledge and all the time in the world in which to learn?" Saint retorted.

"No Saint," Fergus became contrite. "You cannot help it that you are semi-immortal and have a big head."

With great indignation Saint crossed his arms over his chest reminiscent of his older brother. He leaned his body against the sink and waited for the laughter to die down.

"Really now, is it that funny?" Saint asked staring straight at Fergus.

"Yes." Fergus replied.

"Well," Dr. Grey cut in. "I will give you one piece of information our resident genius here does not know." He said as he added more cream to his coffee.

"Listen up Saint," Fergus teased. "Something you don't know, so now you will, which means you will no longer not know it."

Mika squelched to urge to laugh by coughing.

"Are you quite finished?" Saint asked when he felt it was safe.

"I suppose." Fergus said as he shrugged his shoulder.

"Sometimes I do believe you have been inside Ghost's head too long," Saint snorted as he began to leave.

"You may want to stay for this," Dr. Grey's comment took on a serious tone. "It is rather important."

"Obviously not more important than humor at my expense."

"Actually, it is." Dr. Grey said somberly.

"What could be more important than laughing at Saint?" Fergus asked.

Dr. Grey walked forward and placed his hands on the counter in front of Fergus and Mika, his deep gray stare danced from each man to the other before speaking. "How about the fact Charles Stone had a daughter?"

Charles had a daughter.

The words hung above the group's heads like a spectral being. Dr. Grey watched Fergus who stared down at the pattern of the Idad, the Celtic symbol of the Yew tree that adorned the brown leather bracers he wore on both wrists. Dr. Grey couldn't think of a time when Fergus had not worn some form of an archer's protection on his wrist. On anyone else the bracers would seem out of place, but on Fergus they fit perfectly.

The three men before him became eerily still. Yet their stillness gave Dr. Grey little pause. He knew the strength and power that lay beneath the human exterior of their kind. He had been witness to what shape-shifters who allowed their more animalistic tendency to dictate their course of life were capable of doing. Those were the ones that were more animal than human, and the ones humans needed to avoid.

For them it was the thrill of the chase. They enjoyed the kill and took pleasure in watching their prey suffer. Animal or human did not matter to them. All would be counted as a lower form in the food chain.

Luckily for Michael Grey, the four he dealt with daily were not that kind. However, he was no fool. He knew within the time it took to draw a breath, any one of the three men surrounding him could silently kill him, but that would never happen. More than once had he entrusted his life to Fergus and the others and, if need be, he would do it again.

Dr. Grey waited for the weight of his words to settle and for the shifters to finish their private conversation. He had been around the group long enough to note the subtle signs of telepathy. Minute movement of muscles about the eyes played on the faces of both Saint and Fergus.

Dr. Grey studied Mika. He too seemed to be speaking with someone, yet something in Mika's demeanor gave Dr. Grey the impression that he did not speak with Fergus or Saint.

During the first few years of his involvement with shape-shifters, Michael Grey found the telepathic conversations between them to be rather rude, but he soon realized there was little rationale for his annoyance. After all he had been raised in a time where nuance was a language all its own, the slightest glance or gesture could be a complete and secret conversation.

Upon deeper examination, he concluded he was jealous of his inability to use telepathy when all about him could. Many times, he tried and even went so far as to ask for help. After two years with no success, Dr. Grey accepted the fact that telepathy wouldn't be listed as one of his many talents and, at the moment, he was glad for this one particular short coming.

As Dr. Grey suspected, Saint was the first to speak. "I believe we may have heard you wrong. Did you say that Charles had a daughter?"

"I did."

"That none of us knew about?" Fergus asked.

"Her name is Charlie Jean Carson," Dr. Grey offered in way of an answer.

"Carson?" Saint asked.

"Her mother's maiden name."

"But that's impossible," Saint continued. "Charles would have never kept something that important from us. Besides, he would never allow a child of his to grow-up outside of Haven."

"Actually, he did." Dr. Grey said as he leaned a slim hip against the counter.

"I don't believe it," Fergus rose and brushed passed his brother. In frustration, he dumped the content of his cup down the drain.

"How long have you known?" Saint asked.

"The Foundation has known since she was a child." Dr. Grey was met with more silence. Saint and Fergus glanced at the other. "And how long has that been?" Saint continued.

"Charlie Jean is in her mid-thirties." Dr. Grey replied.

"So, for more than thirty years?" Fergus asked.

"Yes. We have," Dr. Grey answered.

"Please explain how you, the Foundation and Charles could keep this a secret?" Fergus asked leveling his tone.

"We could go into detail about this…"

"Let's have a synopsis, shall we?" Fergus crossed his arms and leaned against the sink as well.

"Very well," Dr. Grey placed his cup on the counter and straightened. "Some 30 odd years ago, Charles came to me. He said that during one of his vacations he had met a woman and fallen in love. He wanted to marry her, but the hills of Montana held little enticement for her. Charles said the woman was pregnant and he was sure the child belonged to him. After the baby was born, we watched over her and protected her as best we could. We had our suspicions that she would grow to be a guardian, but since there has not been a female guardian in five generations, we couldn't be certain." He held up his left hand to stem the question he knew was forth coming. "All the same, this child began to exhibit both telepathic and empathic ability around the age of five or so. When she was ten, she began healing wounded animals in her neighborhood."

Saint cut in. "The Foundation has tested her DNA and is certain she is Charles' daughter?"

"There is no question, she is Charles' daughter. There is also no question she is a Guardian."

Again Dr. Grey took time to let his statement sink into the collective. They all knew no female child born with the Guardian gene had made it past puberty in five generations. The Foundation was unable to determine why that should be and, without a female Guardian to supply genetic material for testing, the Foundation was at a loss. But now, there was Charlie Jean and there was hope.

"Charles wasn't the last of the Guardians?" Saint asked.

"No. He was not. However, he swore us...the Foundation and me to secrecy." Dr. Grey glanced toward Mika, who continued to stare at a spot on the counter. Slowly he continued. "It was Charles' belief that the fewer people to know of her existence, the safer she would be."

"Do you understand what this means brother?" Saint asked as he leaned into Fergus.

"I do," Fergus answered. "It means that for thirty years, we were lied to."

The statement did not surprise Dr. Grey. He had expected Fergus would view the Foundation's involvement and subsequent silence as an act of betrayal. He also knew that unfortunately, trust would become an issue between them, but it was a chance he and the Foundation had to take to protect the child.

"You had only been home for a few months, when all this began. It was a troubled time for us, Fergus. Charles did not want to burden you with his problems, not when you were still so weak. We did as Charles requested. No more, no less." Dr. Grey said.

Fergus shot an unforgiving glance to the slender man on his right. A lesser man would melt under the flaming gaze of Fergus Wolfe. However, Michael Grey was not a lesser man.

What was done was done. Nothing or no one could change that. Fergus would understand and come around in his own time. The problem was, with one such as Fergus, that could take years.

"So why tell us after all this time?" Fergus asked.

"Because," Michael Grey explained. "there has always been a Guardian residing at Haven and there must always be one. This woman must be brought here. Not only for the good of Haven and Theriontrope, but for her safety as well."

"And I suppose the Foundation would like for us to go and fetch her," Fergus stated more than questioned.

"Yes. They would," Dr. Grey answered.

The relationship the Foundation had with Fergus and the others had never been clearly laid out. From the outside, it would seem Delta Pack fell under the authority of the Theriontrope Foundation. But ultimately, Fergus had autonomy to pick and choose which assignments they would take.

Seldom if ever had Fergus refused. Yet, Michael Grey realized this might be one of those rare moments when he did. Especially when Fergus came to the realization that for years the Theriontrope Foundation had been in the process of slowly cultivating Charles' daughter to one day take his place.

Her training began in total secrecy when she was a child. Yet another thing Fergus would view as an act of deceit. There were a few other choice items Dr. Grey had left out of his explanation, but the others would learn of them in time. It had been the Foundation's hope that Charlie Jean could be eased into service willingly, but with the death of Charles, Dr. Grey realized its time-line had to be pushed forward.

At the moment, all that mattered was Haven needed a Guardian as much as, if not more than, the Shifters did. There had always been a Guardian and there must always be one. Dr. Grey refused to let his mind wander to what the consequences of not having a Guardian might be. Goddess forbid.

Instead he brought his focus back to the situation at hand. "Have you reached a decision?" he asked.

"Yes," answered Fergus. "She is Charles' daughter and as such her place is here, at Haven. It is where she belongs."

"Good," Dr. Grey agreed. "Now, on the matter of who will go…"

"There is no matter," Fergus stated. "I will go. Surely it will take no more than one of us to bring the woman here." With that, Fergus raised himself and began to walk to the door.

"Actually Fergus," Dr. Grey began. "It has been decided that Mika and Ghost should go."

Fergus stopped mid-stride. "Mika and Ghost? Did something happen of which I do not know? Am I no longer Pack leader?"

"Of course you are still Pack leader. However, the Foundation feels that in this situation a more gentle hand may be warranted."

"Gentle hand?" Fergus cocked his head to one side in a pose similar to his younger brother.

"Maybe gentle was the wrong choice of words," Dr. Grey answered. Try as he might, Michael Grey couldn't read the emotion in Fergus' eyes. Contempt? Frustration? Loathing?

"Then what would be the correct choice?" Fergus asked. His ancient Celtic accent thickening his words.

"Fergus, this operation will require a certain amount of…finesse. Yes, that's the word–finesse."

"Finesse you say?" Fergus crossed his arms over his chest. For a man six foot–five inches, Fergus had a way of appearing ten feet tall. It was an ability Michael Grey normally admired, but at the moment he found it disconcerting.

"Is finesse not required in every action I do for the Foundation?" Fergus stepped toward Dr. Grey. Raw power emanated off Fergus' skin, causing the others to fidget. "Do not let this exterior fool you, Michael Grey. I am, we are," Fergus said motioning to the others, "first and foremost animals built for stealth, finesse and cunning. Are those not the qualities for which the Foundation pays us handsomely?"

Dr. Grey knew there was no clever way around this conversation. He had immediately regretted his choice of words once they had left his lips. Fergus was right. It was his finesse and stealth that made him excel in his profession as Theriontrope's private assassin.

But the Foundation had invested a great deal of time and effort in protecting CJ and guiding her toward this moment.

The last thing they needed was for Fergus to rush in and intimidate the hell out of her.

"Fergus, you must understand," Dr. Grey pleaded. "This situation requires a more delicate approach. After all, Charlie Jean is a woman, not a threat to be neutralized." In desperation, Dr. Grey turned to Saint for help.

"Fergus, I think what Michael is trying to say is..."

"What Saint? What is the good doctor trying to say?" Fergus' words were directed at his brother, but his stare never left Dr. Grey's face.

"I believe what he is saying is this job takes a particular...That what is needed is well...Someone..."Saint stumbled for the correct phrase.

"What? Is the ever-eloquent Saint Wolfe at a loss for words?"

"Fergus there is no easy way to say this," Saint said.

"Then prithee brother, just say it as I no longer have feelings in need of sparing."

"Very well then, what we are trying to tell you..." Saint began again, only to be cut short.

"What both are trying to say, rather poorly I may add, is that you, dear friend may best all of us here in many things, but you are no ladies' man."

All eyes darted to the doorway. Clothed only in blue jeans, Ghost leaned casually against the door-frame. "Face it brother," he continued as he walked toward Fergus, "You can beat me at most everything, but when it comes to women, I'm your wolf." Ghost flashed his million dollar you-gotta-love-me smile.

Fergus regarded Ghost with cool contempt. "I see you are through licking your wounds."

"The mention of a beautiful woman can always bring a man back from the brink of despair," Ghost said.

"Beautiful? For all you know she has two heads and four arms," Fergus said.

Ghost arched his perfect pale brow in thought. "Well, that could be interesting and possibly worth exploring. In the right venue, of course."

"Is that all you ever think about?" Fergus questioned.

"Can I help it if women find me irresistible?"

"Spare me," Fergus groaned as he narrowed his gaze at Ghost.

For a moment, Dr. Grey began to wonder if someone should separate the two of them, but the younger of the two stepped aside to allow his leader passage.

"Fergus," Dr. Grey called as Fergus neared the doorway. "We have not been given your decision."

The leader of Delta Pack stopped inside the door. White edges showed along the back of his knuckles as he gripped the door-frame. "As you wish it, Michael Grey," Fergus said over his shoulder and left the room.

"Very good," Dr. Grey said. "A plane will be ready within the hour. As usual you will find your instructions waiting for you once you board." Reaching for his cell phone, Dr. Grey excused himself from the room.

Ghost rummaged through the warmer. "Do I smell bacon?" he asked, oblivious to the stares of Mika and Saint.

CHAPTER SIX

"Well, you look like crap," the sound of her friend's voice sliced through Charlie Jean Carson's brain. CJ, as she was known by her friends, shielded her eyes and squinted up at her good friend Bethany Rose, who, like CJ, had a mother who thought her daughter needed a double name.

"It's what we do in the south," CJ's mother had told her years ago when CJ asked why she had two names and, since her mother also had a double name, Gypsy Lynn, CJ thought little more about it.

Charlie Jean squinted and ducked her head against the sun's assault on her sensitive eyes. "I'm happy to see you too, sunshine."

"Please tell me it's for a really, really good reason," Bethany Rose lamented as she joined CJ for their standing Saturday breakfast date.

"Such as?"

"Such as one who is about six-two, blonde hair, blue eyes and abs you could lick whipped cream from," Bethany Rose stared into space longingly.

"Who the heck are you talking about?"

"No one in particular," Bethany Rose sighed. "But he sounds pretty good, huh?"

No matter how bad CJ felt she had to smile at her friend. "Do you ever think of anything besides men?" she asked shaking her head.

"Umm, nope. Don't think so," she answered with a devilish grin.

"Well in answer to your question yes, I have a reason and no, by your definition it was not a really good one." CJ tried to seem light-hearted about the situation, but being awakened in the middle of the night with a migraine had a way of putting a girl in a bad mood.

"Hmm…" Bethany began, "a muffin and coffee, dark sunglasses and you wince every time a semi-loud noise is made. And knowing you, this isn't the result of a hangover."

"A hangover would be preferable," CJ said as she attempted to eat, chewing slowly, in hopes her teeth would not hurt as much.

"So no hangover and no man?"

CJ shook her head confirming the "no man" theory.

"Migraine?"

CJ nodded.

"Don't you think you may need to get those things seen about?" Bethany Rose sat down the coffee cup she had been cradling.

"I have. CT scans. PET scans. I even tried Bio-feedback. Nothing stops them completely. I have medicine to take when I know they are coming on, but not when they happen in my sleep."

"What do you think brought it on?"

"I don't know," CJ replied defeated. "I guess I always thought they would stop once I became an adult."

CJ felt put out. Migraines had been a part of her life for more years than she cared to admit. During her time at the University of Florida it seemed she spent more time hidden away in a darkened room with a cold compress on her head, than in the classroom.

"Your last year in undergrad," Bethany Rose said as if reading her mind.

"You have no idea. It was horrible. If the nurse saw me coming, she would have a shot of phenergan waiting for me." CJ snorted as she thought back to the days of being carted off to see the nurse.

"I remember those late afternoon trips to the campus health center," Bethany Rose added sympathetically.

"What?" CJ asked, coming out of her recollection.

"I said I remember. You were miserable."

"How do you remember?" she questioned. "You weren't there."

Bethany Rose stirred her coffee, taking care in placing her spoon on the napkin. "I guess it seems like I have known you forever. I sometimes forget we've only been friends for a few years." She paused. "Plus, I know you have told me about them before."

CJ squinted in concentration as she assessed her friend's statement. The aftermath of migraines never allowed her to think clearly. With a shrug, she let Bethany Rose's comment go. "You're right. I'm sure I've told you before and I know what you mean. It does seem like we have known each other forever."

"Anything stressing you out?"

CJ thought for a moment. Throughout her life, CJ's intellectual side always tried to attribute the headaches to stress. But in truth, stress never seemed a factor.

After all, the migraines began when she was a teenager. CJ thought of her mother and the stupid hypnosis Gypsy Lynn had put her through. Was it coincidence her migraines began after the hypnotic suggestion to forget her dreams was planted inside her head? CJ thought not. In her world, there was no such thing as coincidence.

Stress did not seem a factor. Her clinic was doing well and, in fact, she had been contacted by another veterinarian about joining with his clinic.

Everyone in her life was healthy and happy. True, there were no blonde haired, blue-eyed guys with rock-hard abs hanging about her office, but that would come in due time. At least, she hoped it would. There was the occasional hiccup, but nothing major or life threatening.

"Not really," CJ shrugged. "Everyone and everything seems to be fine."

"What about food?" Bethany Rose prodded. "Too much chocolate or caffeine?"

"Don't go there," CJ warned. "I gave up cheese and wine, but to ask me to give up chocolate and coffee? That's inhumane!" CJ took a gulp of coffee to prove her point.

"Okay. Okay. It was only a question," Bethany Rose gestured with her hands.

The ringing of CJ's cell phone sent invisible shards of glass tearing through her skull as her mother's designated ring-tone sang out.

"Great," CJ groaned. "First a migraine, now Gypsy Lynn." She drew out her words, mocking her mother's accent and flipping open her phone.

"Mom, what a surprise," CJ chirped with much more enthusiasm than she felt. Gypsy Lynn Carson had an impeccable, if not uncanny, sense of timing. Think of all the times you would least like to talk to your mother, and those would be the times when Gypsy Lynn would call.

"Um hmm—" CJ grunted. "Yes ma'am—I did—I'm fine—last ni—yes." No matter how hard she tried, CJ was incapable of uttering more than three syllables. Not that that was unusual. Once her mother got to speaking, she never seemed to breathe.

Bethany Rose rolled her eyes, folded her arms and sat back. A typical call from CJ's mother could take four seconds, four minutes, or four hours and there was never a clue to which scenario it would be.

"Mom," CJ tried to interject. "Mom. Mother!" CJ grabbed her forehead, regretting the energy placed in her voice. "I did not mean—breakfast—Bethany Rose—no—gotta go—I will—um hum— love you too. Bye." CJ closed her eyes in unison with the phone. Her mother loved her and meant well, but sometimes...ugh!

Breathe. The familiar masculine voice inside her head softly commanded. Without question, CJ obeyed. *Again, Little Star. Deeper,* he coerced. And again, CJ obeyed. *Once more,* the voice added and CJ took in a deep breath one last time.

With an audible whoosh, she released the air and opened her eyes, trying to focus on Bethany Rose.

"Better?" Both Bethany Rose and the internal voice asked simultaneously.

"Yes," she answered to both, but mostly to the one in her head.

CJ could sense the concern with the tone of Minky's deep masculine voice. He was her comfort and her rock. In him, she could always find solace.

For many years, she questioned the voice. Was it truly her friend or had she made him up? It wasn't until she was confronted by a psychic, that her anxiety was eased. "He is your protector," a psychic in New Orleans' Jackson Square had told her once. "Listen to him. He will never lead you astray." After that, CJ never questioned the voice again. Her sanity maybe, but not the voice.

"You know, you should let your mom talk more. You are such a conversation hog," Bethany Rose broke CJ's concentration.

"Hmm?" She had half heard the comment. "Oh yeah," CJ huffed. "Yeah, you know me. Never letting anyone else speak."

"Have you ever finished a complete sentence around that woman?"

CJ stopped with the coffee cup mid-way to her mouth. "Good question. I am pretty sure the answer is no." CJ shook her head. "Come to think of it, I'm pretty sure I may have been twelve the last time we had a complete two-way conversation." CJ took a sip of coffee while her mind wandered back to her childhood and age twelve.

That was the year CJ sarcastically referred to as her Clint Eastwood year. It was good, bad and ugly. Puberty hit with a vengeance making her more than a little self-conscious.

Her first kiss came that year at a friend's birthday party. Later she discovered the kiss had been the result of a dare. On the upside, a friend of her mother's introduced her to gourmet coffee. Thus, began CJ's lifelong affair with Juan Valdez. Still, the icing to CJ's Clint Eastwood year was meeting Dr. Gilda Thornton, her first psychiatrist.

Gypsy Lynn had decided it was an excellent idea to take her daughter to see a "specialist" when CJ refused to give up her imaginary friend. How could CJ give up Minky? The thought of giving up the large brown dog with gold eyes broke her heart.

CJ remembered how she would regale her mother with tales of her and Minky. She told Gypsy Lynn about the swirling sparkly doors through which he would take her into mysterious worlds that lay on the other side. In the beginning, Gypsy Lynn would laugh at her daughter's ramblings, insisting that, even though CJ's adventures with Minky seemed real, they were merely "little childish dreams". But for dreams, they seemed so real.

CJ's "little dreams" seemed to start not long after she met Minky. She told her mother about the lanky dog appearing from nowhere, and he sat under a tree and watched her play. She had no idea how long he had watched her. All she knew was one minute he was there, the next he was gone. It seemed he could appear and disappear on a whim.

At first, his visits were sporadic seeming as if he came and went with the changing of the wind. But over the span of a few months, Minky visited more frequently. Still, he simply watched as CJ played.

Though she was a child, CJ remembered finding the courage to approach the animal. Boldly she walked up to the dog. He seemed so huge, yet she had no fear of him. CJ spoke to him and he answered back. However, she heard his voice not with her ears, but inside her head.

Gypsy Lynn did not find it odd her child had an imaginary friend, after all her daughter was gifted with a vivid imagination. Gypsy Lynn was sure over time, her daughter would out-grow her need for an imaginary friend.

However, when CJ was twelve and still talking to Minky, Gypsy Lynn decided enough was enough. She demanded CJ stop her foolishness and grow up. CJ refused.

In her world, Minky was real and there was nothing her mother could do or say to make her admit otherwise. Enter the specialist, or in this case, the psychiatrist.

From the age of twelve to fifteen, CJ saw one psychiatrist or psychotherapist after another. They all agreed the appearance of Minky and CJ's reluctance to give up her fantasy of him stemmed from the lack of a father in CJ's life. The dog was a substitution for a male role model.

Obviously, CJ's subconscious chose a dog since, according to Gypsy Lynn, CJ's father had worked with animals until his untimely death. Even as a kid that sounded like a load of crap to CJ, but her mother listened to the specialist.

To keep CJ from being put on too many medications, Gypsy Lynn had her daughter hypnotized to suppress the dreams. Her rational was "if hypnosis worked to lose weight and to stop smoking, then it could stop those damn dreams." And for the most part, it did.

However, controlling one's thoughts when asleep wasn't easy, and from time to time a dream would sneak through. When they did, CJ would wake with a killer migraine complete with vomiting and myopic blurs.

Hypnosis may have been a way to control the dreams, but it had no effect on Minky. Day after day, he continued to come around. Until, as much as it pained CJ, she confronted her companion. She told him there was no way he could be real and she commanded him to go away.

Obediently, Minky did as she asked, but there was one condition to his retreat. If ever she needed him, if she was in trouble or needed a friend, all she had to do was call his name and he would return to her. It was up to her to make the first move.

After that day, CJ never saw Minky again and she never told anyone else about her imaginary friend. Nor did she admit that his was the voice she heard inside her head. If she was ever in trouble or upset, his gentle voice always guided her to safety and calm.

"Hello?" CJ felt a hand on her arm. "Hello? CJ? You in there?"

"Hmmm? Oh, sorry," CJ replied. "I...um..."

"I know. Off in your happy place," Bethany Rose chuckled.

"Just thinking."

"About?"

"Nothing important," CJ answered.

Bethany Rose noticed the way CJ refused to meet her gaze. "You had one of those dreams again, didn't you?"

CJ sighed. That's what being friends with someone for ten years would get you, your own personal mind reader. CJ had to admit it was her own fault since it was common for her to share one of her dreams with Bethany Rose. For some reason, no matter how strange or fantastical CJ's dreams may have seemed, Bethany Rose understood.

"Maybe," CJ answered sheepishly.

"What was it this time? Mountain lion? Black bear?"

"No. Wolf." CJ tried to hide behind her cup, but caught the questioning glance Bethany Rose gave her.

In CJ's world, there were dreams and then there were DREAMS. Dreams were your regular, run-of-the-mill dreams. The kind you have and by the time your shower is finished, they are forgotten.

Then there were DREAMS—the strange, out-of-the-ordinary, rock-you-to-your-foundation dreams. They stay with you like a speck of dust in your eye, until you are able to wash it out. A DREAM was what CJ had the night before. A DREAM had caused her migraine.

And the wolf was the irritating piece of dust trapped in her mind's eye that would not leave until she washed it out by telling someone. The "someone" in this case was Bethany Rose. Fortunately, her friend was available.

"Was it a particular type of wolf or a regular old timbre wolf?"

Something strange in Bethany Rose's tone made CJ cut a sidelong glance at her friend. "It was an arctic wolf actually. Why do you ask?"

"Oh, no reason," Bethany Rose smiled nervously, fidgeting with her napkin. "Go on," she insisted. "It's going to eat at you until you let it out."

CJ did not trust her friend's nonchalance. There was an edgy biting quality to her tone and actions. With reluctance, CJ launched into the description of her dream, recounting each image as it played over in her mind.

In detail, she described how the large wolf was covered in his own blood and how she healed him with thoughts and words that were not her own. She also told Bethany Rose how the animal's beauty almost moved her to tears.

Nothing within his silver blue eyes spoke of fear or mistrust. He was so brave. There was no whimpering. No trying to bite her. He showed complete resolve and understanding that she was there to help, even though he thought her someone she was not.

Yes, CJ explained, she knew it to be a dream even though the whole incident seemed so real. She had felt the coarseness of his fur underneath her fingertips and caught the smell of the forest when she leaned close to him. The wolf's humanity had moved her most and she needed to know the wolf would live.

"I know I sound nuts," CJ said. Her eyes brimmed with tears.

Bethany Rose placed a reassuring hand on CJ's, giving it a gentle squeeze. "Not nuts sweetie. All of us can be affected by our dreams."

"Bethany, I've had these kinds of crazy animal dreams all my life, but this…this was different."

"Different how?"

CJ pulled her hand from Bethany Rose's and sat back in her chair. "I don't know. Contradictory, maybe?"

"I don't understand."

"It was more real than the others, yet less believable. The room seemed dark but bright. There were multiple voices, but only the wolf and I were in the room. And he seemed more human than animal, yet he was clearly a wolf." With chin in hand, CJ leaned on the table. "See, nuts."

"You say there were multiple voices?" Bethany Rose asked, her dark eyes darted suspiciously away from CJ.

"Seemed to be," CJ answered.

Bethany Rose pressed further. "Male? Female? Did they all sound the same or different?"

CJ cut her eyes at Bethany Rose. There was something different about her friend today. She seemed to ask too many questions and, whether it was her own sense of reason or that of Minky, CJ decided she had already said too much. "I don't know."

"You're a vet Charlie Jean," Bethany Rose emphasized. "Caring for animals is what you do. Of course, it would upset you if an animal were needlessly hurt—even in a dream."

"I suppose you're right," CJ sighed and shrugged off her earlier comment.

"Of course, I'm right," Bethany Rose smiled. "I'm always right."

"You wish."

"I know," she chuckled. "Besides, think of these crazy dreams as a blessing."

"Yeah, vomiting all night is a blessing," CJ snarked.

"Okay. I give you that. But it was those types of dreams that made you become a vet, right?"

CJ paused for a moment. It was dreams like the one the night before that caused her to pursue a career as a veterinarian. That and the fact she was following in her father's footsteps. "True."

"Well then, not such a bad thing."

"Don't use logic on me. My head hurts too badly."

"I know what will fix that," Bethany said as she rose and began to clear away her trash.

"Don't say it," CJ groaned.

"Yep. It's that time—retail therapy and a pedicure."

"Ugh."

"Come on. The day is young and so are we."

CJ watched Bethany Rose as she walked toward the trash can. Maybe her friend was right. A little shopping might take her mind off things.

She did want to get a new shower curtain and re-decorate her bathroom. Wow, the decisions one comes to when on hiatus on the bathroom floor.

Grabbing her belongings CJ stood to leave.

"Thank you for saving my son," came a voice from behind her.

CJ spun around, coming face to face with a tall, impeccably dressed woman. The woman seemed to tower above CJ and CJ had to stop herself from glancing down at the woman's shoes to check the height of the heels. "I'm sorry, did you say something?" CJ asked her.

"I said thank you for saving my son," the woman re-iterated, and with a majestic wave of slender fingers, disappeared into nothingness.

CHAPTER SEVEN

Mika's personal preference for transport over long distances was by spatial shift. Unfortunately, not all shape-shifters possessed that skill-set. Ghost happened to be a member of that group. His inability to travel by wormhole left the pair only one option. They had to fly.

Normally Mika was the epitome of calm. Little could or would work him into a state of agitation, but now he was anything but calm. No matter how hard he tried, Mika was unable to get comfortable. The moment Theriontrope's Learjet took to the air, he began to fidget in his seat.

So far, he had scrolled through the entire library of his mp3 player about four times. It was useless. Mika realized, with the exceptions of Warren Zevon and Steppenwolf, he hated every song downloaded to the player and he made a mental note to wipe the hard drive clean and download all new tunes once he made it back to Haven.

With a great sigh, he pulled the earphones from his head and let them drop into his lap. Reaching into the seat next to him, Mika picked up the manila envelope containing the hotel and rental car information they would need once they landed in Florida. It also contained a photo of CJ. Not that Mika needed one.

The task had fallen to him and Ghost to convince Charles' daughter to return with them to Haven and take her father's place as Guardian. The question was how?

As much as he would have liked to use the direct approach, somehow Mika figured it might not work. He could imagine the conversation.

"Hello, my name is Mika and this is my friend Ghost. We need you to come with us to Montana so you can take over from your dead father who was murdered only a day ago."

CJ would say, "I'm sorry, but do I know you?"

Then Mika would say, "Of course, you know me. I'm the imaginary friend who has watched over you for the past 30 years and by the way, did I mention I'm a 133-year-old shape-shifter?" Mika shook his head and threw the envelope back into the seat. That would go over well.

He had watched over CJ almost every day of her life since she was a child. He had seen her grow from a child to a woman. He had gone through the teenage crushes and bad relationships. It was enough to drive most men to the brink of insanity. But Charles and Grey had entrusted Mika with her safety and it was a job he had not taken lightly.

Through hooded eyes, Mika watched as Ghost reached for the envelope and pulled CJ's photo from the package, studying it.

"Not bad," Ghost muttered. "Wonder if the rest of her is as wild as her hair?"

Without warning Mika lunged toward Ghost, grabbing CJ's picture and the envelope. "CJ Carson is none of your concern." He plopped back into to his seat.

"What the heck, Mika?" Ghost asked, stunned by his friend's actions.

"I know what you were doing and it ends here. You will not lay one paw on her, do you understand?"

"Don't you think that should be her decision?"

Mika leaned forward, his black glaze piercing straight through Ghost. His tone was harsh, yet barely above a whisper. "Do not push me on this Ghost. Charles' daughter is off limits. Are we clear on this?"

Ghost stared at Mika in disbelief. Never had he seen his friend this protective of any woman. Had he not known better, nah, there was no way Mika could have a thing for her. They had never even met her.

"Ghost—" Mika growled.

"Okay. Okay. Paws off. Geesh," he answered putting up his hands in resignation. Without another word, Ghost leaned back to stare out the window giving Mika much needed quiet.

True. Ghost was like a brother to Mika and probably more so than had they been related by blood. But there were times when Ghost could find your one raw nerve and trounce all over it. In every sense of the word, Ghost was the annoying little brother.

Mika had known it was too much to ask to come alone on this mission. Had he been given his choice of traveling companions, it would have been Saint. At least then the only problem Mika would have to face was Saint's inability to curb his urge to share obscure knowledge at the least appropriate moment. He would never have to worry that Saint would try and seduce their assignment.

Mika took in a deep cleansing breath and tried to focus. He knew there was a reason it had to be Ghost. If his suspicions were correct, then Charlie Jean had been the mysterious healer the night Ghost had been wounded. If she could recognize Ghost's animal form, then Mika would be positive she was not only a Guardian, but a healer and a dream-walker with powerful telepathic abilities, a combination that had not been seen in his lifetime.

"We should be on the ground in 15 minutes," the pilot said over the intercom. "Please prepare for landing."

"So," Ghost said trying to break the ice. "What's the plan?"

Mika had a plan, but in all honesty, it wasn't really a good one. Briefly Mika laid out his idea, and as expected, Ghost was less than thrilled at the idea of being in wolf form, but it truly was the easiest way for Mika to confirm his assumptions.

Once on the ground, the guys grabbed their belongings and de-planed.

Ghost groaned as he stepped on to the tarmac of the small private airport. "No seriously, have I ever told you I hate the rain?" he complained.

"Pretty much every time it we have to be out in it," Mika returned dryly, as he scanned the area for the jeep that was to be waiting for them. "You must remember rain is the Great Spirit's way to clean and replenish the Earth. You should be thankful."

"It makes my hair do weird things." Ghost said shaking his head about and trying, to no avail, to make his hair lay flat. "Could we hurry this up?" Ghost asked when he noticed Mika was not moving.

"Hold," Mika whispered, holding up a hand for silence.

Ghost inclined his head to the side, listening for something other than the sound of falling rain and the engines of the small jet powering down.

"What?" Ghost asked as he scanned the area near the hanger.

We are being watched, Mika said using the common telepathic link between them.

Can you see them? Ghost asked.

I am afraid not. Mika walked toward the red jeep awaiting them near the aircraft hangar.

Did Dr. G. mention anything about someone meeting us? Ghost asked following close to Mika.

No. He did not.

How do you want to handle this?

I am unsure if there is anything to handle. Get to the jeep, but keep watch.

Will do, Ghost added as he sprinted toward the vehicle waiting near the hangar doors.

Purposefully, Mika strode across the tarmac. He did not want whoever was watching them to know he was aware of their presence. Mika jerked his head up, as the sound of footfalls thudded across the rain soaked pavement.

Using the acute senses of the coyote, he scanned the surrounding area trying to pinpoint the location of the sound. From the corner of Mika's eye, he caught a quick glimpse of a woman as she ducked into the shadows. Dropping his bag, he ran to the edge of the building where the woman had disappeared.

He could smell the ionic shift in the air as it bounced off the surrounding buildings and trees. The scent was a tell-tale sign of a wormhole being created. Pushing himself to go faster, Mika rounded the side of the building in time to see a petite brunette woman step into the swirling tunnel. With a coquettish wink and wave of her hand, she was gone.

Mika stared in disbelief as the space about her collapsed in on itself, leaving no trace of the wormhole or the woman. Had he not known better, Mika would have sworn he knew the woman, but in the dark and rain, he couldn't be certain.

"What the—that wasn't—was that?" Ghost sputtered from behind Mika.

"You saw her then?"

"Briefly but...yeah. No. Couldn't have been..."

"Impossible," Mika said brushing past him.

"But Mika," Ghost called after Mika, as he kept close behind. "It really looked liked—"

"No more, Ghost. I know what you want to say and I tell you it is impossible. Now get in and speak no more of this."

"Don't you think we need to tell Saint or at least, Fergus?" Ghost asked as he opened the door to the Jeep and climbed inside.

Mika sat silently staring out the window. He probably should and would tell Fergus about the other shape-shifter. For the life of him he couldn't figure out what she wanted or who would have sent her. Turning inward, he asked the Great Spirit for the answers he sought, but was met with silence. The Universe's silence meant only one thing—it was not for him to know.

Mika tapped his thumbs against the steering wheel. "In time, we will tell Fergus what happened. But, we will not tell him the other part."

"You mean she looked like—"

"Enough." Mika's tone was soft but firm. "Remember our oath. In honor of our brother, we do not mention her name. It must not be spoken."

Ghost's jaw tightened. He hated to try and keep things from Fergus. Even when he was a child, Ghost found it difficult to hide anything from their leader. It was as if his mentor resided inside his head at all times. He had no idea why the bond between the two of them was so strong, and took it for granted it was the same between Fergus and the others.

Still to hold such a thing from Fergus seemed nearly impossible, but he would do his best. Without thinking Ghost shook his head violently scattering water across the jeep. His thick blonde hair danced about his head before each hair settled perfectly into place.

The fine spray of water forced Mika to shield his face with his forearm. When he thought, it was safe, he glanced at his companion over the crook of his arm. Ghost was the only member of Delta Pack to keep his hair in any style other than long. As far as Mika knew, Ghost had a standing appointment with the same stylist every four weeks and had for more than five years.

Mika tried to enter the coordinates for their hotel into his GPS system. However, he found the task most difficult with Ghost in such proximity continually shaking his head and rearranging his hair. Stifling a groan, Mika asked the Great Spirit for both patience and control where Ghost was concerned.

For what Mika hoped would be the last time, Ghost flipped the visor back into position and settled back in his seat.

"What?" Ghost asked innocently.

"Finished?"

"Maybe." Ghost drew out his answer.

"You know, it would be far easier for me to program this if you were not bouncing about."

"Want me to do that so you can drive?" Ghost held out his hand in offer to take the GPS.

"No. I want you to stop wiggling about."

Ghost opened his mouth in retort, but Mika could tell he thought better of it.

Ghost faced out the window and watched the rain. "Fine."

Mika shook his head as he finished programming the GPS and mounting it to the wind-shield. "Please drive to highlighted route," the GPS instructed. Mika did as directed, stopping the vehicle at the entrance to the road.

After what seemed an eternity, Ghost spoke up. "What's the problem?"

"There is no problem." Mika stopped the vehicle, refusing to pull out onto the highway.

"Want me to drive?"

"No, I wish for you to give me a moment of silence," Mika said with more agitation than he meant.

"Please drive to the highlighted route," the GPS instructed again, causing Mika to glance at the tiny map on the screen, then back to the road.

"Spit it out," Ghost said.

"Spit what out?"

"Whatever it is that's bothering you."

"There is nothing to spit out. I am fine."

"No, you're not. What's up?"

Mika stared intently through the windshield. "I am merely concentrating on the road," he replied.

"You know, I might, could buy that," Ghost said "if we were actually on the road and not still in the parking lot."

"I am thinking about how to handle our meeting with Miss Carson," Mika said as he finally pulled the jeep onto the highway. "Since you will be in wolf form, I will need to do the talking."

"Oh yeah," started Ghost. "And that's another thing. Why do I have to be the pet?" Ghost made quotation marks in the air around the word pet. "You know women can't resist me." He added as he flipped the visor down again. "See? See?" Ghost said. "My hair is starting to curl. Geez."

Mika decided this was the perfect time to take a page from Fergus' book and keep his mouth shut. It was either that or throttle his younger brother.

Many years before, it was made apparent that women did tend to fall at Ghost's feet and he would be more than happy to tell you so. Women always seemed to faun over Ghost and had done so since he was a boy. But Mika had also seen women fall over themselves to be with other shifters as well. If Saint were there, Mika was certain he would have an elaborate explanation that included the effect of a shape-shifters' hormonal secretions upon the human brain. Pheromones always played a part in attraction, but in the case of shape-shifters, there was more than mere chemistry involved.

For most shifters confidence and power were a natural part of their existence and as easy to them as walking. It took a great deal of internal energy to shift from one form to another. The ability to control that much energy left a shifter feeling invincible as if nothing or no one could ever hurt you. It was a confidence born in the wake of immortality and was most apparent in the older ones such as Fergus and Saint.

Mika once asked a female friend what made certain men more attractive than others. "Power," she told him without hesitation. "Women find power seductive."

The same woman also told him women found chivalry to be sexy. Chivalry and a man who could do home repairs. Mika could understand the part about chivalry. Many women probably did find it appealing. Although, he noted that most allowed themselves to be treated less than chivalrously. He was not so convinced about the other.

But where Ghost was concerned even Mika had to admit there was more to a woman's attraction than chemistry or power or chivalry. Ghost's ice blue eyes and white-blonde hair screamed of his Nordic heritage as much as Mika's own dark coloring and long braids left no doubt of his.

To see Ghost was to view another time and another place. In truth, none of the four shifters known collectively as Delta Pack appeared to belong in this time. They could blend in if they truly wanted, but for Ghost it did not seem so easy no matter how hard he tried to adopt the language and style of each passing year.

Normally Mika could easily ignore Ghost's little bouts of narcissism, but not tonight. Tonight, was the only thing that kept Mika from meeting CJ face to face, and he was finding the wait almost intolerable. Mika had no idea how she would react to the news of her father, or to who and what he was. The anticipation was in fact, pushing him to the edge.

"By the way," Ghost interrupted, derailing Mika's train of thought. "How do you think you will be able to convince Charles' daughter to meet with us?"

"You are not the only one who knows how to speak to women, Ghost."

"I never said I was."

"Not in so many words, but it was implied."

Out of his peripheral vision, Mika could see Ghost's eyes as they followed the length of the two long braids that lay meticulously down his back. Straight and shiny as a panther's coat, the braids did not stop until they touched the top of Mika's belt.

"Wow, when was the last time you cut your hair?" Ghost asked.

Ghost's question caught Mika off guard. "What?"

"When was the last time you cut your hair?"

"I do not know." Mika answered in agitation. "You act like you have never seen my head before."

"Of course, I've seen it before. I just never noticed how long your hair was."

"Does it really matter?" Mika glanced in the rear-view mirror before making a lane change.

"No. I guess not," Ghost muttered. "You know, I have a great stylist back home. When we get back—"

"Ghost," Mika snapped.

"What?"

"Stop being such a woman!" He blurted out.

"You did not," Ghost sputtered.

"Yes, I did."

Ghost muttered something about not believing a friend could say such a thing, then fell silent. If Mika had made his comment to anyone other than Ghost, he would be concerned of offending him or her. However, he and Ghost had been friends many years and he knew very little could or would affect his friend's ego. Within minutes Ghost would be back to his old self with no apparent damage to his self-esteem.

But until then, Mika would revel in the silence—beautiful and glorious—that fell upon his ears. The only two voices to be heard inside the jeep were Steven Tyler's and the gentle tones of the GPS.

Mika thanked the Great Spirit for getting them safely to the hotel before Ghost had a chance to speak again. Pulling into a parking space, Mika turned off the engine and sat silently.

"You getting out?" Ghost asked as he grabbed his gear.

Mika tapped a soft rhythm on the steering wheel as he sat in thought. He knew the best thing to do would be to check in the hotel, get some dinner, lay out his plan and start fresh in the morning. But this was the first time in many years he had physically been in the same city as CJ, and all sense of reason was being over ridden by his desire to see her.

"Hey. Are you going to sleep out here or what?" Ghost asked again. Mika stared blankly at Ghost. All it would take would be to drive about ten minutes and he could be at her door. He would not even need to use a spatial shift to get there.

He reached for the keys still in the ignition, feeling the cool metal beneath his fingertips. As much as Mika longed to see CJ this evening, he realized it would be best to wait. After all, he had waited seventeen years, what was one more night?

Grabbing the keys and his bag, Mika locked the jeep and joined Ghost in walking toward the hotel. His reunion with CJ could wait. Tomorrow would come quickly enough. Besides he still needed to speak with Fergus and convince Ghost that wearing a dog collar was a good thing. *Great Spirit, give me strength.*

CHAPTER EIGHT

"They saw me," the woman muttered as she dropped her satchel onto the table.

"It makes no matter," answered Lucas as he poured her a drink. "They, you said?"

Hissing curses in several languages, the woman took the offered glass from his hand. Slowly she swirled the golden liquid in the glass. She inhaled using all her senses to take in and savor the aroma before taking a sip. Lucas always did have the best of everything and that included Scotch.

She had not meant for either Mika or Ghost to see her. Not really. Okay, maybe, she thought as she swirled the Scotch across her tongue reveling in the taste and the small burn it produced in the back of her throat. But she had been hidden too long. It was hard to stay under the radar of Theriontrope and Delta Pack. Had it not been for her present employer it would have been impossible. Then again, had it not been for her present employer, she would not have to.

"Yes. They. Mika and Ghost."

"So, the white wolf lives." Lucas spoke more to himself than to his companion. "Do you think they recognized you?" Lucas asked.

"There was recognition." She thought back to the confusion on Mika's face. "But, I doubt they will say anything. My name is all but forbidden especially to Saint." Taking a deep gulp from her glass, she tried to push away all thoughts of Saint Wolfe. She hated the statement "you never forget your first love", but in the instance of Saint, she began to think it was true.

"Besides," she sighed, casting her thoughts to the side. "To the rest of the world, I'm dead."

"Yes," Lucas said. "Yes, you are, and that is what makes you such an asset in this situation."

"What is it you wish of me my Lord?"

Lucas studied the petite woman before him. Eyes the color of coal stared back at him without fear. A trait he both admired and loathed.

"You know you don't have to call me that, Bethany Rose."

"And you do not have to call me Bethany Rose. I hate that name," she spat. "It is so... common."

Lucas found her pouting quite adorable. There was something about her which brought out his fatherly instincts. More so than did any of his own children.

"We have been over this. Bethany Rose is better for the situation than Bridget. " He placed a comforting hand on her shoulder, drawing her underneath the shelter of his arm.

"But," she protested.

"But we couldn't take the chance of Charlie Jean mentioning your true name around that coyote and raising his suspicion." He could see the small woman mull over his words. In the end, she would agree with him. She always did. "At the moment," he said. "I only wish for you to watch and report. Keep a close eye on the Guardian and her keepers."

"And how am I to keep them from seeing me?"

"My advice? Stay in the shadows."

CHAPTER NINE

"Brother, what are you doing?" asked Fergus, as he strode into what would soon become the study of the new Guardian. That was, if Mika and Ghost were successful in their journey.

Fergus remembered the day Charles took over the position as Guardian from his father Ian. The study seemed to grow overnight. Expanding upward, the room grew adding a second floor. Each shelf filled automatically with volumes and volumes of leather bound books ranging in topic from biography to fiction and varying in languages throughout.

The lower floor contained reference books pertaining to Theriontrope Foundation and the Shifter population. Behind the desk and tucked well beneath the landing, sat a glass enclosure with antiquated scrolls kept there to protect them from the elements.

Saint was dwarfed by Charles' desk and the stacks of the huge books and scrolls that surrounded him. Saint skimmed each page with lighting speed, soaking in each word and placing it in his mental super computer.

Fergus could tell his younger brother was a wolf on a mission and should probably not be disturbed. Yet as the older brother and leader of Delta Pack, Fergus needed to know what had Saint so enthralled. At least, that was his rationalization for disturbing his younger brother.

There was no way Fergus would ever admit he hated being left out of the loop. Luckily, he was a patient man and it would be only a matter of time before Saint came up for air.

While he waited, Fergus tiptoed up the stairs to the second story landing. He let his fingers and eyes peruse the titles of the books he found there. Many times had Fergus ascended this staircase. There wasn't a book resting upon the shelves he hadn't read.

As Fergus skimmed the shelves, one title caught his attention: The Three Musketeers by Alexander Dumas. He pulled the heavy volume from the shelf and thumbed through the time worn pages.

Absently, he studied the room and its contents. There was no denying the study felt like Charles. Its dark wood gleamed from the moonlight that streamed in from a bank of large windows opposite the wall of books. Charles had known what every book was and where each one was located. He had once told Fergus it was in his genetic make-up to know, kind of like being a homing pigeon for books.

How he would miss his old friend. Fergus cursed under his breath. Being a shifter came with perks and drawbacks. To seemingly live forever could be counted as both, he supposed, but it was the part he hated most about being whom and what he was. People whom= he loved came and went. Yet, he would always remain.

Left behind. The words reverberated deep inside his soul, as the image of indigo blue eyes beneath long black lashes swept across his mind. As always, Fergus shoved the feelings further back into the recesses of his mind and slammed the door shut on them. He had no time to feel anything or think about haunted blue eyes. Not with killers on the loose.

Being the one left behind had become daunting for Fergus. Over the past few years, he tried to convince himself it was only fatigue. He was exhausted from fighting and watching those around him die. True, he had Saint and Mika and Ghost, but no matter how much he loved his brothers, in the end he was still hopelessly alone.

More than two-hundred years he had walked the Earth. For almost as long he had cleaned-up other people's messes. Long ago he had lost count of the missions. Countless wars and even more countless bodies had piled up along the way. What did it matter? He scoffed. It was as the Goddess willed it.

Fergus ran his hand down the spine of the book, before placing it back upon the shelf. *Ah, to have been a Chevalier.*

"And a fine one you would have been," Saint said.

Fergus leaned over the railing above Saint's head and peered down. He had not meant for his brother to hear his thoughts, least ways, not consciously.

"Did you say something?" Fergus asked. Of course, he had heard every word Saint had said, but he figured this would be his best entry into a discussion.

Saint pulled his attention from the large book. "I said you would have made a fine Chevalier."

"Thank you. I have always been fond of the rapier." Fergus added as he trotted back down the staircase.

"And I would have guessed it was because of the hose," Saint mumbled and went back to reading.

"Saint?" There was no answer. "Saint?" Fergus asked with more emphasis. Still no answer. "Aodhàn?" He finally said, calling Saint by his given name.

"Yes?" Saint answered, his attention still firmly planted amongst the yellowed pages.

"Mind telling me what you are doing besides emptying the whole of the library?" Fergus waved at the stacks of books laying upon the desk and about the floor.

"Research, dear brother. Research." Saint picked another book off the floor and thumbed through it.

"Are you going to tell me or do I have to take a walk through the jungle of gray matter you call a brain in hopes I may discover what lurks there?" The proposition was not a fun one for Fergus. He hated to try and read another person's mind, especially Saint's.

Unlike most wolves or humans, Saint's brain contained a complex maze of thought patterns. It was worse than any jungle Fergus had ever tried to traverse. Luckily, he had only been forced to do so a couple of times. However, if that was the only way to get an answer then so be it.

"What did you say?"

"You know exactly what I said Aodhàn Wolfe. Don't make me…what does Ghost call it?" Fergus stopped to think for a moment. Ghost had lots of names for things. "Oh yeah, the Vulcan mind melt."

Saint blinked up at his older brother in confusion. "Vulcan mind…" Saint let the words trail off in his thoughts. "I believe the word is meld not melt."

"Are you sure? I would have sworn it was melt."

"Quite sure. It is meld," Saint clarified flatly.

"Either way. What are you working on?"

Saint put down the book he cradled in his hands. "Something has bothered me since speaking with Ghost after he was attacked."

"Speaking with Ghost can be bothersome," Fergus grumbled noting Saint's look of exasperation as he took a seat across from his brother.

Undaunted by Fergus' stare, Saint continued. "As I was saying, Ghost said the men that attacked him and Charles mentioned a pennant or pendant. There are a few references to family crests, rings and such, but nothing about a pendant per se."

"Maybe, he misspoke?" Fergus suggested.

"Do you actually believe he misunderstood?"

Fergus stared as his brother. One of Ghost's most irritating, yet useful qualities was his ability to quote any spoken line he had ever heard. If Ghost said his attackers asked about a pendant then they did. "No," Fergus conceded. "If he said it, he heard it."

"Exactly," Saint agreed as he stood and pulled yet another book from the bottom of a pile. He flipped the pages furiously until he came to rest somewhere toward the back of the book, and handed it to Fergus.

"I did find a rather obscure reference, in Latin of course…"

"Of course," Fergus agreed sarcastically.

Saint paused and tilted his head. "Really Fergus. Do you want to know what I found or do you not? The choice is yours," he asked.

"Please forgive," Fergus acquiesced as he took the book from Saint.

On the left side of the book, written in florid script, was a rather lengthy ode and as Saint had promised, it was indeed written in Latin. He was not as up on dead languages as Saint, but he could understand it well enough.

"It alludes to the calculus carus or beloved or dear stones," Saint began explaining. "One to represent each of the four elements. I believe that is what the drawing on the facing page represents."

Fergus examined the drawing opposite the poem. It depicted the world or the ancients' version of the world. At each of the four cardinal points was the image of a woman. Each dressed in Classic Greek style and each with a different item in her hands. Fergus took each woman to represent a different Goddess.

To the north, the goddess held what appeared to be mountains. In the south, a goddess stood her hands formed a "V" above her head as flames danced above them. The western goddess held an urn with water pouring from it, and finally, the goddess of the east, who appeared be surrounded by swirling leaves.

"Obviously, you are better at translating these things than I," Fergus said as he placed the book on the desk. "What do you think it means?"

Saint leaned back. "I am not sure, but I did take the liberty of scanning the writings of Breathag, Charles' great, great grand-mother and first known guardian of the Stone family."

"And?"

"And it would seem for the Haven to function there must always be a guardian."

"We already knew that." Fergus agreed.

"Yes, but we did not know that without one, Haven will die."

"That seems a bit fatalistic, especially for you," Fergus smiled wryly.

"Not really. According to Breathag, Haven is a living, breathing entity, sustained solely to protect shape–shifters. But to do so Haven needs a human protector–the Guardians. It would seem guardians are more for Haven then they are for us. Without one, Haven dies and if Haven dies then we, as a race, shall die."

Fergus pursed his lips. Could this be the true reason for Charles' death? Could someone want to destroy shifter–kind?

Surely Saint was over reacting. This rumor was one of the many wives' tells that had beseeched their kind since the beginning. All cultures had such tales. Armageddon. Ragnarok. Call it what you like, it was all the same.

"A mere fable," Fergus said with his normal nonchalance.

Saint shook his head. "I am not so sure. Did you not ever wonder why and how Haven is what it is?" Saint motioned about the library. "This room is or was Charles Stone. Remember how it changed when he took over from his father? The size changed. The arrangement changed." Saint waited for an answer. When none came, he continued. "Think of your room or Mika's or Ghost's. All three rooms are very different. None of us decorated the rooms. Yet each represents who we are in essence. Even mine differs from yours and we are blood. I did not choose the furnishing or the linens. Did you?"

Fergus mulled over Saint's words. It was true. Mika's room held artifacts from the Lakota tribe and Ghost's room was decorated with artifacts from the Viking era. It never occurred to Fergus where the items came from. They simply appeared.

"I never thought of it before. I just accepted it as what was," Fergus finally answered.

"As have we all, but I fear unless Mika and Ghost are successful, then the fable will come to a reality."

"Can we not appoint someone as Guardian? There are many who know of us and would be willing to do so."

"I do not think so. According to the journal, selection is at the will and whim of the Fates, not us." Saint paused, wandering deep into his own thoughts.

Fergus rose to his feet and stretched. Melancholy pulled at him, pushing him close to the brink. He couldn't think about the end of Haven. For him to walk down that road, might take him far pass the edge of reason.

The fur beneath his skin itched and burned to be set free. He did his best thinking while running and it had been days since he ran free as a wolf.

"How about a run, little brother?" Fergus asked.

"A run? On the eve of our possible destruction?"

"You are supposed to be the optimist in the family and I the pessimist. Do not change thy temperament. It might confuse Ghost."

Fergus knew his brother's demeanor all too well. As a child, he had seen it many times when their mother was displeased with him. Again, sadness flooded him as he thought of his mother and father. What he would not give to see them once again.

"Has Ghost wronged you in some way?" Saint asked.

"Not only me. Ghost has wronged all of us," Fergus insisted. "It was he I left to watch over Charles. Had he done his job, we would not be in this predicament."

"Your mood did not come about in one evening. For more than a fortnight you have treated him ill."

Fergus' jaw tightened. How was he to tell Saint the true reason for his treatment of Ghost when he did not understand it? Over the past couple of weeks, Fergus began to sense the psychic probe Ævar continually sent in search of Ghost.

At first, he tried to ignore the feelings and pass them off as paranoia, but as time went on, he realized the true danger Ghost was in. That was why he gave the order for Ghost to stay with Charles. He thought of all the places in the world his protégé would be safest, it would have been Haven. That was his mistake and one he would not make again.

He could feel Ghost's pain and it was not good. He knew there was no way to truly save Ghost from being found considering his status as a member of Delta Pack. The identities of its members were no longer a secret. Mika had even told Fergus there was a web-site devoted to the Pack, but at the insistence of Theriontrope, the site was quickly removed.

Acid gnawed in the pit of Fergus' stomach. "I treat him like the irresponsible child he is," Fergus said, not wanting to share his true thoughts with his brother.

"In case you have not noticed, Ghost ceased to be a child more than ninety years ago."

"I believe it is Ghost who needs to realize he is no longer a child," Fergus grumbled as he crossed is arms over his chest.

"Now who is acting like a child?" Saint moved to Fergus' side. "Was it not you who taught him what it is to be a shifter?"

Ignoring his brother's agitation, Saint continued. "If it were not for you Ghost would surely have died as a child. It was you who traveled to Iceland to bring him back here. It was you who nursed him back from the brink of death. It was you who taught him to hunt as both human and wolf. And it is your blood that flows through his veins. You are more father to him than brother."

When Theriontrope called upon Fergus to go to Iceland and retrieve a child, he obeyed without question. He was given very little information, except the child's life was in danger and the child's mother had asked the Foundation for sanctuary for her son. As always, once sanctuary was asked for, Theriontrope and Haven were bound to fulfill that request.

Fergus reasoned the rescue would not be a hard one. He planned to transport into the village, get the child and transport back. Simple. Quick. Clean. But there were problems with his plan.

The first problem was Fergus' ability to spatial shift and transport cleanly. Although he was well over 100 at the time, his ability to bend space and walk the wormhole it created was relatively new. The process could be done, but the amount of physical energy he would have to expend was staggering, especially if he were to bring another with him. But pride overtook his sensibility and he assured Dr. Grey and the others he could do it. Piece of cake, he promised and it should have been.

At the time, Fergus formed his plan little did he know the child he was sent to retrieve lay near death. Transporting a healthy child would be difficult. Transporting one as sick as Ghost was near impossible. The strain to the boy's body would be too great.

Fergus remembered with complete clarity the moment he first saw Ghost. The family who had taken the wounded child in was kind and sympathetic to shape-shifters, but they had no idea how to care for a child whose wounds were as extensive as Ghost's. It truly was the will of the Goddess he survived.

Before Fergus could knock upon the door, a woman stooped and bent with age opened the door to him. Without so much as a word, she motioned him into the small house. Barely had he stepped foot across the threshold before the putrid smell of decay and infection assaulted his senses.

Silently, the old woman led Fergus across the dimly lit cottage and into a tiny backroom. There he found a makeshift cot placed close to the fire. The bed was so piled with elk skins, he was barely able to make out the spectral face peeking out from the shadows. Fergus walked to the bedside and pulled the back the pelts.

Taking an oil lamp from the mantle, he held it near to better examine the boy. Almost doll-like, the boy was the most fragile thing he had ever seen. Dirty bandages caked with blood were wound about the child's neck and still appeared to be oozing blood. Deathly pale, the boy appeared little more than the ghost he would later be named for.

"His name is Æger Thorolfur. He is the first-born son to king Balder." Fergus remembered the woman of house saying.

The bed creaked with Fergus' weight as he sat to inspect Ghost's wounds. Fergus watched Æger's breathing to see if the child was even alive. Each breath seemed more shallow and labored than the one before.

Gently he pulled the child into his lap to unwrap the bandages. Once freed, a large gaping slash slit Æger's throat from under his right ear, diagonally across the front of his throat to stop near the collarbone of his left shoulder. On closer inspection, Fergus could make out the impression of teeth marks. What had happened to this child?

It wasn't until later that Fergus learned Æger's younger brother and twin, Ævar, had attacked him. Not only had Ghost's brother slit his throat but also bit into the wound once it was formed. Fergus remembered thinking how barbaric that had been even for a wolf.

During Fergus' inspection the child opened his eyes. So, moved by the child's ethereal beauty, Fergus speculated if angels truly existed then he gazed upon the face of one. It was still hard for Fergus to think about the state in which he found Ghost without becoming emotional.

Fergus knew the child to be approximately the same age as Mika, yet Æger seemed much younger. By the gods, the child was ten years old, yet he barely weighed four stone. Fergus could only hope once they were back at Haven and under the watchful eye of Ian and his wife, the child would grow as healthy and strong as Mika.

Æger could barely breathe yet he fought in vain to speak. The knife had sliced deep into his larynx making it impossible for him to speak. To this day, Fergus did not know what the child was trying to say, but he did not need to.

Æger's eyes said it all. Many times had Fergus seen the fear and surrender in eyes of men whose lives he had held in his hands, and it asked but only one thing—mercy. Never had he expected to see such defeat on the face of a child. Maybe it was Ghost's beauty or the pain that racked Ghost's tiny, fragile body, but something within Fergus seemed to break, though he would never admit it.

No matter how hard he tried to wrap his mind around the situation, Fergus couldn't fathom a parent throwing away a child. Even though, his own mother had done exactly the same thing when she took her own life and left him and Saint to fend for themselves.

He had refused to let his own brother die, so it would be with Æger. But how was he to get this child strong enough to travel?

In desperation, Fergus sought answers from Ian Stone and Saint. Their solution? Fergus was to transfuse a portion of his blood into the child. No one knew whether or not it would work, but it was the only option they had. Little did either of them know, their solution was one that would have greater repercussions than any could imagine.

Either way, there was a chance the child would die, but the chance of death was greater if Fergus did nothing. The equipment used was rudimentary compared to today's technology, but it worked. Over a course of three days Fergus replaced Æger 's missing blood with his own. When he felt, the child was strong enough, Fergus took him in his arms and transported the two of them back to the gardens at Haven.

Somehow, though weak from loss of blood and little nourishment, Fergus found the strength to get both him and Æger safely back to Haven. He vaguely remembered Saint and Ian rushing from the house to greet them upon their arrival. Both men tried to take Æger from him, but he couldn't bring himself to give the child over to the care of another. He had gotten them this far, he would continue on.

Without ceasing, Fergus strode through the manor house, up the grand staircase and into the room that would forever belong to his newest brother. The moment Ghost was safe and in his new bed, Fergus collapsed.

He awoke a few days later. A pair of ice blue eyes peeked out at him from behind a mane of white blonde hair. Fergus could see the wound was still raw and red, but it was completely closed and the healing had begun. The transfusion worked. Fergus' blood had healed the child.

"Why did you not let me die?" A small voice asked.

"Your death was not an option," Fergus answered wearily.

"But…was it not the will of the Goddess I die?"

Fergus pulled himself to a seated position to see the child better. "Did you ever consider it was the Goddess' will for you to come live here?"

Æger seemed to consider Fergus' statement thoroughly. With a nod, the child accepted Fergus' theory. "You know how to shoot a bow?" Æger asked, changing subjects as children often do.

It was then Fergus noticed the boy held a pair of his archer's bracers in his hands. Fergus watched as Æger traced the Celtic pattern with his tiny index finger.

"Yes." Fergus answered, watching the child carefully.

"Bal…my father promised to teach me how to shoot, but he did not have time." The boy paused in thought. "I will never see him again, will I?"

The tone in Æger's voice gripped the warrior's heart. He had felt the same way when the day realized Saint would grow up without having their father to teach him the ways of their people or how to hunt or shift form.

There was no reason to lie to the boy. "No, you will not," Fergus answered. "But I will always be there for you and, when I am well, I will teach you."

Æger's expression grew serious. "Promise?" he asked.

"I give you my solemn oath."

My solemn oath. Three little words that for Fergus held great weight. He had meant what he said when he told Ghost he would always be there no matter what. But if the feeling in his gut was any indication; the 'what" would one day prove most difficult. And, although he found it hard to admit it, Fergus knew that in his mind, Ghost would always be a tiny child, lying half-dead in his arms.

"I did only that what had to be done to insure his survival. No more, no less."

"Maybe so," Saint retorted. "But you should know your opinion matters greatly to him."

Fergus snorted. "Since I am not of the fairer sex, I truly doubt my opinion means that much." He placed the book back on the desk. "Rarely if ever does he listen. He is impertinent, boisterous, narcissistic and a general pain in the arse."

Saint shook his head. "Bark all you want dear brother. I will always know better."

Fergus was restless. Since being awake before dawn, he had been in meetings with Michael Grey, taken inventory of his personal arsenal, as well as taken target practice with his longbow and crossbow. There was nothing for him to do but wait. Wait, think and remember.

Fergus groaned. He did not want to think about anything now. He only wished to run and feel the soft earth beneath his paws. "Brother, too long have I been trapped inside this form and wish to do so no longer," he said, his hands going to the snaps that held the bracers tightly about his wrist.

"As you wish," Saint added as he walked past Fergus to the other side of the room and opened a door to the outside. "I will run with you," Saint said, unbuttoning his stark white dress shirt. "But you must do something for me."

"And that is?"

"Agree to speak with Ghost when he returns. Whatever lies between the two of you needs to be gone. You, best of all, know it is imperative to trust the others in your pack. The repercussion of not doing so puts all our lives in jeopardy."

Fergus did know well the backlash that could come from not trusting the man next to you. It was a lesson he learned the hard way and did not wish to repeat. And, whether Saint believed him or not, he did trust Ghost. But Ghost could be foolish and impulsive and...and Saint was right. Damn him.

Ghost was more son to him than brother, but recently Fergus had questioned his own need to continue on. His dreams of late had led him down a very dark path. What if he chose to take that path? What if he were the one who left people behind?

"Fergus?" The fearfulness in Saint's voice brought Fergus back from that dark path and he bit the inside of his cheek to keep from saying something he would later regret.

"Did you hear me?"

"About Ghost? Yes. Yes brother, I heard you. I will speak with him upon his return," Fergus said then pulled his black t-shirt over his head.

"All shall be well then," Saint agreed. "Meet you at the fallen oak." Fergus heard Saint's voice become faint. The air charged with energy as his brother's body shattered into millions of points of light that spun and swirled to converge into the form of a large red wolf.

"It will be I that meet you there," Fergus called out as he launched himself into the air. Landing completely transformed into a creature almost identical to his brother. Bolting outdoors, he shot past Saint. *Let us see who gets there first!*

CHAPTER TEN

Ísold lifted her head and listened. Off in the distance she could hear the distinctive whump, whump, whump of helicopter blades beating their way across the sky. A slight chill ran through her and she pulled the heavy robe of bear fur more closely about her shoulders. It was too early for the supplies transport, which could mean only one thing. Her captor was on his way.

Rising, she walked out onto the balcony in time to see the helicopter fly overhead and behind the great walls of the old keep. Snow fell in soft drifts spiraling ever downward to land about her. She had not realized night had fallen, but time was not important anymore.

"Your private Ice Palace," he teased the day he locked her away there. She had only enough freedom to allow her entry into any part of the old fort and grounds, but never beyond its walls.

Ísold knew here, amongst the snow and ice, no one would ever find her. To shout into the night would be useless. Her screams would be swallowed by the winds and any who did hear were paid well for their silence. They were in his employ and loyal to him even if their loyalty was bought by money, fear and blood.

Tilting her face skyward, she stared off into the darkness at the tiny flakes of white coming down. One for each of my tears, she thought. Ísold closed her eyes and made the same wish she had made every day since being brought to vígi hvítur litur, the Fortress of White.

Returning to her bedroom, Ísold went to the ornate writing desk that sat in the center of her room, completely covered by a myriad of hourglasses. Often, she found it ironic that each little timekeeper should be a gift from him, her jailor. It was one of his little twisted jokes since time mattered so little here.

"Ah," she said when the perfect one was found. After thirty or so years of being locked away, Ísold knew how long it would take for him to get from the great hall to the top of the turret that housed her bedchamber.

Gilded with turquoise sand inside, the hourglass she chose was not big since his journey up the stairs would take only fifteen minutes. Intricately etched on the band at both the top and bottom were tiny stars, her favorite of the ancient timekeepers would keep guard of each precious minute for her.

Flipping over the hourglass, Ísold picked up the book she had been reading and sat down to escape for a few moments more from her prison. Her body may have been held against its will, but her imagination couldn't be.

One of the few pleasures afforded her were books from around the world. Just as the hourglasses all came from him, so had the books. One small kindness against his many injustices, she thought, as she traced the outline of the gold embossed letters on the front.

The book's broken spine had long ago refused to hold its yellowed pages. In rebellion, its brittle contents fell at her feet and scattered about the floor. Ísold knelt before them, tenderly taking up each page and placing them, one by one, back between their covers. How many times had she read and re-read the words between the dilapidated covers of her favorite book, The Tales of the Brothers Grimm? She lost count years ago.

Maybe it was the kinship she felt with Rapunzel at being locked away in the tower that made Ísold return to the book time after time. In another time and place she thought she had found her own Prince Charming, but unlike Rapunzel, Ísold's prince would never come to take her from the prison tower.

Absently, Ísold's hand went to the braided torc about her neck. Designed in the old Norse style, the torc was adorned with two wolves' heads. But unlike a traditional torc, hers was not left open. Instead, the jaws of the wolves were interlocked, forging an unbreakable seal. Neither the bronze clasp nor the braided rope encircling her neck showed signs of wear. Both held as strong today, as the day they were first fastened about her throat.

Ísold was told a witch had made the torc and the power it held was granted by the Gods. The rope, supposedly made from the mane of Sleipner, Odin's eight-legged horse, could work whatever magic had been placed upon it and neither the clasp nor rope could be destroyed in any way. Only by the grace of her captor would she ever be set free.

The torc worked its magic well, binding Ísold's hame, or spirit, to her physical body. No longer would she be able to leave the physical realm and allow her spirit to walk the in-between. The spell was simply too strong for her to break.

Ísold was also considered to be a seiðr or seer by her people. She was young when her powers of second-sight began to develop. Within a few years, she learned to walk the dimension that lay between reality and dreams. She called it the In-between.

It was a place few dared to go, and thanks to the torc, neither could Ísold. The torc had taken everything from her, except for her gift of second-sight. After all, it was the ability he found most useful.

As a child, Ísold's hame had been free to wander where it liked. There she too could shift form becoming any animal she so chose. It was an ability she had been testing the night she stumbled across the one she named hana rau dòglingr, her red prince.

The picture of their meeting would forever be etched into her memory. Though covered in blood and barely able to stand, he was the most beautiful creature she had ever seen.

His deep amber eyes allowed her a glimpse into his pain-filled soul. His intense longing for freedom ripped at her heart. She could feel how he ached to shed his human form and shift into the powerful wolf she instinctively knew he could be. She could sense the wildness in him and it was easy for her to imagine how beautiful he must have been racing with abandon through the wilderness.

Ísold understood that yearning. She had lived in a prison without walls from the day her family had discovered her to be a seiðr. Her mother, so elated at her daughter's gift and in need of finding favor with the ruler of her people, gave Ísold into his hands for safekeeping.

Little did her mother know the extent of their ruler's cruelty or possessiveness. Rarely did he allow Ísold to leave his side. At the time, she had been too naive to understand his need for her to be near was not born from love, but out his need for control.

Only in the nighttime did he allow her privacy. It was then she would drift off to sleep only to dream the strangest of dreams. In those dreams the young witch discovered she could walk into the shadow-lands and be somewhere else. Nighttime became her respite and joy.

Ísold became proficient at controlling her decent from one reality into another, except when she was fatigued. On those occasions, her hame would forsake its mortal ties to wander without her guidance. It was on such occasion, she met her red prince.

Her King had demanded much from her that day. One after another the questions came. With each question, no matter how he worded it, the answer was always the same—there was another such as he.

That evening, in a state of exhaustion, she collapsed into bed. Ísold felt the gentle warmth tingle throughout her body and she recognized the signs of a spirit that wished to wander. No matter how hard she tried, Ísold couldn't fight the pull of the invisible tide. The more she fought the rising energy, the more her body ached until finally she gave in, letting the current sweep over her.

Shadows swirled about her finally giving way to light. Ísold found herself standing a few feet from a man. His wrists were wrapped in thin silver ropes used to suspend his body from a large hook in the center of a damp prison cell.

His long red hair was matted to his face by partially dried blood. Along his torso angry red whelps dripped crimson onto the gray stone floor near his feet. He did not move and Ísold thought him dead.

Warily she crept closer, until she stood slightly beneath the shadow of his body. To a young girl, the man seemed a giant. Intently, she watched him for any signs of life and found herself relieved to hear an audible breath escape his lips. She had no idea how long she stood there, studying every detail of his face. Neither the tiniest of lines about his eyes, nor the faint auburn shading of whiskers along his jaw-line escaped her attention. He was breathtakingly beautiful, and so different from the other men about her.

Slowly he opened his eyes. Even shaded by pain and exhaustion, they were the brilliant amber of the rising sun. In that moment, she felt an inexplicable connection to him. She could almost see the silver threads of her life being intertwined with his. In that moment, the stranger became her rau dòglingr and she loved him with an intensity her young mind couldn't yet fathom.

Most times he was half out of his mind from the pain or drugs the king ordered for him. Ísold took great care with him, trying to relieve the clouds of doubt she could see roll through his mind. To him she was little more than a specter of the night.

Yet despite his misgivings, Ísold sat by his bedside. She sang him ballads of times gone by or entertained him with tales of her people. Eventually, she trusted him enough to tell him of her walks through the shadow lands. Of how only in her dreams, did she become a changeling like her mother and brothers. Her own ability to transform was in question since she was born of a union between a human and a shifter and, even though she was nearing her twentieth year, she still showed no signs of shifting.

For five years, Ísold watched as her prince was tortured day after day and left for dead. Still, night after night, she would go to him. She had to be near him, to assure herself he still lived. There was so much she told him and he spoke not at all. Still, she loved him. Her heart would never belong to another. It was the will of the Goddess.

With a sigh, Ísold rose. She let the book open to the page containing the wood-cutting of Rapunzel's prince kneeling at the base of the imprisoned princess' tower. Gently she ran her fingers over the prince's nondescript face and imagined another in its place. One with a high, broad cheekbones and eyes the color of the burning sunrise.

How young and foolish she had been to believe that one such as he would keep his promise and come back for her? "If you are not my dream," he had whispered to her, "then by the Goddess I swear I shall return for you." Those were the only words he had ever spoken to her.

His voice was raspy and dark with an accent she could never place. She wrapped his beautiful words around her soul and wore them as a mantle to shield her from the king's cruelty.

She now knew the stranger to be dead. The king had been sure to tell her as much. Though there were rare times when Ísold thought she felt him move across the spaces that separated them, but those times were as fleeting as a snowflake upon the tongue.

As the last grain of sand fell upon the others, Ísold heard his footfalls outside her door. He would knock as always—one of the few shows of respect he still held for her. Ísold closed the book and left it this time. He would take all of her attention, he always had.

The knock was the same. Three swift raps, a pause, three more and a final pause while he awaited her answer. She could make him wait an eternity if she wanted, but it would only raise his ire.

"Enter," she called and sat upon the thickly covered bed.

"There you are," he said as he entered the room.

"Where else would I be?"

"Where indeed," he answered and allowed the same smug smile to cross his face that he had sported since Ísold had known him. "I have a present for you," he said, holding out a box wrapped in bright red and gold.

"I did not know freedom could be placed in such a small package." Ísold smiled sweetly.

"It can...if it contains a key." He shook the package playfully at her.

Optimism sprang in her so quickly she could hardly contain the feeling. Leaping to her feet she grabbed at the package, which he quickly placed above her and somewhat out of reach.

"Ah, ah ah..." he teased. You know the deal. You give me something, I give you something. He let his gaze wander downward to where her robe had gaped open while she tried to grab the package.

Ísold suddenly stopped. Of course, how could she be so stupid to think he would want nothing for his "kindness"? She stared into his cold blue eyes; the humor that showed on his lips touched nowhere else. Especially not within his soul, since he couldn't possibly have one.

"What is it you wish from me?" she asked, pulling the robe closed.

"That which I always ask of you and that which you have always freely given."

Ísold took a deep breath. Since childhood, she had done as he asked. Why should she expect this visit be any different from the others?

With resolution, Ísold went to a small table near the balcony doors and picked up a large silver chalice. "As you wish," she said and flung open the doors. Stepping out onto the snow-covered balcony, she scooped the white powder into the cup. Taking the cup to the fire, Ísold held it above the flame, allowing the snow to melt. She motioned for him to take a seat across from her. "The doors must remain open. The cold will not bother you." Her words were more statement than question.

"Not at all," he said.

Ísold watched as he unbuttoned the jacket to his dark blue suit and remove it. Meticulously he placed the jacket on the back of a chair and slid into the one opposite hers. The deep blue of his suit was a stark contrast to his nearly white complexion and silver hair. She had never quite gotten used to his fairness and how it contrasted greatly to her own deep black hair and midnight blue eyes. Like the father. The statement brought her both comfort and pain.

"Drink, but only three sips," she ordered when the snow had melted from the heat of her hands into the chalice. He took the chalice and did as she asked. Taking the cup from him she stared into it deeply. Scarring was the only gift of divination she had left thanks to him.

Luckily, it was simple. The difficulty came in knowing what not to tell him.

As a child, Ísold was so excited with her ability to predict the future and see what others did not, she told everything without censure. Knowing very little of the history of her family, she did not know certain items were best left unsaid. It was a lesson found out too late.

Ísold stared down into the water, pushing her vision past the tiny waves and ripples, into the silver beneath, then further still into the place few had the ability to see.

She saw a large white wolf as it ran across black sand beaches. He was light against dark. The animal skidded to a stop the moment he caught sight of another, identical wolf. The second wolf stood beneath a flaming Yew tree atop a hill overlooking a beach.

The two wolves regarded each other, neither backing down from his position. Instantly they charged toward each other. She could hear the rip and tear of flesh beneath strong jaws. The sound of bone crushed loud in her ears. The second wolf picked up the first and threw it with all his might against the burning tree. There it was consumed by fire.

Words flowed from Ísold's mouth. It was her voice, but as usual the words came from some distant place.

Blood at last an enemy makes.

Tide and time an enemy takes.

When first is last and last is first,

Thor's own blessing quenches not the thirst.

The Yew tree fear, take head you must,

Lest its flame turn bone to dust.

Ísold gasped and tore herself from the chalice.

"What? What does that mean?" her captor asked.

"Two wolves stand in battle, only one shall live."

"Two wolves! Impossible!" He shouted and rose quickly, upending the table and scattering its contents. "Ghost is dead."

"The white wolf lives. You have failed...again." Ísold found comfort in her last word, but her joy was short lived as delicate yet strong hands wrapped about her throat, pushing her to the floor. The pressure around her neck increased with each passing second.

She gasped for air, but breathing was impossible. Finally, she thought. Finally, he is going to kill me. Sweet Freyja, grant my wish. Take me to Fólkvangr. Allow me to walk free again even if it is in death.

Darkness tinged her world as Ísold began to slip from consciousness. She silently prayed mercy would be given and her decapitation would be swift.

Slowly the world became right again as her limp body fell to the floor. Her lungs burned as they filled with oxygen and her pulse returned to normal. *No. No. No.* Her mind screamed. This wasn'twhat she wanted. She wanted death. Yet again, her Goddess had betrayed her.

"What else did you see Spá?" He spat out the Norse term for witch.

"I..."she coughed. "I told you. Your brother will be your downfall."

He stared menacingly down at her. "How?" He asked as he took a step toward her.

I do not know." She answered and pulled herself off the floor. "I did not see that."

He towered over her. "You said I would be victorious. For that to happen all protectors of Haven must die, starting with that cur."

"Did you learn nothing at the feet of Balder?" Ísold asked.

"You are not worthy to speak his name in my presence," he hissed. "You knew nothing of him."

"Mother told me..."

Not possessing the speed of a shape-shifter, Ísold couldn't move quickly enough to avoid his wrath. She could only feel the sting from the back of his hand as he slapped her across the face, splitting her lip and sending a shower of blood across the room. The hot, metallic taste filled her mouth.

"My mother..." He hissed.

"Our mother, Ævar," Ísold cut in. "She is my mother as well."

"Our mother..." he continued through gritted teeth, "is no better than a common bitch after she took your father into her bed. Worse yet he was human, which makes you a mongrel, little sister." His acknowledgment of their relation filled with venom.

"In fact," he continued, "you are very much like our mother–a common bitch in heat. Lest you forget the prisoner you helped escape."

Ísold cast her glance downward. She remembered him all too well. It was her orchestration of his escape that landed her in this place.

A menacing laugh, cruel and cold as the arctic wind, rolled all too casually from her brother. "See what love gets you?"

At Ævar's words, something inside Ísold snapped. She pulled herself to her full height and walked to him—unafraid. What more could he do to her? All that she loved had been taken from her at his hands. Her home. Her mother. Her prince. There was no way he would ever kill her. It was a much better torture to keep her alive and hidden away from the world.

Ísold wiped the blood from her mouth and stared down at the crimson streak against her ivory skin. Her eyes met his and with a quickness she did not know she had, Ísold rubbed the blood across his cheek then kissed him there.

"Why do you hate so much, Ævar?" she whispered near his ear. "Or would you rather I call you Ivan?" Ísold felt the stillness that moved across her half-brother and, in that instant, she realized she no longer feared him or his retaliation.

"My hatred is my own concern," he answered calmly, his implacable stare never leaving her face. Silence passed between them. Each watching the other, unbending in their own defiance.

"Well," he began as he walked to the chair to retrieve his jacket, "this has been enlightening as always."

Ísold stood ridged, waiting for him to leave. He would go and once again, she would be alone with her books and memories of what it was to have once been free.

"Ísold?" he called to gain her attention. She was not blinded to his sickeningly sweet tone. To its harsh cruelty.

"Yes my lord, what do you wish?" she asked.

"I almost forgot your gift," he said as he placed the long-forgotten package upon the table.

Ísold's hand went again to the clasp of the choker about her neck. "I know what I long for most cannot await me in that package."

"That depends, does it not?" He waited on her to answer, but she refused. "As you wish it." He opened the door to leave. "Come, come. Did what I say of your ex-lover hurt so much? Surely in all these years I have said or done worse."

"He was not my lover," she confessed.

Ævar's laughter came from nowhere, catching her off guard. "Then that makes it all the sadder. Still, I can see where it would have been a challenge when he could hardly stand."

Ísold listened to the whisper of the wind and snow as it swirled outside the open doorway. Maybe if she ignored him, he would go.

"Maybe…maybe I should take back the gift. In light of your confession." He reached tauntingly for the package, but Ísold snatched it from the table and ripped the paper off before he had a chance to retrieve it.

It took a moment for her to recognize the image in the gold gilded frame. Though it had been thirty years since she last saw him, the man's long red hair and amber eyes would forever be as much a part of her as any memory could. Ísold blinked and then again.

She reached for the edge of the table to hold herself upright. "This cannot be," she said. Her eyes welling up with tears.

"I thought you might like a real face to pine over at instead of the ones in your books." Ævar leaned against the doorframe.

"What type of trickery is this?" she demanded as she fought back her emotions. She looked again at the photo of the man in the long black coat. He appeared to be a man without a care in the world. A free man without the memory of a promise made to a foolish girl.

"There is no trickery. That is truly Fergus Wolfe. He is very much alive and well, for the present."

"Rau dòglingr," she whispered. "but you told me…you told me he was dead."

"It seems both of us have a ghost to contend with."

Anger rose from deep within Ísold. She had never talked back to Ævar or fought for her own freedom. How could she have fought? She had no powers. No means of protection. Nothing. Without conscious thought, words hissed from between gritted teeth.

"Of Earth and Water, of Fire and Air,

the Universe bore four daughters fair;

Spread cross time, scattered through space,

Earth alone knows her place.

One by one each shall be found,

four by four they shall be bound.

Four daughters born, know not of each other,

Each to be found by grace of the mother."

"Wonderful!" Ævar exclaimed, clapping his hands together. "I do love when your little prophecies rhyme. It was very touching and poetic. In fact, it was one of your best yet." Ævar mocked her. "Tell me, what does it mean?"

Ísold was not sure what it meant. She wasn't even sure where the words had come from. As before, the voice was hers, the words were not and she stood speechless before her captor.

"See little mongrel, even you do not know everything." With that, Ævar left, leaving the door to her room ajar.

CHAPTER ELEVEN

Ævar bounded down the spiral staircase that led from the bedroom of his half-sister to the great hall of vígi hvítur litur. He had acquired the fortress over seventy years ago in a "battle of supremacy" with a rather nasty and aggressive shifter.

It was a battle to the death. The sheer fact Ævar held all rights to the old castle stood as testament to his ability as a warrior.

"What is wrong?" asked Cassius, Ævar's second in command, as Ævar entered the castle's great room.

"How can you stand so close to that fire?" Ævar asked. "By the Goddess you were born a son of ice and snow. You should embrace your essence."

"I do embrace my essence," Cassius said. "But as you can see I am dressed in Armani, not animal," the larger man said making a small bow and gesture toward his clothing.

"Humph." Ævar strode to the sideboard. Not giving the impeccably dressed shifter a second glance, he poured himself a glass of brandy.

"What has put you in such a poor humor?" Cassius asked as he warmed his backside, keeping an eye on Ævar. "I take it your visit with Ísold did not go as you hoped?"

Ævar gulped the amber liquid from the glass and poured another. This one he sipped slowly savoring the warmth and taste.

"You could say that." Ævar watched Cassius. It had always intrigued him that a man of such dark coloring, could become stark white when he shifted from human to animal. Then again, Ævar was sure there were stranger things in this world.

"My brother lives," Ævar said, his eyes boring into Cassius.

Most usually shrank from Ævar's icy stare, Cassius, however, did not fit into that group, which was why Ævar felt the need to keep him near.

That and the prophecy Ísold had made only days before their meeting. It was one of the few Ævar could remember verbatim.

"As dark of night and light of morn,

So be the man who takes bear form;

Of cold and ice and moon and sun,

Of noble birth comes this one.

Friend he be or foe he make,

The first one offered you must take."

Ísold was barely twelve when she spoke those words. Ævar did not always understand his half-sister's prophecies, but to him this one became clear the moment he met Cassius. The two had met more than thirty-five years ago, and Cassius had been at Ævar's side ever since.

Cassius was born a prince among the Clan of Snow Bear, though he did not want to take possession of the throne. Dark skin and eyes belied the massive polar bear that lay beneath a human exterior.

If Cassius was surprised by Ævar's pronouncement of Ghost's existence, he did not show it. Then again, the bear showed little emotion most of the time. Yet another reason Ævar liked having him around.

"I was under the impression that little project was completed," Cassius stated and walked across the room to join Ævar for a drink.

"So was I."

"Never send a human to do a shifter's job," Cassius commented.

"Humph," Ævar snorted and took another mouthful.

"That changes things a bit, does it not?" Cassius inquired.

Taking inventory of the room, Ævar moved to sit in a large wing backed chair behind a great mahogany desk. The great hall held row upon row of book-lined shelves running the entire length of the room and towering at least twelve feet toward the sky.

His gaze lingered on a worn chaise lounge tucked away in the corner. He could see the permanent indentation left by many years of Ísold lying there reading each and every book he had brought her. The thought occurred to him that maybe he should send her a new one. After all her birthday was coming soon.

"Regret?" Cassius asked.

"No," his answer was frost upon the air. "Regret is for the weak." Ævar thumbed through the pages of a book left upon the desk. "I agree."

"You do?" Cassius raised an eyebrow. "About what?" He asked as he sat across from Ævar.

"To kill a shifter, you need a shifter."

"Who do you suppose to send?"

A cruel smile crossed Ævar's face. "I was thinking maybe a woman this time. Æger seems to have an affinity for women and vice-verse."

"Any female in particular?" Cassius asked, eyes narrow.

"This calls for cunning. Skill. Cat like reflexes wouldn't hurt either." Ævar stopped and waited for Cassius to catch up to his line of thought.

"You're not thinking...not Apple-y?" Cassius seemed shocked.

"None better. She is all that and more."

"You've got the more part right. She is the walking definition of hellcat. That witch almost took my face off for saying good morning!"

"I'm thankful we do not scar easily or I would have some explaining to do," Ævar chuckled.

"Do you not think Fergus will recognize her?"

Ævar stopped laughing at the mention of Fergus Wolfe. "Fergus the virtuous," Ævar spat the name as he thought of Theriontrope Foundation's resident hit-man/savior. He dismissed the thought with a graceful wave of his hand. "It has been years since their last meeting. She has changed quite a bit since then," Ævar said.

When Ævar first found Apple-y she was completely feral. Life had been hard for her. She was one of the unfortunate few Theriontrope had no idea existed. Abandoned as a child, Apple-y was left to fend for herself on the streets. No one taught her right from wrong or how to handle the shifting process and the sexual energy that accompanied it.

Prostitution became her means of survival. While entertaining a client, Apple-y shifted. Confused and scared, she did what most wild cats do and lashed out at the nearest living creature. That had been her first kill. After that, her mind splintered, and she began to live more and more as an animal, and less and less as a human.

News of savage murders by a wild animal in the alleys of Moscow began to surface. Ævar knew there was no way a stray animal could wander the streets of Moscow undetected. It took a great deal of connections and money, but he finally found entrance into Moscow. There he tracked Apple-y, a crazed

Siberian tiger, living in the sewer system. She had become his own Pygmalion triumph. Sort of.

"You are really thinking about calling Apple-y to do this?"

"Why not? As she would say, she's purrrrrrrrrrrfect." Ævar rolled the "r" in imitation of Apple-y's accent.

"The woman speaks of herself in third person," Cassius mumbled into his glass.

"We are still working on that," Ævar said and moved to place his empty glass back on the sideboard. "We leave in twenty minutes." Ævar started for the door.

"Going to say good-bye to Ísold?"

"No," he answered, not stopping. "I need to speak with the caretaker and cook about provisions."

Cassius nodded his head and continued to sip on the bit of brandy left in his glass. When the last of Ævar's footsteps echoed out of range, he turned toward a large tapestry that hung along the west wall. It depicted a fierce Dragon being brought down by two wolves while others in the pack waited their turn. The hanging was a remnant of the original owners from centuries ago.

"You may come out of hiding," Cassius said to the tapestry. "He is gone."

"Are you sure?" a tiny, slightly muffled voice came from behind the wall of fabric.

"I am sure. He went to speak with cook."

The tapestry swayed slightly and Ísold stepped from her place of hiding. "How long have you known I was there?"

Cassius rose to greet her. "Since your feet landed upon the last stone. I must say your stealth has gotten better over the years."

"I have had time to practice," she said nervously changing from one foot to another.

Cassius smiled affectionately and opened his arms wide. Ísold ran to him, her heart almost bursting from the elation at seeing her old friend. She so missed the touch of another and it felt wonderful to be in someone's arms.

"Is it true?" she asked as she clung tightly to Cassius' chest.

"Which part?" he asked, resting his chin atop her head.

"Rau dòglingr. Is he truly alive?"

"Yes," Cassius whispered. "He is as alive and well last I saw."

Ísold slowly released her hold on Cassius and pulled back from him. "You...you have seen him?" The elation in her heart was replaced with pain.

Every night since being locked away she prayed to Freyja to let her die, to take her to be with her prince. No wonder the Goddess never answered her plaintive cries. Fergus lived and had forgotten about her. But he promised, her gullible heart whispered.

"I have not spoken with him, nor he with me."

Tears stung the back of her eyes. "But all these years," she whispered. "How could you know and never once tell me?"

"I did what I had to do." Cassius took a step forward and placed his hands upon her shoulders. Ísold tried to pull away but he held her tightly, forcing her to acknowledge him. "Please little sister, do not be mad at me. I did it to protect you, to protect your heart."

She did not wipe her tears away. "Protect me? How were your lies my protection?" She wanted to shout, but knew to do so would bring Ævar.

"That night. The night before I took Fergus through the tunnels of prison, I heard his promise to you."

Ísold dropped her face to stare at a spot on the floor. Nothing he had to say could interest her. Cassius had been her one and only friend, and he was a traitor.

"That night, Fergus barely knew his own name. We walked until we were out of your line of sight, then he collapsed. I carried him to the end of the tunnel. Half-crazed from pain and starvation, yet he asked me to watch after you, no matter what that took, until he could return for you."

"Obviously, neither you nor he are the men I believed you to be. I am a fool," she whispered.

"I cannot speak to Fergus, but you are no fool. Fergus did not have time to fully regenerate before Ævar had you bound by a witch and thrown into this place." He motioned to the castle walls.

"Ævar told no one. Not even me." Cassius. "After Fergus' escape, he trusted no one. I couldn't risk everything that we had worked so hard for."

"But surely the Foundation…"

"Due to your lineage, they do not classify you as a shifter. You are off their grid. To this day, Fergus has no idea who you were or that it was Ghost's own brother that held him captive all those years."

Realization landed heavily on Ísold. "No one knows I exist?" Her eyes pleaded with Cassius. They begged him not to confirm her fears. "Not Theriontrope? Not Fergus?"

"No," he answered flatly. "Considering everything, I thought it best to let sleeping wolves lie."

"No one knows of me," she whispered again.

Cassius sniffed the air. "Ævar comes. Quick. Hide," he ordered, pushing her toward the tapestry that had been her hiding place.

Ísold trained her ear toward the door of the great hall. She could hear faint footsteps as they made their way down the long hallway from the servants' area. Doing as she was told, she skittered toward the tapestry, but pulled to a halt.

"What is it?" Cassius whispered.

Ísold darted back to him. Standing on tiptoes, she kissed Cassius gently on the cheek. "I forgive you," she whispered, then disappeared once again, beneath the giant dragon.

CHAPTER TWELVE

Mika stopped the jeep as he pulled into the parking lot of Carson Animal Clinic. He knew his hesitation would bring Ghost's attention. Mulling over the situation, he tried to decide what should be their next step.

"What's up?" Ghost asked.

"We need to find you someplace to change. Unless you want to change out in the open. After all, I know how much you love the rain."

Ghost leaned forward, and the rain beat against the windshield. "I would love for it to stop."

"Keep your eyes open for someplace secluded." Mika drove toward the open country in hopes of finding a more private spot.

"Over there." Ghost said and pointed to an abandoned gas station.

The building was falling down, but there was an awning attached that seemed to be in decent shape. It would be sufficient enough to shield Ghost from the rain and hopefully anyone who might be watching.

Actually, humans had seen shifters change form many times. There were hundreds of videos on ur_vids.com that showed shifter transformations. Aspiring visual effects artists submitted the bulk of the videos, but there were ten or more Mika knew to be legitimate.

He found the comment section after each video most amusing. By all implications, the general populace found the faked videos to be more realistic and the real videos most fake. Even so, the last thing Mika wanted was for Ghost to be another video on the web.

With that in mind, he pulled the jeep into the old gas station and as deep into the shadows as possible. Ghost was already bare to the waist and in the process of removing his shoes when the jeep came to a halt.

Ghost opened the door and climbed out of the jeep to remove the rest of his clothing before he shifted.

Mika fidgeted with his mp3 player and waited for the familiar rush of energy that accompanies the change. Anyone within twenty feet could feel the change of negative ions in the air that occurs when a shifter transforms. Another shape-shifter would know immediately what had taken place. A human would notice they were becoming calmer.

But at the moment, nothing was happening. "Why haven't you changed?"

"Because."

"Ghost, we have no time for games. We are almost late as it is."

Ghost said as he climbed back into the jeep. "We may be much later if you don't tell me what is really eating at you."

"There is nothing eating at me, and there is nothing I would like to spit out. Would you please shift so we can continue our task?" Mika blew off Ghost's statement and began to disconnect the GPS.

"Um hmm, our task. And what is it about this task has put you in such a grouchy mood?"

"I do not know…"

"Don't give me the I-know-not routine. I'm not buying it."

When Mika did not answer, Ghost shifted in his seat to stare out the window.

Mika could tell by the tightness of Ghost's jaw that he was becoming upset, but what could Mika do? When it came to Charles's daughter, Mika knew many things about who she was and what she could possibly be.

Hiding his knowledge from the others had been difficult. It's not easy to keep secrets when you can share thoughts with another. Luckily, his pack never ventured into those secluded places.

It wasn't that he wanted to keep the information from Fergus and the others. Over the years, Mika had repeatedly asked for permission to tell them about Charlie Jean and his assignments. However, Charles and the Theriontrope Foundation refused his request, placing him under a gag order.

No one could know. Maybe the day had finally come when he could disclose the secret he had carried more than thirty years.

Mika hoped Fergus would understand his betrayal. If not, then the two of them would deal with that when the time came.

Currently he had other issues at hand. Like a partner who refused to do what was asked of him. Mika knew Ghost could literally be like a dog with a bone and not let things go. In short, Ghost was incredibly stubborn.

"I know both you and Fergus think I pay little attention to things which do not directly affect me," Ghost said, picking at a frayed spot on his blue jeans. "Which, I admit, may be a bit true. Fergus thinks me little more than a child, and I know at times I push you to your limits." Ghost held up a hand to stop Mika from butting in. "Please, let me finish."

Mika waved his hand for Ghost to continue.

"Despite what anyone thinks, I do pay attention."

"Such as?"

"Such as, you have acted strange since we found out about Charles' daughter."

"Why do you say that?"

"I heard the conversation from the kitchen. Everybody had something to say except you. Care to tell me why?"

Mika silently stared at the turquoise and silver rings that adorned his hands. This was one time he wished Ghost had not paid attention.

"Fine," Ghost said as he slid out of the jeep. "Don't tell me." He angrily threw his jeans into the back seat. "Maybe when I'm over two-hundred you guys will think of me as grown."

Before Mika could voice a rebuttal, the air began to thin and he heard Ghost's voice cry out, "By the power of Greyskull. I am pooweeerrrrrrr!" Electricity zipped along every nerve ending as each molecule of Ghost's body moved and shifted in an intricate dance separating, rearranging and converging. Within mere seconds, the transformation from man to wolf was complete.

"Well that was subtle," Mika said flatly.

I've been trying out different catch phrases. That one isn't bad, but still...Ghost answered using their common telepathic pathway.

Mika shook his head.

What? Ghost asked as he leapt into the passenger seat.

"We should have taken away your remote-control years ago. Remind me to speak to Fergus about that when we get back to Haven." Mika answered as he got out of the vehicle and shut the passenger side door. Glancing in Ghost's direction, he wondered how it was possible for a wolf to seem dejected and pissed off at the same time?

Getting back in the jeep, Mika placed his hand on the key, cranked the engine and sat there. He couldn't get Ghost's statement out of his head. Was it possible he and Fergus treated Ghost as a child? Surely not.

Fergus called Ghost a child, and Mika had snapped at him earlier. But that was different. Fergus had been upset about the death of Charles, as had they all. As far as Mika's outburst, to say Ghost could be exasperating was somewhat of an understatement.

Would it take until Ghost reached two hundred before they thought of him as grown? Mika had no answer for that.

He and Ghost were not that different in age, but for some reason Ghost always seemed younger. Maybe it was because he was the last member of Delta Pack to be raised in the Haven. If they truly thought of themselves as a family, then Ghost had to be the "baby brother."

"Ghost?" Mika faced his companion. Still Ghost stared straight ahead. "Okay you win," Mika said to him. Ghost peered at him from the corner of his eye. "You are right. There is something that bothers me."

I knew it! Ghost whipped his head toward Mika.

Mika felt the need to qualify his statement. "I am not at liberty to share at this moment."

Fergus doesn't want me to know?

"No," Mika answered.

See I was right. Fergus doesn't trust me.

"Do not blame Fergus. He knows nothing and neither does Saint."

Ghost was shocked. *Fergus doesn't know? Whoa...*

"Exactly. And at this moment, it is more important for you to have as little knowledge as possible."

But...

"But," Mika jumped in. "When we are finished here today, I promise you full disclosure."

Everything?

"Everything. Agreed?"

Ghost sat in thought for a moment before speaking. *Agreed,* Ghost chirped. *Let's go.*

"You know, you really are like a woman. Hot one minute, cold the next," Mika commented.

My ancestors were from Iceland. You know, land of fire and ice. It only stands to reason.

"Of course, I should have known," Mika said as he drove the jeep from its half-hidden position and back onto the highway. Out of his peripheral vision he could see Ghost's paw try and adjust the radio.

"What are you doing?" Mika asked.

This is a great song.

Mika's mind had been so far away, he had not being paying attention to the music. He never thought of Ghost as one to like "Talking Heads," but who was he to argue, so he turned it up. *Take Me to the River* was a great song. The Al Green version was best; but this one was more in line with the others on this playlist.

Mika had to smile. He could only imagine how ludicrous it must be to see a member of the First Nation and a large white wolf singing, and howling, rock music at the top of their lungs. Soon the Talking Heads were replaced by Bon Jovi and, without missing a beat, the two continued to sing.

The jeep bumped along the short drive to the Carson Animal Clinic. The music played only long enough for the duet to finish their rendition of *Lay Your Hands On Me*. It was times like this Mika felt he and Ghost truly were brothers.

"Oh, I did forget one thing," Mika said as he leaned into the back seat and pulled out a plastic bag with the name Doggy Doodles stamped on it in bright pink letters.

Oh no. No. No. No. Ghost protested when he saw the black leather collar Mika pulled from the bag.

"Come on Ghost, think of it as part of the uniform."

We do not wear uniforms. Ghost's eyes widened as he watched Mika attempt to place the collar around his neck. A low growl issued from the wolf's throat as he snapped at Mika's hand.

"You did not try to bite me!" Mika drew his hand back.

Yes, I did. And I'll do it again if I have to. He snapped his jaws again to punctuate the statement.

"Come on Ghost, be reasonable."

I think not wanting to be choked is rather reasonable! Leather collars could be fun, but not here, not now and not with you!

"I cannot believe you said that," Mika responded. "Wait, yes I can, but that does not change the fact we need to appear credible." He reached toward Ghost once again. This time Ghost quickly snatched the offending piece of leather from his hands and held it tightly between his teeth.

No.

"It will be okay," Mika said trying a less aggressive approach.

Since when is humiliation ever okay? Besides, this is the wrong color. It needs to be violet.

"I know I am going to regret this, but why does the color matter?"

Because violet brings out the blue in my eyes.

CHAPTER THIRTEEN

Through the downpour, CJ could barely make out the forms of a man and a large white dog as they sat inside the red jeep parked in front of her office. She stood inside the glass door to her clinic and watched with curiosity as the two figures waged a battle over whatever the dog held between his teeth.

Occasionally the scuffling would halt and the man would talk to the dog. Then the tug of war would begin again. To CJ it appeared the man was attempting to reason with the dog.

"What's going on?" asked Arial Schoemann, CJ's all around helper and, in CJ's humble opinion, the best veterinarian assistant in the known universe.

"I'm not sure," answered CJ as she took the cup of coffee Arial offered. "Thank you."

CJ shook her head as she sipped hot liquid from her favorite coffee mug. Since every worker at the Carson Clinic seemed to be addicted to coffee, each had a personal cup so no one would get confused and drink another's coffee.

CJ still used her favorite 'X-Men' mug. It had been a gift from an old boyfriend in college, and though she had long since parted with the man, parting with the mug seemed impossible. After all it was the perfect size and shape and sported a picture of Wolverine in blue and yellow spandex. "Mmm, hazelnut. You're the best, Arial," she said glancing over her shoulder at her assistant.

Arial stood on her tiptoes, watching over her boss' shoulder. One hand held her mug that had a cartoon of a rabbit decked out as Mae West and the slogan "I'm not fat, I'm, fluffy." The other held onto the door to help her keep balance.

Arial was, in her own words, "taller than she appeared." Which may have been true considering she only appeared to be five foot three and, like the rabbit on her coffee mug, slightly fluffy.

The two women stood by, watching ensuing battle between man and wolf. "Sorry I had to call you in this morning." CJ apologized.

"Don't be. It's not like I had anything to do," Arial said.

CJ heard the sadness creep into Arial's voice. It had been almost six months since Arial's divorce had become final and the process had been a difficult one to watch.

Arial's demeanor changed drastically in a matter of days. She went from being the first person in the office every morning to not coming in at all. When the others in the clinic wanted CJ to fire Arial, she refused. Instead, she stood by her friend and allowed her to take time off to collect herself.

When it came to Nick Schoemann, CJ always felt something was amiss. She had told Bethany Rose that he made her "spidey senses" tingle and not in a good way. CJ had always found Nick to be shady at best, but it wasn't until he cleaned out Arial's bank accounts and fled the state that CJ discovered how much of a jerk Nick Schoemann had actually been.

Nick made business deals with less than reputable characters and dragged Arial's credit along for the ride. Once the investigation began the authorities found a trail of false identities and scams across the country. Unfortunately, they had also found enough documents with Arial's signature forged on them to choke a Clydesdale.

Luckily for Arial, Florida was an equitable distribution state, meaning she would be responsible for what the courts deemed fair, unfortunately that amount was still more than she could afford on her salary.

CJ helped by securing Arial a good attorney, but that was the best she could do. Short of winning the lottery, there was no way CJ could help momentarily. Besides, she knew Arial would never accept money from her.

Nick's infidelity also came to the forefront during the divorce. He conveniently blamed Arial's weight for his transgressions, although her weight had not changed the whole-time CJ had known her. Thinking about him filled CJ with anger.

One day, CJ thought. One day that rat bastard will get what is coming to him, and I hope I am there to see it.

Nick's leaving had broken Arial's heart, but CJ was sure her friend realized it was the best thing that could have happened.

"How long are you going to let this go on?" Arial asked glancing at CJ.

"Hmm. Sorry." CJ took her attention back to the jeep and its occupants. "I thought they would have stopped."

CJ squinted her eyes in an attempt to focus on the man inside the jeep. She was under the assumption he was the same man who had called in earlier that morning to the emergency vet line. According to him, he was only in town for a few days, and his dog, who normally traveled well, seemed to have taken ill on this trip.

Usually it took more than something so minor to make CJ open the clinic on a Sunday, but the man's voice held an eerie familiarity that CJ refused to ignore. Suspicions lurked in her mind, yet the thought was too ludicrous and utterly impossible even to her.

CJ took one last sip and handed her coffee cup back to Arial. Grabbing her rain slicker from the tree stand next to the door, she charged out into the weather. Quickly she jerked open the passenger side door to the jeep.

"What are you trying to do to this animal?" She snapped as she popped her head inside the door. Both Mika and Ghost ceased their fighting.

He is trying to choke me to death, Ghost grumbled.

"I am not," Mika replied.

"Are not what?" CJ noticed the dog's muzzle was merely inches from her own face. She pulled back slightly to see that he held a black leather collar in his jaws. "You were fighting over a collar?" CJ asked, rolling her eyes as she took the collar in her hand. "Give," she commanded to Ghost.

Without so much as a tug, Ghost relinquished the collar Mika had fought so valiantly to acquire. "You don't need this, do you?" She shot a quick glance at Mika, locking onto his gaze the moment her eyes met his.

The world tilted under her feet as waves of calm and peace washed over her. Somewhere inside she felt a connection to this man that rocked her to the center of her being. Without warning, her eyes filled with tears as her heart recognized the one who sat before her.

It was as if she could see past his long braids and ruddy complexion to see who he truly was. Inside CJ's mind, the realist wrestled with the dreamer, confusing her. She tried to speak, but words couldn't form in her brain.

Ghost leaned forward and gently touched his cold, damp nose to CJ's cheek, bringing her back to the present.

"Wha...?" She asked as she rubbed the moisture from her cheek. CJ stepped back from the jeep trying to ignore her rising panic. "Come on boy," she said to the wolf. "Let's go inside."

Willingly Ghost obeyed, running quickly into the dry comfort of the clinic, closely followed by CJ. Being a gentleman, Ghost trotted across the waiting room before shaking to remove the water from his fur. When he was done, he walked back to the door.

"Ummm, Doc?" Arial asked, admiring the large white dog next to her.

"Yes?"

"What kind of dog is this? He's beautiful. Big, but beautiful."

Ghost leaned his body against Arial's legs. *You're not so bad yourself,* he thought and sat down at her feet.

CJ knew without a doubt what type of "dog" Ghost was. It was the same type of dog from her dream the other night. She removed her rain-gear, glancing at the animal.

"He isn't a dog actually. He is Canus lupus arctos," CJ answered.

"Arctos? As in Arctic?" Arial asked in surprise.

"Yep," CJ answered as she hung the gear back in place. "In other words, an Arctic wolf."

"What the heck?" Arial burst out. "Is it, you know, safe to be this close?" Ghost jerked his face toward her. "Sorry baby," Arial apologized as she gently rubbed the velvety fur of his ears between her fingers. Ghost, not being one to ignore attention, leaned his head into her hand.

"He seems perfectly tame where you are concerned," CJ replied. In fact, if CJ's assumptions were correct she knew Arial would be okay.

"What is he doing here? An animal like this shouldn't be owned by anyone. He's not a poodle you know."

Thank you, Ghost said. *I couldn't agree more.*

CJ did not agree with wild animals being kept as pets, but she knew there could possibly be extenuating circumstances where this one was concerned. Although, she couldn't fathom what would lead two diverse beings as the man in the jeep and an Arctic wolf to be together. CJ waited for Arial's normal rant about her views on wild animals being kept in captivity, but none came.

"You okay?" CJ asked as she noticed Arial continued to stare down at the wolf, her gaze locked on his.

"That was weird," said Arial.

"What was?" CJ asked, running her fingers through her hair in a vain attempt at removing the tangles that insisted on staying there.

"I would have sworn—I thought—he thanked me," she blurted out.

"He did," CJ said, trying to appear undisturbed by Arial's statement since she had heard it also.

But for CJ, hearing an animals' thoughts was a way of life. She had done so since childhood. However, there was a difference between this wolf and the animals she treated in her clinic.

Unlike the wolf at Arial's feet, most animals thought in pictures not words and definitely not complete sentences. CJ quickly thought of Minky and how he, too, thought in complete sentences. It was a fact that confused her greatly as she grew-up.

Swallowing hard, CJ fought to tamp down her rising anxiety. "Where is the owner?"

"Still in the jeep." Arial took a sip of coffee and resumed petting the white wolf that seemed determined to lie against her.

CJ returned to the door. Sure enough Mika remained seated behind the steering wheel, his body straight and eyes staring foreword. "Geeze Louise, don't make me have to go get him too."

Mika, get in here. Ghost sent the message to his friend. He even barked to get Mika's attention, but there was no movement from the jeep.

"Arial," CJ began. "Could you please take our patient into exam room one?"

"Uh, sure." Arial touched Ghost between the ears to get his attention. "Come on boy. Let's go."

Ghost looked up at her, then back at the jeep. *Mika, this isn't funny. They are calling me boy and you know how I hate that,* Ghost pleaded.

"Do you know his name?" Arial asked as she started across the room. "I don't think he likes to be called boy."

"No. His owner never told me," CJ answered, biting back the urge to call out the name of the wolf from her dream— Æger. It danced on her tongue longing to be set free.

Again, CJ's rational mind told her it was only a dream. Yet her heart knew it to be true. Still she questioned the possibility.

Ghost, my name is ghost. He sent his thoughts to her.

"Okay, then I'll call him Ghost." Arial chirped and continued to the exam room.

Ghost stopped motionless and stared at Arial.

When she realized her companion was not longer at her side, Arial stopped. "Come on," she cooed. "I won't hurt you."

Lady, that's the least of my worries. Ghost's gaze narrowed as he scanned Arial from top to bottom coming to rest at her feet. *Did you know you have on two different color socks?* He sent the thought out to Arial, who immediately adjusted her pant leg in order to see her socks.

"Funny, wolf, very funny," Arial smiled down at Ghost. "You keep that up and I'll start calling you Fluffy," she teased.

Ghost took a step back. *What the—Lucy, you got some 'splainin to do!* Ghost called out to Mika.

"What did you say?"

"Nothing," Arial shook her head. "Fluffy here is being difficult."

Hey!

Arial smiled sweetly and ignored Ghost's protest.

Out of the corner of her eye, CJ could see Ghost and Arial retreat into the examination room. When CJ was alone, she released her calm façade and her body began to tremble. She crossed her arms, holding tightly to her body, trying to stop the tremors. The rain had nearly stopped and she could see the man in the jeep better. He was definitely Native American, though not of Seminole heritage. That much she could tell.

Even if she had not seen him up close moments ago she would still be able to tell he was incredibly handsome. There was always something about dark men that made her weak, but with this man there was more than inherent good looks. The instant her eyes met his was the instant CJ had taken momentary leave of her senses. She recognized him or something about him yet she was positive they had never met before.

CJ was not the best at remembering names, but he was a man who would never escape her memory. However, it was not his physical appearance she inwardly acknowledged; it was his soul. A soul wrapped not in the form of a man, but in that of a dog.

Sunmanitu. The voice she had come to know and love all these years shimmered in her thoughts. It was her protector, friend and confidant. Coyote, it translated. Not dog.

CJ gasped. This is crazy, she thought. I'm crazy.

Say it Cikala Wicahpi. He urged. *Say the words I long to hear fall from your lips.*

CJ felt light headed. Only he had ever called her by the name, Little Star. When she was a child she thought the words he taught her were a made-up language.

I cannot come to you, unless you speak my name. That was my promise to you, remember? The voice reminded her.

This isn't real. You are not real, she stressed.

Know that I am as real now as I was then; do not let others fear cloud what you know in your heart to be true.

Not since the day she pushed him from her life had CJ spoken Minky's name aloud. A simple five letter word, it became a powerful talisman she carried close to her heart. Even in the darkest times, she refused to utter it aloud for fear he would come. That had been his promise to her. Should she dare? What if the man seated merely a few feet away was truly the living, breathing incarnation of her guardian angel?

What if she called out to him and he did not respond? She would feel the fool, and the little part of her that held onto hope of his being more than a trick of light and shadow, would die in the wake of the knowledge she had truly made him up.

Trust your heart, the voice continued. *It speaks only truth to you.*

CJ took a deep breath. Summoning all her courage, she whispered into the mist four little words that alone seemed so benign, yet in concert would change her life forever. "Minky, I need you."

Barely had the words time to form upon the wind, before Mika was there. He stood silently before her in the haze of the fading rain. "Is it really you?" she whispered.

Mika nodded slowly in confirmation to her statement. The shock that a man, this man, could be her imaginary friend was too great for CJ's mind to accept.

She rocked on her heels. Her body becoming lead as the world swirled about her, dragging her into darkness. She fell into something solid and warm. It was there against her back, cradling her. The scent of the rain and earth flooded her nostrils, calming her.

CJ did not fight against the feeling. Instead she allowed the comfort of the darkness to carry her further and further down. It spun and whirled like a tornado in her mind. One after another the images of people and animals flew by quickly, eventually stopping on the face of the man who claimed to be Minky.

Slowly her tunnel vision widened and CJ found herself on the banks of a large crystal blue lake. Snow capped mountains reflected in the mirrored waters. The solitary cry of an eagle took her attention skyward and she watched as the powerful bird dove at break-neck speed towards the water. With graceful strength, the eagle plucked his dinner from the lake and flew off toward the mountains.

Words were not strong enough to describe the emotions running through CJ. She felt drunk and sober, anxious and excited, yet calm and serene. There was no physical pain only the sensation of floating. She searched the deep recesses of her mind and came to the only logical conclusion.

"Am I dead?" She directed the question to the man at her side.

"No," he answered with a hint of humor. "You are not dead."

"Then...am I dreaming?"

"No, not a dream either."

"Then where are we and who exactly are you?" she asked.

"Do you not know me?" Mika spoke directly to her, yet continued to stare out into the middle of the lake. There was sadness in his voice, and CJ was unsure if the sadness belonged to her or to something else.

Did she know the man at her side? Her heart said yes, but her mind said no. Without shame or guilt, CJ stared at her companion.

He was taller than she by maybe four inches, no more. The earrings he wore were made from real feathers, wrapped with silver wire. The one closest to her swayed gently from the beating of his heart. Her gaze followed the long length of his braids to where they ended slightly above his belt.

The sleeves of the scarlet shirt he wore were rolled up exposing his forearms. Try as she might, CJ couldn't stop the woman in her from wondering if the skin beneath his shirt was the same deep sun-kissed color as the part she saw.

A laugh, deep and masculine, echoed across the lake. She would have thought it her imagination, had the sound not been followed by the plopping of frogs as they scattered into the water in surprise.

CJ's lifted her gaze to Mika's face. Still he stared ahead, unwavering. "Are you going to answer me?" she asked.

"The answer is yes," he said.

"Excuse me?"

"Yes, my skin is the same color all over."

"I did not mean...How did you..."

"I have been inside your mind since you were a child. It is easy for me to slip in and out of your thoughts without your notice."

CJ grunted and crossed her arms over her chest in defiance.

"Forgive me. I did not mean to embarrass you," he whispered.

"You didn't. I, uh…" Okay, she thought. I am embarrassed. Dang it! "You still did not answer my original question," she said trying to change the subject.

"Does that mean you have finished taking inventory?" he asked with a hint of male smugness.

CJ blushed, but felt no true remorse. "You asked if I did not know you. I was only checking to see if I recognized you. Which, I am sorry to say I did not."

"Very well," he said, facing her.

Though there was little emotion in his voice, his eyes held a pain and longing CJ did not understand, yet felt compelled to erase.

Mika took her hand in his and placed it over his heart. Her pulse quickened at his touch.

"What…uh…what are you...?" She stammered.

"Do not speak, Charlie Jean," he said. "Only trust."

CJ peered deep into his caramel eyes. Gold flecks twinkled and danced in a way that was mesmerizing. If he asked her to walk on a bed of hot coals at this moment, she would do it for him.

"Close your eyes," he requested as he brought up his other hand to cover her eyelids with his palm.

If any other man had tried to touch her in such a way, CJ would have pulled away, but she ignored her mind's protests and did as he asked. With eyes closed, CJ allowed Mika to guide her wherever he wished.

"I need to know that you trust me, Wicahpi. Truly trust me."

CJ nodded her obedience. "I do," she whispered. "I don't know why, but I do." Even with her eyes closed, she knew her statement had made him smile, and that made her happy.

"This is real CJ. I am real. I need you to open your mind," he instructed her. "Open you mind and your heart. Allow them to guide you to our Mother. She gives us all the answers. It is our job to know how to receive them."

Time held no influence over the events that were taking place. For CJ, it seemed to be both an eternity and mere seconds. The heat of Mika's body radiated though his shirt to penetrate her hand, and the rhythm of his heart pulsed strong and steady through her fingertips and into her body.

"Listen. Can you hear it? Can you hear my heart beat?

"Yes," she whispered.

"As my heart beats, so does that of every living thing upon the Earth. Every creature. Every plant. Even the water. Can you hear those?"

Timidly, CJ opened her heart and her senses to the world about her. She heard the breeze as it whispered through the pines and recognized the songs of the different birds that sang along its branches.

The world around her buzzed and thrummed. Each sound blended with the next to create a symphony that played in time to the beat of Mika's heart.

The hum surrounded her. It permeated every pore and cell of her body. It intermingled with the beat of her heart and joined it with that of the world about her.

"You feel it. Don't you?" Mika asked.

"I feel it, but—but what is it?"

"Connection," he explained. "Connection to the Universe and all she has to offer you. Do you believe me?"

CJ nodded her acceptance of his words.

"Then speak to her, for she is your mother."

CJ felt a moment of panic. "I don't know how."

"Merely ask with your heart and listen. Whatever comes to you, no matter how strange or odd it may seem, is the truth. Mother cannot lie."

Again, CJ nodded. She had trusted him so far, so why not all the way. She licked her lips to speak, but instead she did as Mika instructed and asked with her heart. *Who is the man before me and why do I trust him so?*

Why do you ask such a question? A voice not quite feminine, yet not masculine answered her. The answer seemed to come from inside as well as out. *Your heart already knows him, does it not?*

But what my heart thinks cannot be true, CJ argued.

And why is that?

*Because, that would mean he is...*CJ paused. She couldn't bring herself to voice her assumptions, even in her own mind.

Is what, my daughter? What must he be? The voice urged CJ to answer.

It would mean the impossible. That he is, that he is an animal, yet he stands before me as a man...

Do you think that your own heart would lie to you? The Universe asked.

No, CJ answered.

Then trust your heart. Believe in yourself.

Trust - a small word with enormous implications. CJ trusted very few and often questioned her own actions. In the whole of her life there had been, and was, only one being she had ever trusted, and she had sent him away.

Uncontrollable sadness washed over her. If only she had not been a child, she would not have sent him away. Tears stung the back of CJ's eyes. How could she have hurt him so? How could she have let her mother hurt her so?

In all these years, no man had ever come close to possessing Minky's strength and compassion. True, he had stayed close to her. Still, even though he was a constant shadow inside her mind, it was not the same as having him physically near.

Many times, she had thought herself crazy to compare all the men she met to an imaginary dog. But Minky had a pure and beautiful soul, much like the soul of man whose heartbeat lay beneath her hand. *Can it be? Is it possible?* CJ questioned.

It is all possible, my daughter.

Then tell me what it all means. Why am I here?

If CJ had not known better she would have sworn the Universe smirked at her question. *My child,* the voice answered patiently. *You are here because it is time for you to take your rightful place as Guardian and protector.*

Protector of whom?

CJ had become so entranced by the slow steady rhythm of the Universe, she had not noticed Mika's release of her hand nor that he stepped away from her.

Open your eyes my daughter. The disembodied voice called to her. *See the one before you for who he really is and allow yourself to accept the gifts a mother has to offer.*

As the last words faded into oblivion, CJ did as asked. She opened her eyes. Barely three feet away stood the coyote from her childhood. "Minky?" She whispered as she fell upon her knees before him.

Yes and no, answered the coyote. *My true name is Mika, but you have long called me the other.*

As she beheld her long-time friend, CJ felt an understanding creep deep into the core of her being. It was as if she unlocked a hidden door and stepped inside. Without a doubt, she understood who she was and what she was to do.

All the years of strange dreams and voices inside her head had led her to this moment and this man. Gingerly she reached her hand toward Mika's muzzle and did as the Universe asked.

With an open heart and mind she viewed the creature before her. Briefly an image of his face morphed from that of a coyote into that of a man. To most the superimposed image might have seemed strange, but not to CJ. For once in her life all was as it should be.

"It truly is you," she whispered as she pressed the palm of her hand against his cheek.

Yes. He answered telepathically.

"And this place," CJ said glancing about. "What is this place?"

This is Haven. He said as he pushed his forehead against hers. *And soon it will be your home.*

CHAPTER FOURTEEN

"Dr. Grey," Mina Greer chirped as he walked into the front door of the old Victorian that housed the main offices of the Theriontrope Foundation.

He took the small slips of paper from her hand. "Greetings, Mina. Anything of interest?" Dr. Grey smiled kindly at his assistant as he shuffled through his messages, reading each briefly as he did.

"Nothing exactly, doctor," Mina fidgeted in place. "Except..." she paused.

Something in her tone brought Michael's attention away from what he was doing. He looked at her over the top of wire-rimmed glasses. "Except?" he coaxed.

Mina cut her eyes nervously and pointed toward his office door. "She's here," Mina whispered, shielding her mouth with her hand.

Dr. Grey stiffened. Even without Mina saying his visitor's name, Dr. Grey knew exactly who "she" was. "You do not have to whisper, Mina," he chided playfully.

"I can't help it. She scares me."

Dr. Grey leaned forward and gave Mina a fatherly kiss on her forehead in an attempt to alleviate her anxiety where Theriontrope's benefactor was concerned.

The Theriontrope Foundation belonged to Michael Grey. He had taken it upon himself to oversee the day-to-day operations and care of the foundation which encompassed the guardians, shifters, Haven and of course Delta Pack.

It was a large job and, over the years, he learned to rely on a network of human observers and helpers. The network was comprised of people from every walk of life and all were friends of shape-shifters. But no matter how large the network was, there was only one that held the purse strings and as with all companies, the one with the money held the real power.

With the recent developments at Haven, the death of Charles Stone and the near death of Ghost, Michael knew it was only a matter of time before she contacted him. He had not, however, expected her to come to Theriontrope offices in person.

"How long has she been here?" He asked.

"She was here when I came in," Mina said. "It always un-nerves me when she pops in like that."

"Hmm. I guess I had best not keep her waiting then," he said and patted Mina on the arm. "I will send for you if need be."

"Yes, Doctor."

Taking a deep breath, Michael straightened his jacket and headed to his office. "Forgive me," he said as he entered the room. "If I had known you were coming, I would have been here sooner."

"I have all the time in the world," she said crossing her long legs. "There is no rush."

"Of course," he replied. "To what do I owe this honor?"

The beautiful blonde smiled up at him. "Do not play coy with me, Grey. You know exactly why I am here." She paused briefly adjusting the buttons on her jacket. "No matter how often I journey to this world I will never get accustomed to these bindings," she spoke aloud, but mainly to herself.

Eventually, her attention came back to Michael Grey. He shifted under her weighted gaze. Though he had known the woman across from him for more centuries than he could count, occasionally she would look at him in a way he had yet to decipher.

"Tell me Grey, the shape-shifter called Ghost, he is fully recovered?"

"He is in perfect health."

"Healed by the dream-walker?"

"Yes."

"And soon she will take her father's place in Haven?"

"Both Mika and Ghost have gone to retrieve her and bring her back to Haven. If she will come," he added.

"You worry too much, Grey. The girl knows her place. She may not fully understand, but she knows."

Michael watched his benefactor as she rose and walked to stand before the oversized mirror that covered the length of wall behind his desk. The mirror was made of obsidian and framed in silver, with the images of a bear, wolf and cougar intricately carved into the white metal. The three stood as silent watch guards over his every move.

He was thankful the relief could neither see nor hear what took place in his office, but there were times that he was not so sure.

"I have always liked this mirror," she said.

Grey remained silent. What was there to say? Of course, she liked the mirror. It had been made and placed in his office at her command. Besides, he knew that where she was concerned silence was normally the best option.

"The question becomes what is to happen to those responsible for the death of Charles? They have broken Haven's gravest law." She said, adjusting a twig of hair that worked loose from ornate combs.

Dr. Grey cleared his throat before he spoke. "According to Ghost the assailants were human, not shifter."

"It matters not," she countered. "The puppets may have been human. The puppet master, need I remind you, is not." She paused amid preening to watch him for a moment. "You do know of whom I speak?"

"I have an idea."

"I'm sure you do." She smiled. "I have always trusted you, Grey," she said as she trailed her fingers across his jaw line. "And always will."

In the eons Michael Grey had served the benefactor of Theriontrope Foundation, she seldom if ever gave praise. Silently he bowed his head in acknowledgment of her statement.

"How long do you think it will take?" he asked to forget the feel of her touch upon his skin.

"Until?"

"Until Haven begins to start changing?"

"I do not know. She, like all females, can be fickle, but you should know that as well as I." She laughed softly. The sound wrapped around him like a blanket. Warm. Soft. Completely inviting. "Tell me, Grey. Do you remember when I placed you in charge of what you refer to as the Theriontrope Foundation?"

Michael Grey stood for a moment, wondering if he was being tested in some way. Of course, he remembered the day she placed him in charge of watching over the Guardians and shape-shifters. At the time, he had no idea what his life would be like and on more than one occasion, he had to ask himself, would he do it again? Unfortunately, the answer was always the same—a thousand times yes.

The woman waved her hand before the mirror, turning the black surface translucent, revealing her personal doorway to and from the land of the Gods.

"Elskede," she said using a term he had not heard in centuries. "Beloved one. I know you grow weary from this job and it is my solemn oath to you, that once this is sorted out, you shall be rewarded."

"My reward is but to serve my Goddess."

"The words of a compliant servant," she sighed. "After all this time Valborg," she called him by his ancient name. "I thought..." the Goddess let the words drop and stepped through the glass to the other side. "It is you alone I trust Grey. It is you who must keep safe my children." With another wave of her delicate hand the portal closed.

His heart almost soared the moment he heard his true name fall from her perfect lips. He had forgotten how much a simple word could mean. The Goddess had given him his name when he was but a child. How funny that the name she chose came to represent so much in his life, Guardian to the Guardians.

Michael exhaled slowly. Try as he might, he couldn't get the feel of her flesh against his out of his mind. Her scent. The soft lilt of her voice. That and much more would remain etched in his mind for all time.

CHAPTER FIFTEEN

Charlie Jean opened her eyes to find herself lying on the smoke colored sofa in her office. Made of leather and overtly masculine, the sofa was the one thing she had splurged on since opening her practice. She envisioned it as the type of thing she might have inherited from her father had she known him.

A pair of silver blue eyes amidst solid white fur stared down at her. Slowly CJ reached out her hand and caressed the velvety soft fur of the animal's muzzle and chin. Recognition passed between her and the wolf, and without doubt she knew that this was the wolf she had healed in her dream.

"Æger Thorolfur," she whispered to him. The white wolf closed his eyes and dipped his head slightly in a show of affirmation. CJ smiled. She was not crazy. Ghost was not some image she had conjured up from her subconscious. She had walked through dreams and healed him.

"My beautiful boy," she said. "It really is you."

A gentle pressure against her legs took CJ's attention from Ghost. Mika was seated next to her. His left arm braced against the back of the sofa, the other gently touching her leg.

He is real, she whispered into the corners of her own mind. Her heart leaping with joy. This is all real.

Mika leaned into her slightly, his eyes penetrating deep into her soul. In her hidden thoughts, CJ doubted that anything could shake him. Her heart warmed at the memories of her childhood and the coyote that watched over her.

He is a coyote. This beautiful man, with eyes the color of toffee was actually an animal. The thought sounded foreign in her mind.

Her head throbbed and the room swirled slightly as she pulled her body upright. Automatically, Mika adjusted his position so CJ could lean against him.

"You are not well," Mika said. Concern may not have shown in his face, but it did in his voice.

A small, but sharp pain began above CJ's right eye. Yippee. Another migraine. Sunlight, what little there was, assaulted her sensitive eyes. Unable to focus, she screwed her eyes tightly shut.

"What is this?" Mika asked. She felt his hand reach underneath her hair and begin to gently massage the back of her neck.

"Migraine," she winced. "They happen every time I go into that dream world thingy."

Mika looked to Ghost who immediately left the room.

"Where is he going?" She asked softly.

"To get your friend," he answered and continued kneading the knot that had formed at the back of her neck.

"How can he..." CJ stopped her question. Things in her world were starting to change and something told her that if she could hear Mika when he spoke to her mind, then it might be possible for Arial to hear Ghost.

Before Mika could answer Arial appeared in the doorway.

"I believe your friend is in need of something to eat," he stated. "Do you have anything here? Preferably something with sugar."

"I'm sure I can find something," Arial answered and left the room with Ghost close at her heels.

"I don't think I can eat anything," CJ said. The mere thought of food made her stomach lurch. "Especially anything sweet."

"You must," Mika said. "To walk the In-between takes much energy. You need to replenish your energy and sugar works quickly."

The pair sat in silence and waited for Arial. Through her pain, CJ noticed Mika's thumb tracing a lazy pattern along the inside of her wrist, just above her pulse. The motion was hypnotic and CJ found her breath synchronizing with the rhythm of his movement.

You aren't gonna believe this, Ghost said as Arial handed Mika a familiar box.

"Twinkies?" Mika stared at the item in disbelief.

"She's addicted to those things." Arial stated. "It is almost as bad as her coffee addiction."

Even though Mika said nothing aloud as he pulled the Twinkie from its wrapper, CJ could tell a conversation passed between him and Ghost. Maybe if her head had not been about to explode she would have cared. She ignored the spongy cake that Mika pushed toward her, trying not to throw-up.

"How can you be sure this will help?" she asked, taking the item offered.

"Something your fa...a friend once told me," Mika explained.

CJ gagged as she tried to eat the Twinkie. "Really, I can't."

Really you must. Mika gave a mental push to his statement.

Looking at those around her, CJ realized this was a battle she would not win. Reluctantly, she ate. "Is he?" she pointed at Ghost who once again pressed himself against Arial who had taken a seat on the floor.

"Is he what?" Arial asked protectively, her arm wrapped around his body.

"Is he...still acting strangely?" CJ tried to cover her almost blunder.

"At the moment, I find him acting quite normal," Mika mumbled aloud. But, he continued on the telepathic line between them. *Ghost is like me.*

What do you mean like you? He's not a dog? she asked.

Ghost sighed in frustration. *I...am...a...wolf.* He spoke slowly. *Mika tell her. I'm a wo-hoa...wait, I can hear her.*

Yes, and she can hear you. Mika glanced up at Arial, then back to Ghost. *Ghost is both man and animal. For us the two halves reside within the same body, whether we are in human form or animal form.*

But you are not a wolf? CJ stated.

No, Ghost, Fergus and Saint are wolves. Mika explained.

Fergus and Saint?

The others. You will meet them once you move to Haven. He answered, gently tucking a stray curl behind her ear.

"Okay y'all," Arial broke in. "I don't know what is going on here, but for some reason I feel like a third wheel or something." She said as she pushed herself off the floor. "Sweetie, you feeling better?" Arial placed a hand on her friend's shoulder.

"Much. Thank you."

Arial shot a questioning glance at Mika then back to CJ. "I'll be in the front if you need me, okay?"

"I'll be fine," CJ answered as she squeezed Arial's hand. Arial nodded and started to leave the room. Ghost rose to follow.

"No Fluffy, you need to stay here," Arial said as she placed a hand down to stop him.

"Fluffy?" Mika asked as Arial closed the door.

"Don't ask. It's something between them." CJ said.

"Fluffy?" Mika seemed stupefied by the word.

Let it go. CJ heard the annoyance in Ghost's voice as he sat before the couple.

"So, let me see if I can get this straight," CJ said. She leaned a bit forward and propped her hands on her knees. "The two of you are what? Were-wolves?"

"Most of us prefer the term shape-shifter or simply shifter, since we are not all wolves or canines for that matter," Mika answered.

"Okay." CJ gave time for Mika's answer soak in. "Then why are you human and he is a wolf?"

He made me. Ghost accused.

"It did not hurt you," Mika said to Ghost. "Besides, I thought it would be the best way for us to gain entry into your clinic."

Rising, CJ walked to her desk and leaned against the edge. Her strength was returning and the spots behind her eyes began to disperse.

"Couldn't you call me or something?" She asked trying to wrap her brain around the events going on around her.

"This isn't a dream, CJ. We are not an apparition of your imagination."

"Why now?"

"Because," Mika answered and rose from the sofa to stand before her. "It is as it has to be."

"That isn't an answer," she said.

Mika pleaded with Ghost for help.

You're on your own here pal. Ghost answered and jumped up on the couch.

Mika took in a deep breath. "There is much about this Universe that is not understood or explained. Many things simply are."

"Like you and Fluffy being shape-shifters?" She asked.

"Yes, like me and Fluff—"

Hey! Ghost blurted out.

"My apologies, old friend," Mika addressed Ghost, before answering CJ's question. "But yes, like Ghost and me, we are all shape—shifters. You know this to be true."

As much as it confused her, CJ knew he was right. He spoke the truth. She had seen Mika both as man and animal and, as strange as her world was becoming, it was as it should be.

It was obvious to her that for some inexplicable reason, her life was tied to the man before her. To be with him, where ever that may be, was the right place to be. The thought brought her both fear and excitement.

But she had so many questions.

"All your questions will be answered in their time," Mika broke into her thoughts.

"If we are going to have any type of a relationship, you have got to stop reading my mind," CJ smiled up at him.

"My apologizes, Little Star. I have done it so long, it is a part of me."

CJ let it go. How could she argue with the truth? Mika's being inside her mind was as much a part of her as her own heartbeat. She wondered about the difference between human and animal. How could a man change into a wolf? True, Ghost was inordinately large for a wolf, but still… "Can I see it?" CJ asked.

"It?" Mika seemed confused.

"It. You know the change. I want to see you change into a coyote."

Mika seemed momentarily shaken at her request, but any distress quickly disappeared. She watched as he crossed arms over his chest as he pondered the question. A rather muscular chest she noted, and a tiny part of her jumped for joy at the thought of possibly seeing him without a shirt. After all, one couldn't switch into an animal while wearing a collared shirt and Levi's could they?

"Ghost," Mika called.

Hmm? Ghost asked. Yawning.

"Shift."

What? Here? Now?

"She knows in her heart. She must see it with her eyes," Mika explained.

*Do you realize what you are asking? I mean, I'm going to be...*Ghost paused.

"Be what?" CJ asked.

Naked, Ghost answered bluntly.

"And this is a problem for you?" Mika asked.

Not for me, Ghost stated as he climbed down from the sofa.

"I have seen naked men before," CJ added.

You are not who I am worried about. Ghost said. *You're sure about this?* He asked one last time to Mika.

"It is what must be."

As you wish, Ghost said as he prepared for the change to come.

"Oh, and Ghost?"

Yeah?

"No catch phrases this time," Mika requested.

You know you really take all the fun out of this. Without another word, Ghost took his place in the center of the room.

Images of were-wolf transformations from old movies ran through her head. The movies always seemed to depict the shifting process as violent and painful. However gross and gory, CJ was ready for the worst nature had to offer.

She watched the wolf close his eyes and lift his head toward the sky as if he were about to bay at the moon. The change within him began subtly. Light radiated outward from the core of his chest. Energy flowed along his fur causing a change in the charge of the ions in the air, and CJ felt the fine hairs along her body begin to rise.

Ghost's body became a translucent ball of light, growing brighter with each passing second, until without warning he burst into a million tiny particles of light. CJ covered her mouth to stifle the small scream that rose in her throat.

Like glitter upon the wind, the tiny points of light sifted and danced in the spot where the wolf once stood. The particles expanded upward and outward, then quickly contracted one last time into the form of a man. Definitely not like the movies, she thought.

Unashamed in his nakedness, Ghost stood before her, his head tossed back and arms outstretched. The visage of exquisite ecstasy played upon his face. Slowly he tilted his head forward until his ice blue gaze met hers. A roguish smile crossed his face and he winked playfully at her. A crimson blush rushed up CJ's neck, flooding her cheeks.

Speechless, Charlie Jean pushed herself away from the desk and walked toward him. She allowed her eyes to roam over his body as she circled him. He was as tall as Mika, but that was where the similarities ended. Where Mika was darkness, Ghost was light.

Front to back Ghost's body was perfection. She was amazed by the sight of the fine platinum hair that dusted lightly tanned flesh along his chest and arms. He was as sleek and trim as his wolf counterpart. With a cursory glance, CJ noted Ghost's body was without blemish. Not even a freckle or birthmark covered his skin.

"As you can see, we are as much man as we are animal," Mika stated.

"I'll say," CJ whispered breathlessly, not taking her gaze from Ghost's body. Had she not seen the transformation for herself she would not have believed it. Mere inches separated her from Ghost, and she became mesmerized by the knowledge of what was. His hair was an odd mixture of white and gold, similar to that of the wolf he had been before, and it fell in perfect layers above where his collar would be, if he wore a shirt. The slight indention in his chin caught her off guard, but in retrospect was as it should be. He appeared angelic, almost childlike.

CJ studied every inch of his face. That is where she found Ghost's one imperfection. A ragged scar ran beneath his chin and along his throat. When in wolf form, the scar was imperceptible. It had faded over time, but CJ could tell it was meant to be fatal. Involuntarily, her hand came up to trace the line of the scar.

"Do not touch him," Mika growled.

She had not seen Mika move, yet his hand firmly gripped her wrist, halting her fingers and their exploration of Ghost's body.

CJ blinked up at him confused and embarrassed. "I only wanted to examine his scar." Aggravated by the overwhelming need to explain her actions, CJ tried to wrench her arm from Mika's grasp.

Why should she care what this man thought? She would touch whom and what she pleased.

"Humph," Mika grunted as he released her.

If CJ was honest with herself, she would admit that Ghost truly was one of the most beautiful men she had ever seen. But even naked, he was nothing compared to her Mika.

Her Mika? CJ faltered for a moment, then re-gained her composure. It was perfectly valid to consider him to belong to her. After all, Mika had been with her most of her life. It was only right that she felt some possession over him. Before the thought could take hold, CJ plucked it from her mind and cast it aside.

Without warning, Ghost sprang toward the door. CJ jerked back to avoid being plowed over. She watched as he leaned his head against the door and held up his hand for silence. CJ had no idea what had captured Ghost's attention. Without thought, she reached for Mika. Comfort and peace surrounded her the moment she took his hand.

The sound of arguing voices could be heard rising from the outer office. "Rat bastard," CJ hissed under her breath.

"Who?" Mika asked.

"Arial's ex-jerk," she answered.

"No!" The group heard Arial's shout, followed by the sounds of scuffling. CJ reached for the door and pulled hard, but it did not budge. In her anxiety, she did not realize Mika had placed his body between her and Ghost, his shoulder holding the door firmly in place.

CHAPTER SIXTEEN

"Open the door!" CJ commanded.

"I cannot," Mika answered calmly.

"What?" she shook her head. "Why not?"

"Ghost needs to shift."

Confused, CJ glanced from one man to another. "What?"

"Ghost must be wolf, not human when that door opens."

Without another word, Ghost called forth his wolf form. The bright light that accompanied his transformation forced CJ to shield her eyes. What seemed to take minutes before, took mere seconds. When there was time, CJ would ask, but Arial needed her.

As soon as Ghost's transformation was complete, Mika pulled the door open.

Without thought of consequence, Ghost raced down the hallway and toward Arial's voice. The slick tile floor made traction difficult, but he maintained control as best he could.

Ghost, slow down. He heard Mika's command inside his head, but he did not obey. His one driving thought was Arial's safety.

"Stop!" Mika demanded. "Ghost, Stöðva," Mika hissed in Icelandic.

Despite his urge to charge ahead and rip out the man's throat, Ghost slowed and stopped beyond the hall's doorway and stuck his head around the corner to get a better view.

Arial stood with her back to the hallway door and Ghost. Her body rigid. Unfortunately from his vantage point, Ghost was unable to see the man on the other side of Arial. Tension surrounded the pair causing the fur along the ridge of his back to bristle. *Come on, baby. Step to the side,* Ghost telepathically requested.

To his surprise, Arial stepped to her right, allowing him a better view. She held both hands tightly around a stapler, wielding it like a gun. Had he not been so concerned with her safety, Ghost would have found the scene amusing.

Weasel was the first word that came to Ghost's mind when he saw Nick Schoemann. Ghost was sure he could add a few more adjectives to the list, but before he had a chance, CJ pushed past him to stand next to Arial.

"You are not welcome here," CJ said to Nick.

"Arial asked me here," he retorted.

"I doubt that," CJ snorted.

"Tell her," Nick demanded of Arial.

"It doesn't matter." CJ said as she placed her hands on her hips in defiance. "This is my clinic and I am telling you to leave."

"My wife and I have things to discuss."

"Ex-wife," Arial emphasized. "And we have nothing to talk about."

For Ghost, the time for talk was over. Arial had tried her way. It was time to try his. With teeth bared, Ghost sprang from the doorway, inserting his body between Arial and Nick, forcing the man to take a step back.

Making his stand, Ghost watched and waited. All he wanted was for Nick to twitch the wrong way. Go ahead, make my day, Ghost thought and backed his haunches against Arial's legs.

After a few seconds, he became aware of the minute tremors along her body.

"You have been asked to leave." Ghost heard Mika's voice and knew his friend stood near.

Nick's eyes darted from one person to the next, then came to rest on the white wolf.

"It's not smart to stare a wolf in the eyes," Mika said. "They take it as a challenge." At Mika's prompting, Ghost took a step forward. An almost imperceptible growl of warning rolled in his throat.

"Okay," Nick conceded. "I'll leave." He walked to the door. "But this isn't over." Nick mumbled and left.

Ghost watched Arial's ex drive out of sight. He heard the thump of her body as she collapsed, weak kneed, into the closest chair. Her hands trembled violently. She pulled the clip from her dark red hair and ran her hands through shoulder length tresses. CJ bent down and spoke softly into her ear. Mika, as usual stood back with his arms across his chest, observing.

A small sob escaped Arial's throat, before she began to sob uncontrollably. The agony of the sound pierced Ghost's heart much like the arrow had done previously. Unable to take the sound of her tears, he pushed past CJ to lay his chin upon Arial's leg.

Her body shook from the release of tension and tears. *If only I was still a man,* he thought. If he were then he could put his arms around her, whisper soothing words in her ear and do whatever she asked if it would stop her pain.

Ghost took a mental step backward. It was not that he was without sympathy for others, nor was it unusual for him to want to comfort a woman, but not like this. This was different.

He wanted to ask Mika for guidance, but what was the question? He felt Arial's hand burrow deep into the fur on his back. Involuntarily, his skin rippled from the scruff of his neck to the tip of his tail.

Arial's face was merely inches from his. Her deep brown eyes were still wet with tears and her face was flushed from crying.

Ghost became confused when she placed both hands on either side of his head, making it impossible for him to move his face. Not that he wanted to. "Thank you for coming to my rescue, Fluffy," she said. "You were very brave." Gently, she stroked the velvety fur along his ears.

"Ummm, Arial?" CJ caught her assistant's attention. "Maybe petting him isn't such a good idea."

"Why not?" Arial asked.

Yeah, why not? Ghost reiterated.

Amusement played across Mika's face. "She may pet him if she likes, but" he added so only CJ could hear, *You may not.*

CHAPTER SEVENTEEN

"Come with me," CJ requested as she stared across the Formica table at Mika and then to Ghost who was presently in human form.

Once Arial had calmed down enough to leave, Ghost kept complaining about being hungry, so the group ended up at King's Diner. CJ had about 400 questions that needed answering. Including the difficult ones about her father. To her surprise, both Mika and Ghost were extremely understanding and patient in answering them.

She found comfort in the knowledge Charles Stone had been held in such high regard by the men that sat across from her. She could see it in their eyes and hear it in the tone of their voices when they spoke of him. Yet there was something CJ felt she was missing when it came to the discussion of her father.

Mika and Ghost spoke of him as if his death had been recent, not thirty years ago. *If only I had a chance to have known him.* CJ let the thought go. She needed to think of her future and what it held for her.

According to Mika, the Theriontrope Foundation already had another veterinarian lined up to take over her practice. He also explained that, when she was ready, her home in Navarre would be packed up and shipped to Haven. Haven–her new home. She had not seen it, and yet, she loved it.

The Theriontrope Foundation seemed to have thought of everything. Too bad they hadn't thought of someway to notify

Gypsy Lynn for her. Obviously even they did not feel up to that challenge.

"Mika, please come to Mom's with me," CJ asked.

Mika seemed to ignore her request as he stared blankly out the window. CJ couldn't hear what he was thinking, but she could tell by his demeanor that he was deep in thought at her suggestion. Without an answer, he continued his assault on the extremely rare steak.

"Mika?" she asked when she did not receive an answer.

"I am sorry Little Star. You may ask many things of me, but this I must decline."

There were still a few loose ends she needed to tidy up before leaving and what she asked of Mika was the biggest task of all.

She glanced to Ghost who busily chatted up the waitress of the small diner where they had chosen to eat. No help there.

The thought still seemed foreign to her. Especially when she considered the fact that her house-mates would be shape-shifters, but most importantly Mika would be there. Stubborn, irritating male that he was. Was it too much to ask for him to go with her to her mother's house so she could explain why she was leaving?

"Why not?" CJ asked, taking her attention back to Mika.

"Because it is best that I do not. Besides, this battle is between you and your mother."

"There won't be a battle," she said. "Gypsy will understand."

CJ watched Mika purposefully place his utensils beside his plate. Determined not to let him see how hurt she was by his refusal, CJ leaned back against the red and black striped vinyl seat. Her arms crossed beneath her breast.

"Do you truly believe you will be able to tell your mother you are leaving everyone and everything you have known since childhood, to live and work in Montana and she not have anything to say about it? Do not fool yourself, there will be a battle." Mika continued eating.

Irritation shot through CJ. Mika didn't know everything. Gypsy Lynn might surprise him. She might be okay with everything. Yeah right.

"I'll tell her I was offered a fantastic job to work for a wild life preserve out west and the offer was too good to pass up." CJ could read the doubt written across Mika's face at her suggestion. If truth be told, even CJ found her own rationale hard to accept. Gypsy Lynn Carson was anything but a pushover, especially where her daughter was concerned.

CJ continued in her explanation. She was unsure who she was trying to convince more, Mika or herself. "Seriously, if Mom thinks I am making good money, she won't care. Oh, my..." CJ suddenly stopped her explanation. "I will get paid, won't I? I mean how do I pay off my debts or buy food or clothes?"

"All your needs will be taken care of by the Foundation," Ghost chimed in as the waitress sashayed away.

"Nice of you to join us," CJ snorted.

"Hey, I've been listening the whole time," Ghost said. "I, unlike my brothers, am very adept at multi-tasking." He wiggled his eyebrows as he took a bite of his hamburger, which like Mika's steak, was way too rare for CJ's taste.

"Okay smart guy," she challenged. "What were we talking about?"

"Pass the ketchup and I will tell you. Please." Ghost asked, smiling his million-dollar smile.

CJ took the bottle and held it slightly out of Ghost's reach. "Nope," she said taunting him with the ketchup. "Not until you tell me what we were talking about."

"That's easy," he said and grabbed the bottle from her hand with a quickness she did not expect. "Mika's fear of your mother," he answered and popped a french-fry in his mouth.

"I am not afraid of her mother," Mika protested.

"Whatever." Ghost shook off Mika's rebuttal. "Don't worry CJ. If you need a man around, I'll go."

"You?" CJ and Mika asked simultaneously.

"Sure. A gentleman never leaves a damsel in distress and I am nothing, if not a gentleman."

CJ stared across the booth. She was unsure if she should take Ghost seriously or not. He may have looked like an angel, but mischief lived in his eyes. Out of the corner of her eye, she could see Mika as he gaped at Ghost.

Ghost winked at her playfully, then went back to his hamburger. Whether it was her intuition or a mental push from Ghost, CJ figured out the game her new friend was playing and decided to join in.

"You know, Ghost, I think that is a great idea. I'd love for you to go with me."

"You cannot be serious," Mika shot back.

"Great," Ghost agreed, completely ignoring his partner. "We can go after we finish here."

"Mom will love you," CJ beamed. Both she and Ghost ignored Mika's snort of protest as they planned their trip to see Gypsy Lynn.

"Is there a florist nearby?" Ghost asked.

"Actually, there is one on the way. Why?" CJ hoped her innocent act was working and if Mika's face was any indication, the answer was yes.

"I thought flowers would be a nice touch. What do you think? Roses?"

"Nah, Gypsy Lynn is more the Tiger Lily type."

"Fine. Tiger Lilies it is then."

"No flowers," Mika slammed his glass against the table to drive home his point.

"I'm sorry. Did you say something?" It took all her acting ability not to burst into laughter at the incredulous look on Mika's face. She hated to admit it, but it made her a bit giddy to see that something ruffled his perfect feathers.

"There will be no flowers," he reiterated.

"If Ghost wants to buy my mother flowers then that is fine with me."

"No flowers. No Ghost. I will go with you."

"Excuse me, but you said..." CJ questioned.

"I said I will take you," Mika stated.

"That's okay. Ghost doesn't mind. Do you Ghosty?" CJ asked batting her eyelashes.

"Not at all," Ghost answered.

"You..." Mika directed to Ghost. "You need not concern yourself with going to see Charlie Jean's mother. I said I would take her and I will."

"Only if you insist," Ghost said.

"I do," Mika said.

"Okay," Ghost shrugged.

CJ could tell from the smug smile on Ghost's face he was pleased with the outcome of their little game. CJ couldn't help but smile. She and Ghost had only known each other a few hours and already she had an ally, and where Mika was concerned, she might very well need one.

CHAPTER EIGHTEEN

"Zounds!" Fergus bellowed as he bolted upright in his bed. He had pushed himself to extremes during his workout and fallen into bed for a quick nap after his shower.

Quickly, he rose and slipped on his black jeans before striding from his bedroom. Whoever was making that infernal racket was about to get a good piece of his mind, and he knew it was hard to take a man seriously when he was naked.

"Saint!" he yelled as he descended the grand staircase. "What in the devil are you doing down here?"

Fergus' vision adjusted in the dim light of the hallway chandelier to see Saint standing calmly near the bottom step, a mug of tea in each hand.

"I am waiting for you. Here have some tea," Saint said, thrusting the cup toward Fergus.

"I do not want any tea," Fergus scowled. "And you know that is not what I meant."

"Then you are referring to the banging and such?"

Fergus fought the urge to groan or throttle his brother, and at the moment either was a good option. He had always considered himself a patient man and rarely could one fluster him. But there were times that Saint's innate ability to take things literally pushed him a bit too far. If Fergus had not known better, he would have thought Saint did such things on purpose.

"Yes, Saint," Fergus held a tight grip on his frustration and his tongue. "The banging and such. Where is it coming from?"

"Ah, yes. That, my brother, is the sound of construction," Saint answered, forcing Fergus to accept the mug.

"Who ordered work to be done on Haven?" Fergus grumbled as he took the cup from Saint's hand and walked into the den.

"I do not believe it was a who."

Fergus stilled his motion before the cup had time to reach his lips.

"You mean..."

"Haven," Saint finished his brother's statement.

Fergus took a sip of the warm tea. The perfect amount of milk and honey. How did Saint do it? He always knew exactly what Fergus needed before he did. Another of Saint's irritating qualities, but this one Fergus could live with.

As the tea began to calm his nerves, Fergus tilted his head to listen. The large manor house moaned and creaked under the weight of construction. Sounds of wood splintering and slapping against the side of the house seemed to echo through the forest.

"So, it has begun," Fergus commented.

"It would seem so," Saint answered as he opened the French doors that led to the courtyard and the back of the house.

"Destruction or restoration?" Fergus followed out onto the balcony.

"Who can tell? The sounds are the same."

Both men stared upward to the window of what was once Charles Stone's bedroom. "Surely it is construction," Fergus said.

"That would be my guess."

"Have you been in there?" Fergus asked as he took another sip of tea.

"No," he answered.

"Have you tried?"

Shock covered Saint's face at Fergus' question. "I would never!"

Fergus cut a sideways glance to his brother. A small smile tweaked the corner of his mouth. He knew Saint too well to believe his brother would let something as important as Haven's reconstruction go by without as much as a glance. "The door was locked, wasn't it?"

"Yes," Saint conceded. "And before you ask, there is some type of…well, for lack of a better word there is a force-field within the walls so I could not walk through them."

"So, we wait and see."

"Yes. I suppose we do."

CHAPTER NINETEEN

CJ hugged her arms tightly around her mid-section as she and Mika sat in the driveway of her mother's condo. Not until this moment had CJ ever considered she might have an ulcer.

"I can remain in the car if you wish," Mika said, taking her hand gently in his. The pain in her stomach subsided, and she wondered if it was possible that he had taken the pain away.

"No, I want you with me," CJ said, taking a deep breath. "Where my mother is concerned, I will need all the moral support I can get."

"If you insist," Mika said as he got out of the jeep.

CJ watched as he walked around the car to open her door. Reaching in, he helped her from the jeep. His touch was warm and gentle and she was shocked by how much that small act of kindness meant to her.

"Are you ready?" he asked, shutting the door.

"No," CJ said trying to tamp down the fear that rose in her throat. "Why is this so hard?"

"It is always hard to leave those that you love behind," Mika said.

The sadness in Mika's voice tugged at CJ's heart. Though he had not told her as much, she knew the sadness was her doing. "I am sorry," she said lightly stroking his cheek. "I never meant..."

"You did only what was asked of you."

"But I hurt you."

"A hurt that is easily mended now that you are here," he said.

CJ smiled up at him. She wanted to believe him. To believe that he had absolved her of any wrong doing, but she could see the tiny bit of hurt that still lingered in his eyes.

"Hey!" CJ exclaimed as Mika pulled her hand from his face and pushed her toward her mother's door. "Don't be so pushy!"

"You cannot put his off any longer. We are here and this must be done."

CJ cringed at the determination in his stance. "You know, I'm beginning to think Ghost would have been a better idea."

"Then your thoughts would be wrong," Mika snorted and opened the door.

"You!" Gypsy Lynn Carson yelled.

CJ and Mika had barely stepped foot into her mother's home before Gypsy Lynn picked up a vase and hurled it toward Mika's head. Quickly, he deflected the incoming object.

Before they had a chance to straighten, Gypsy Lynn hurled another vase in their general direction, and CJ found herself thankful her mother had terrible aim.

"Mother, stop!" she cried out, using her body to shield Mika against her mother's assault. With any luck, she could stop Gypsy Lynn before any other vases became projectile missiles. "What is wrong with you?"

Gypsy Lynn grabbed a nearby book and pulled back, ready to sling it toward the door and Mika. "I said stop it." CJ snatched the book from her mother's hand. "What is wrong with you?"

Gypsy Lynn said nothing. She merely stared at Mika with contempt.

"I will wait outside," Mika said and started back out the door.

"No," CJ commanded. "You will stay right where you are. And you," she pointed to her mother. "Will tell me what the hell is wrong with you." She could see tears of anger begin to well up in her mother's eyes.

"I thought I got rid of the whole lot of you," Gypsy Lynn spat. "You and that Dr. Grey."

CJ helped her mother to a chair. "How do you know Mika?"

"Mika?" Gypsy Lynn asked. "That's right. I remember."

"What do you mean, you remember?" CJ knelt next to her mother's chair. "What are you talking about, you thought you got rid of the whole lot of them? Who's them?"

CJ had always been envious of the color and shape of her mother's eyes. Doe eyes, she had heard them called. The description even sounded romantic. Much more so than the drab green she had inherited from her father.

CJ had only seen one photo of her father. It sat on the dressing table in her mother's bedroom and had for as long as she could remember. Over the years men had come in and out of Gypsy Lynn Carson's life, but none had been able to completely push Charles Stone from her thoughts. The photo was a testament to that.

To love a man that much. Quickly, CJ censored her thoughts. Inside, she prayed he had not heard her. The last thing she needed was for him to know how she felt about him. Wait. How do I feel about him? CJ shook her head. She needed to take care of one thing at a time and at the present moment that would be her mother.

CJ's attention went quickly back to her mother. "Mom, tell me why you attacked Mika."

"You have your father's hair you know," she said, gently stroking CJ's curls. "And his eyes."

"Yes ma'am. You've told me."

Gypsy Lynn stared out the window and breathed slowly. The room became eerily silent as they waited for CJ's mother to say something. Anything.

"If you are here, then—Charles?" Gypsy Lynn addressed Mika.

"Is dead," he answered.

The way her mother was acting led CJ to think her father had been alive all these years which meant her mother had kept his existence secret. CJ followed her mother's gaze to Mika.

Was it also possible that her mother had somehow known about the Theriontrope Foundation? How else would Gypsy Lynn have known about Michael Grey after CJ had only learned of him earlier?

CJ could feel the heat begin to rise in her face. This wasn't possible. Her mother would never lie to her about something that important. Would she?

Mika? CJ used their private link.

He crossed his arms and leaned against the door frame. *Yes, Little Star?* As usual, his voice revealed little of his emotion.

Tell me I am wrong.

There is much your mother needs to tell you, he answered.

You tell me. Somehow having her fears confirmed by Mika did not seem as treacherous as it would coming from her mother.

I told you, this is between you and your mother.

"She doesn't know?" Gypsy Lynn asked.

"I have told her nothing," Mika said.

"Know what, Mom?" she asked taking her attention back to Gypsy Lynn. "Was Charles not my father?"

"Of course, Charles was your father, but..."

"But what?"

"I should have known this day would come," Gypsy Lynn whispered as she stared away from CJ.

CJ felt Mika move closer. Amazingly, merely knowing he was near helped to calm the fear that had begun to overtake her.

"All these years, my father was alive and you never said anything."

"No," Gypsy Lynn whispered.

"Why didn't you tell me?"

"You never asked, so I never found a reason to bring it up."

CJ leaned away from her mother. "I never asked because you told me he was dead." CJ could feel the anger rising in her. "But why. Why did you not want me know?"

"I didn't want you to go after him. I wanted more for you than a life spent taking care of ...of the likes of him." Gypsy Lynn waved toward Mika. "No matter what you think, that man isn't normal."

"I know exactly who and what Mika is," CJ said in Mika's defense.

"Did you know that he's not human!" Gypsy Lynn snapped as she rose quickly and walked into the kitchen.

"Get back here, Mother," CJ yelled and followed closely at her mother's heels. "You knew that shape-shifters existed? That my father was a Guardian and you hid it from me?" She clenched her fist tightly trying to stop the small tremors that shook her.

"Yes. I knew." Gypsy Lynn spat as she poured a glass half full of vodka. Without batting an eyelash, Gypsy Lynn drank the clear liquid down and poured another. "I knew all about shifters and that place out west somewhere. Your father tried to get me to move there when he discovered I was pregnant with you."

"Wait. You told me my father was a veterinarian. That he died in a plane crash before I was born."

"Minor untruths. I only did it to protect you, Sweetie," Gypsy Lynn said, reaching for her daughter, but CJ pulled back from her mother's touch.

"You lied to me. For thirty years, you lied to me. Why?"

"Those damn stories of yours and that stupid dog," Gypsy Lynn mumbled, cutting her scalding gaze toward Mika.

CJ could feel him stiffen at her mother's words. Briefly, CJ worried he might say something in his own defense, but she knew that was not his way. He would wait and see how matters were to unfold before stepping in.

"Mika is a coyote, not a dog!" CJ blurted out. She knew her statement to be the truth, yet, it sounded strange to her ears, and she wondered if she would ever become accustomed to the thought.

"I didn't care if he is a dog, coyote or a goat. Either way, I had seen him with you, then I saw. Being your mother, it was only natural for me to watch. I saw what happened when he was alone." Gypsy Lynn pointed to Mika.

An odd pang of jealousy flashed through CJ at the thought of her mother having seen Mika transform. It seemed an invasion of their privacy. "You saw him change?"

"Yes. I saw him change, and I knew Charles had sent him. They were going to take you away from me. I couldn't let that happen."

164

"You knew," CJ whispered.

"Yes! Yes! A thousand times yes! I knew!" Gypsy Lynn snapped.

CJ took a step back. Pain gnawed at her insides as the realization of her mother's betrayal hit hard.

"The therapist? The pills?" CJ began to shake from the anger welling up inside her.

"I had to, Sweetie," Gypsy Lynn crooned. "It would have been wrong for me to move you across the country to live in that God forsaken wilderness and be raised with those creatures."

"Mika isn't a creature."

"How do you know?" Gypsy Lynn pounded her fist against the counter. "Do you know what he is capable of when he isn't dressed as a human?"

"No. But neither do you." CJ shot back.

"It was not the life I wanted for you. To grow up in a house full of animals. That was no place for a child."

"My father would have never let anything happen to me," CJ said. She pushed her hands against her face trying to stop the tears.

"I couldn't take that chance," Gypsy Lynn stated and took another sip of Vodka.

"Let me get this straight," CJ said as she took a deep calming breath to stop from becoming hysterical. "My father has been alive all these years, and you lied to me because you were afraid the creatures, as you call them, would what? Kill me? Rape me?" The pitch of CJ's voice began to rise.

She felt Mika's presence as it moved across her mind helping to calm her rising frustration and anger. She had touched not only his mind, but his heart as well. She knew that neither he nor any who lived at Haven would have ever harmed her or her mother.

You are our guardian, Wicahpi. It is against our laws for any to harm you. She heard him whisper in her thoughts.

"They would have never hurt me, Mother. Like the father you never allowed me to meet, I was—I am their Guardian."

"I loved Charles. Don't you think it was hard for me to live without him?"

"No. I don't," CJ answered with more composure than she felt. "I think you loved yourself more. You would rather your daughter be raised without a father, and think of herself as crazy, than make any type of sacrifice." CJ spat the accusation at her mother.

"That's not true. I would do anything for you," Gypsy Lynn cried.

"Except tell me the truth." CJ's heart ached. No matter what Gypsy Lynn had done to her, CJ could always justify her mother's actions, but no more.

Without thinking about her actions, CJ found herself standing before Mika. "Please take me home, Mika. I need to pack."

Gypsy Lynn ran after her daughter. "Pack?"

"Yes, to pack. I'm leaving, Mother. I'm going to go live with those creatures, as you put it."

Gypsy Lynn grabbed her daughter's arm. "You can't be serious."

"Oh, I am very serious." CJ jerked her arm from her mother's grasp.

"But...but what if..."

"But what, Mom? What are you so afraid of?"

"What if you.... what if one of them..."

CJ stared at her mother and wished for once she could read Gypsy Lynn's mind because at this moment she wasn't making very good sense. "Spit it out mom. What iiiif ..."

"What if you get pregnant?" Gypsy Lynn blurted out.

CJ blinked as her mother's question soaked in. Pregnant? Where on Earth had that come from? "Then I guess you'll have to get used to having puppies for grandchildren."

CHAPTER TWENTY

Whoosh. Clank. Whoosh. Thud. The sounds of metal beating against metal carried across the open field. Bared to waist and clad only in leather breeches and knee boots, the two men made a striking silhouette against the backdrop of sherbet colored evening; one man the color of midnight, the other as pale as the snow he loved.

"Arrrgh," Cassius grunted as he sliced through air with a Viking Dane axe. Its razor-sharp blade came within inches from Ævar's neck, who ducked quickly to avoid decapitation.

Ævar swept at Cassius' legs with the staff of his spear. The larger man leapt nimbly out of the way, belying his great size. Cassius found it amusing that many, including Ævar, thought of polar bears as massive lumbering creatures, not quick and surefooted. Yet, he was always able to use that quickness to catch Ævar off guard.

Again Cassius swung his axe, this time coming dangerously close to Ævar's mid-section. The cold iron thudded against the wooden shield, that bore an emblem of a great white wolf, held high by Ævar. The force of Cassius's blow sent Ævar stumbling backwards. The smaller man regained his footing and raised himself to his full height of six feet, which still did not bring him eye level with his adversary.

The two men regarded each other. Cassius watched Ævar closely. He could see the muscles along Ævar's shoulders begin to tighten and ripple as he fought the urge to shift and take on his animal form.

Since their earlier visit with Ísold, Cassius had noted Ævar's less than pleasant mood. It took a great amount of coaxing, but Ævar finally admitted Ísold's visions had been more cryptic than normal. Ghost was alive and well, and still within the care of Delta Pack and Haven. Not that Cassius was surprised. It seemed the Goddess had always smiled on the members of the Delta Pack.

The small hairs along Cassius arms lifted in response to the change in the air about him. He could see the faint glow that emanated from Ævar's abdomen.

Cassius rolled the handle of his weapon over and over in his massive hands. "What ails you?" He placed the handle of his weapon on the ground and leaned against it.

"Do not waste my time with talk. Fight!" Ævar commanded. His voice gruff with the strain of holding back the change.

"No," Cassius said, yet he remained vigilant to Ævar's mood.

"I...said...fight!"

"Not when you are in such a foul mood."

Ævar refused to drop his weapon. Instead he raised it higher, poised to strike at a moment's notice.

Cassius shook his head. With lightning speed, he swung his axe upward, hitting the underside of Ævar's shield to send it flying from the other shifter's hands. Charging forward, he pushed the head of his axe against Ævar's chest, driving him backwards and slamming his opponent's back against the brick wall that surrounded Ævar's home.

"Do you yield?" Cassius snarled, applying pressure to the shaft of his axe.

Ævar gripped and flexed his hand around the handle of his spear. Out of the corner of his eye, Cassius could see Ævar's finger nails as they began to lengthen and bore into the shaft of the spear he held. Yet, he did not take his eyes off Ævar's face.

"Decide well your next course of action, Ævar." Cassius suggested. Now. Cassius thought. Now would be the perfect time for me to kill Ævar and end this blood feud before it goes any further.

Cassius' thoughts were broken by the sound of clapping. It echoed across the lawn taking his and Ævar's attention to the top of the wall directly above their heads. A man, dressed in immaculately tailored chinos and broadcloth shirt, perched atop the brick wall. His golden red hair was gathered neatly with a leather thong at the nape of his neck.

"Interesting," the man commented. His deep green eyes flashed with amusement. "For a moment, I debated as to whether you were actually considering the demise of your employer. You weren't, were you?" the man asked as he stepped from the top of the wall and floated gracefully to the ground.

"Lucas," Cassius growled.

Lucas Dark water smirked. "Dear Cassius, your enthusiasm overwhelms me."

Cassius watched him though narrowed eyes. Lucas Darkwater was the epitome of Viking ancestry. He could imagine Lief Ericson and Lucas as one and the same person.

Lucas was one of the few that could stand eye to eye with Cassius, and the big bear had often wondered if pushed to battle, which man would win? There was arrogance about the other man that grated on Cassius' nerves. But whether he liked Lucas or not, there was little he could do about it.

"To what do we owe the honor?" Asked Ævar pushing the axe away from his chest.

"Rumor has it, your brother still lives. Is that true?"

Cassius could see the muscles work beneath Ævar's jaw line at the mention of Ghost's resurrection.

"An unfortunate situation and one, I assure you, I will rectify."

"Hmm," Lucas commented and nodded. "Cassius, could you be a good little bear and saunter off somewhere? I need to speak with Ævar privately."

"Of course," Cassius bowed courteously and collected his things.

"That will not be necessary." He heard Ævar say. "There is nothing that cannot be said in front of Cassius."

Lucas studied one man then the other before speaking. "As you wish." He shrugged, then walked across the grass to a long sword that had been discarded earlier in the battle. Its point driven deep into the ground by Ævar. Effortlessly, Lucas pulled the sword from its resting place.

Cassius and Ævar watched as he rotated the sword in his hand, testing its weight and balance. Deftly he sliced the blade through the air and into an imaginary foe. "Now, about your brother," the Viking began, his attention not leaving the sword. "Do you have any idea how he survived? After all the guardian was not in a position to help, and the others were too far away to get there in time. Yet, he miraculously survived." He continued to spar with an invisible partner. "Suggestions? Anyone?"

Ah, here it comes, thought Cassius. Since the moment Lucas had popped in from above, Cassius wondered the real reason for his visit. With Lucas, there was no such thing as a social call.

Lucas had always been a partner, if not chief instigator where Ævar and his hatred for all things related to Haven and his older brother were concerned and, though Ævar never discussed it openly, Cassius knew Lucas was also his financial backer.

"Well then," Lucas said. "Allow me to enlighten you. Does the word Dream-walker mean anything to either of you?"

Ævar hissed. "I have heard the stories of a female spirit that travels the In-between to save poor wounded shape-shifters. We all have, but she is merely fantasy."

"The woman you speak of is neither a spirit, nor a fantasy. She is very much real and the reason your brother still lives.

"Preposterous!" Ævar exclaimed. "That would mean that she was a Guardian and my men saw to it that the Guardians are no more."

"And yet, your brother lives. How do you explain that?" Lucas asked.

Cassius stilled. He had heard the rumors about the one who walked the In-between to help shifters in need. Before Ævar had Ísold stripped of her powers and sealed away, Cassius entertained the idea those rumors spoke of her.

After all, she possessed the ability to walk the spaces of the netherworld, but after her exile, the rumors continued. Cassius knew if there was such a person, then the Theriontrope Foundation would surely do everything possible to keep them safe.

"Then the tales of the dream-walker are true?" Cassius asked.

"Balderdash!" Ævar laughed and waved away the thought with a gentle brush of his hand.

Cassius saw the wave of anger as it washed over Lucas. Without notice, Lucas raised the sword above his head and drove it back into the ground, burying the blade completely to the hilt. "There is no time for your laughter," Lucas spat. "The Guardian still lives, and at this moment, she is in the company of two Delta Pack members, one of which is your brother. And soon, very soon, she will take her rightful place at Haven." Lucas took a calming breath and walked back to the wall.

Okay, maybe I won't be able to take him in battle, Cassius reasoned.

"Which means," Cassius heard Ævar begin, but his words were quickly cut off.

"Which means," Lucas whipped back. "The newly appointed Guardian must die," Lucas said as he raised his arms outward. An unseen hand seemed to levitate him back to the top of the wall. The space next to Lucas began to swirl and shift, becoming an open doorway.

"Lucas," Ævar called out before the Viking had a chance to disappear. "Might you help me in my search by giving me a clue as where to find this new Guardian?"

"Find your brother, find the Guardian," Lucas answered as the wormhole closed around him.

CHAPTER TWENTY-ONE

"Hey, you guys are back, "Ghost said, rising from CJ's sofa where he had been firmly ensconced watching her collection of Blade movies. Without so much as a word, CJ stormed past him and Mika, heading straight to the back of her house and slamming the door to her bedroom.

"I take it that didn't go well." Ghost addressed his comment to Mika as he turned down the volume on the television.

"One might say that." Mika glanced back towards the hallway.

"What happened?" Ghost asked, as he too listened to the bangs and slams emanating from CJ's bedroom.

"Suffice it to say CJ's mother did not take to well to the idea of her daughter moving to Haven."

"Why?"

"It seems she is concerned for her daughter's virtue."

"Really, what did she say?"

Mika chuckled lightly. "You really are a girl you know that?"

"Ah, come on Mika," Ghost pleaded, climbing over the back of the sofa to face the hallway and Mika. "I've waited here like a good wolf all afternoon. The least you can do is throw me a bone."

Mika stopped for a moment, listening to the sounds coming from CJ's bedroom. He had known the outcome of CJ's visit before she went to her mother.

The few times he had dealt with Gypsy Lynn, she had been anything but obliging. That is why he wanted CJ to go alone, but when Ghost piped in and said he would go, Mika had to step in. He couldn't abide the thought of Ghost going in his stead. No matter how irritating his comrade could be, he did not deserve Gypsy Lynn's wrath.

Mika continued to stare after CJ. He only hoped she was not mad at him. She had sat across from him in the jeep, her arms wrapped tightly around her mid-section and he could tell it was taking every bit of will power she had to hold her emotions in check. He had wanted to touch her, to comfort her in some small way, but he was unsure how she would handle the intrusion.

He looked back to Ghost, who waited patiently. "Very well, I shall tell you," Mika conceded. "CJ's mother asked what would happen if CJ became pregnant."

"Pregnant? How would that...oh, you mean by one of us?" Ghost asked.

"Yes, by one of us."

"Whoa...and?"

"And... CJ told her mother she would have to become accustomed to having puppies as grandchildren."

Ghost howled with laughter. "You've got to be kidding!

"I would not joke about something as serious as this," Mika said flatly. He most definitely would not joke about something as serious as CJ's children, especially since he would be the father. But that was not something he was about to tell Ghost.

"That's incredible!" Ghost continued his laughter. "Whoa....wait...puppies? You mean she...CJ's mom knows about us?"

175

"Yes. She knows about us," Mika commented, continuing to fight the urge to go to CJ. "But she has never wanted us to be a part of Charlie Jean's life."

"What do you mean she never wanted us in CJ's life? How long have you known about this?" Ghost nodded toward the back of the house.

Mika rubbed silver ringed hands across his face. To answer Ghost's question would be an admission of the secret he had kept all these years, but the truth had to come out eventually, didn't it?

"That is a good question and one that I would like to have an answer to," a voice said from the other side of the room.

Both Mika and Ghost spun quickly. Fergus stood barely beyond a set of French doors that opened onto the deck.

"Uh oh," Ghost said under his breath and jumped to his feet. "Fergus...I... we didn't notice you come up."

"Obviously." Fergus said as he strode into the room. He was dressed in black from head to foot, sporting rivet studded black leather bracers and, as usual, he did not appear to be in good humor.

Mika swore to himself. Normally he could feel when another shifter transported within a 50-yard radius of him. Had he been so distracted by CJ that his senses were impaired? Surely one human woman couldn't do that to him?

But Mika could fool himself no longer. CJ was not any woman. She was his woman. The other half of his soul, and he had waited over a century for her.

He had seen the images of her at his side, sharing his life and giving him the children that he dared not voice he wanted. No, Charlie Jean Carson was not any woman, nor was she merely a Guardian. She was his mate. Wakatanka had spoken.

The realization of this had not been an easy one for Mika. After all he had been her protector for many years, watching her grow from a child, to teenager and into the beautiful woman she became. With each passing year, he had grown to love her more and more.

At first, it had been hard for Mika to admit what was happening to his feelings where CJ was concerned. He thought it best to deny them. After all, she was Charles' daughter and on his honor, Mika would rather die than hurt her or endanger his friendship with Charles. It had taken all his will-power to think of her as merely an assignment.

Having touched her mind day after day, he knew her in a way more intimate than that of a mere lover. He knew the beauty that lay within her heart and soul. He knew her gentleness, and her unwavering devotion to even one such as him. She was everything he ever wanted in a mate and she was destined to be his.

"Is there something you would like to share with the rest of the class?" Fergus asked, leaning black denim clad hips against the edge of the sofa.

"In truth, there is much I need to tell you," Mika answered, leveling his gaze on Fergus. "However, I am not sure this is the best time to do so."

"And when do you propose there will be a better time?"

"Damn her!" CJ cursed as she slammed the bedroom door, stormed down the hallway and into the den. She pulled up short at the sight of Fergus, who stood up when she entered the room. "I... I'm sorry," she stammered. "I did not know...." she glanced from Fergus back to Mika.

Mika placed his hand protectively in the small of her back. "CJ, this is Fergus Wolfe, our leader."

"Leader?" she questioned.

"You've heard of the big, bad wolf, haven't you?" Ghost asked, studying CJ. "Well, that's him," Ghost said with a nudge of his head in Fergus' direction.

Fergus raised an eyebrow at Ghost's comment. "I believe I should resent that statement, but in fact little brother, I seem to actually like it," Fergus commented.

"Told you," Ghost added, winking at CJ. "Wow, did you hear that?" He rubbed his stomach. "I'm famished. Mind if I raid your fridge?"

"Uh...no. Not at all. Make yourself at home," she answered.

Fergus waited for Ghost to leave the room before silently striding across the room to stand before CJ. Wide-eyed, she gazed up at him.

Deep auburn hair fell mostly about his shoulders, with only the front being held back from his broad face by a clasp she couldn't see. Two days' growth of beard, the same exact shade of red, colored his jaw-line, adding depth to burnt orange eyes. For lack of a better term, Fergus was mesmerizing.

"It is an honor to meet you," Fergus said, bowing gracefully to CJ. "And despite what my little brother says, I am not quite that bad."

"Depends upon who you ask!" Ghost called out from the kitchen.

Fergus closed his eyes tightly, and CJ wondered if he was silently reprimanding Ghost, or trying to keep from throttling him. If she was a betting woman, she would have put her money on the latter. As charming as Ghost could be, CJ was sure that someone who seemed as serious as Fergus might have a bit of a problem with Ghost's almost juvenile sense of humor.

"Excuse me," Fergus said and walked toward the kitchen and Ghost.

"I...um.... I need to get some fresh air," CJ said pointing towards the door.

"Of course." Mika stepped away from her. "I will be right here if you need me."

"Thank you," she whispered, gently rubbing her hand along his bicep. She felt his body go rigid under her touch. Quickly, she pulled back her hand. Embarrassed, she walked out into the damp night air.

The heaviness of the Florida evening seemed to parallel the heaviness in her heart. With a sigh, CJ sat in one of the white plastic lawn chairs on her patio and stared out into the open night sky. Closing her eyes, she stilled her breathing trying to connect to the Universe as she had done earlier.

She had so many questions about her life and what was to be. In her soul, she knew that Haven was where she belonged. It was her birthright no matter how much her mother tried to shield her from that. "Damn, Gypsy Lynn," CJ cursed under her breath. Why did she have to lie all those years?

It does not matter. A voice whispered through the night. *You cannot hide from your destiny.* It spoke to her in the soft, calming tones of a parent trying to soothe a child's fears.

"But I don't know if I can do this. I don't know how." CJ insisted.

The knowledge of how lies in the knowledge of your ancestors.

Her ancestors? But she had never been given the chance to know her ancestors. Anger roared through CJ. How could her mother have kept Charles Stone a secret? She would never forgive Gypsy Lynn for that. Never!

No matter how CJ cut it, her world was about to change in ways she couldn't yet imagine. It was about to become a world of shape-shifters and men that could walk through thin air and carry on complete conversations without speaking a word. It all seemed so crazy and yet, the craziest part of all, was none of that scared her.

What did scare her was the fact that, somehow, she was charged with caring for them. Not only Mika or Ghost or Fergus, who kind of frightened her, but all the shape-shifters that roamed the world.

How many could there be? Hundreds? Thousands? The thought of what lay before her was daunting. "I wish I had known my father," CJ whispered into the fading sunlight.

All is as it was meant to be–is. I brought you to this place. I will carry you through.

CJ's chest felt tight with fear. "I don't think I can I do this alone." She spoke again into the breeze.

"You will not be alone," Mika said from behind her.

CJ closed her eyes, savoring the warm comfort of his voice. She had not heard him walk up or open the door. For all she knew, he could have 'poofed' in or out, as the case may be.

Mika's sheer presence made the world about her suddenly seem to come alive. Tree-frogs began a slow serenade from their hiding places among the big leafed elephant ears that grew close to her home, and soon their symphony was joined by the rustling of the palm fronds swaying gently overhead.

Her breath stilled as Mika stepped closer. She could feel his gaze wander over her face and along her body. She shifted self-consciously under his scrutiny. What if she did not meet with his approval? Not that she needed his approval. After all this was her imaginary friend come to life. He would approve of her regardless. Right?

Ambient light leaked out of the windows of her home allowing a better glimpse of his face. Soft shadows blanketed his high cheekbones and shaded his jaw line bringing her attention directly to his dark eyes.

Never could another compare to the beauty and grace she found in him. Neither Ghost's ethereal beauty, nor Fergus' old-world charm could ever do to her what one glimpse of Mika Elkhart could do. Mika was now back in her life, and she could never, would never, let him leave her side again. Of course, he might have something to say about that.

CJ sucked in a deep breath. Until this moment, she had not thought of his abandoning her once his job was through. It was possible that he was merely doing his duty where she was concerned and playing the game, as it were, to get her to join Haven. For all she knew he had a wife and children somewhere.

Without warning, tears stung the back of her eyes as unfamiliar pain sliced thought her heart. How could the thought of Mika sharing his life with another make her heart physically ache? *My god, Carson. Get a grip!* her inner voice demanded.

"Forgive me, Little Star," Mika said, taking a step closer. "I did not mean to startle you."

"No. It's okay," she said, wiping away a rogue tear.

He motioned to an empty chair nearby. "May I join you?"

A stilted smile crossed her lips. "Sure."

"There is little need for your fear," Mika began as he pulled a seat to face her and sat down.

"Fear? I'm not afraid." She said, trying to shield her thoughts from him.

A whimsical smile crossed Mika's face. He knew she was scared, but how could she admit that to him?

"You will have help," he said, answering her unspoken question.

CJ followed Mika's gaze back toward the interior of her house and to Fergus and Ghost.

"Are those two always like that?" she asked, trying to get her thoughts on anything other than the way the man across from her made every nerve in her body stand at attention.

"Like what?"

"I don't know," CJ sighed. "Ghost seems... well...like an extremely irritating little brother."

Mika laughed at CJ's statement, catching her off guard. His laughter made her think of the chocolate truffles she became so fond of on her trips to New Orleans, deep, dark and completely decadent.

"What's so funny?" she asked.

"Forgive me, but you have no idea how accurate your statement actually is," he said. "Sometimes, I believe the Great Spirit put Ghost in Fergus' life simply to see how far Fergus can be pushed before he snaps."

"I can see that," CJ said, glancing over her shoulder again. "But Fergus seems like he could put an end to Ghost's button pushing if he truly wanted to."

"You are probably right, but they are both too old to change at this point."

CJ felt the confusion cross her face. Too old? Ghost did not appear to be more than twenty-five or so. "You make them sound like relics. How old is Ghost? 25 maybe 30?"

Mika swiped his hand across the back of his neck. It had never occurred to him that their ages would ever come into question. He wondered if that would be a problem for her? It certainly wasn't for him, but then again, he wasn't human. "Actually, Fergus is considered an ancient among us, Ghost and I are both children compared to him and Saint."

"Ancient?" CJ looked again into the kitchen where Fergus and Ghost were deep in conversation. Either she was really bad at telling a person's age, or Mika had a strange sense of what was considered old. "Wow, if that's what you think about him, you must be ready to put me out to pasture. Fergus can't be much older than me. 40 maybe?"

Mika cleared his throat. "Fergus is roughly 277 years of age. Give or take ten or so years."

"Wait a minute," CJ said sitting up in her seat. "You expect me to believe that that guy in there who could be a model is almost 300 years old?"

"A model?" Mika asked. "You really think Fergus looks like a model?"

"Are you kidding? All of you guys could be models."

"It is a well known fact that women find Ghost, how shall I put it...."

"Hot," CJ said without thinking. Crap. "I'm sorry. Sometimes my mouth goes before my brain." She could tell that Mika was doing his best to mask his irritation at her words.

"You said nothing I have not heard before. All within the pack are aware of the way women think of him. As for Fergus and I, we are nowhere near that caliber."

CJ stared wide-eyed at Mika. Did they not have mirrors where he came from? It was easy for her to imagine him with his hair down, chest bare, wearing only buckskin. She envisioned him, bare-chested, straddling a horse and pictured on the cover of some romance novel. He was the stuff fantasies were made of.

CJ felt heat rise in her face at her wanton thoughts of Mika and what she would be willing to let him teach her, no matter how old he was. "By the way," CJ began, trying to find a subject to keep her mind off Mika's shirtless body. "I thought you said we shouldn't pet shifters, yet you said nothing to Arial. She was rubbing all over Ghost."

A brief smile spread cross Mika's lips giving CJ a glimpse of perfect white teeth. "I believe I said you could not pet shifters," he answered as his hand came up to stoke her cheek with the back of his fingers.

Tiny volts of electricity seemed to trickle from the backs of his finger straight into her body, and her stomach went into free-fall at his touch. CJ closed her eyes, reveling in the pleasure of the warmth of his skin against hers.

Opening her eyes, CJ allowed her gaze to dance from Mika's gold-flecked eyes to his full lips. She couldn't help the feeling of sheer anticipation that flooded her at the thought of those lips pressed against hers. Does this man have no idea what he does to me?

"What...uh...what do you mean I cannot pet shifters?" She asked trying not to sound as out of control as she felt.

"It is a simple enough statement. Arial may touch any, or all of my brethren, so long as they agree to it."

"But..."

Mika placed his finger against her lips to stop her from speaking. "Even so, you may not," he finished.

The first-time Mika told her she couldn't touch another shifter, CJ truly thought he was joking, but there was a stillness about him that brought home the seriousness of his statement. "Mika, that's crazy," she said, pulling his hand from her lips, but not letting it go. "If I am to be a Guardian and healer for your people, at some point in time I will have to touch them."

"Forgive me," he complied. "You are right. As a healer, you have my permission to touch others."

Surely, she had heard him wrong. Permission? Slowly, CJ leaned back. Her brows furrowed in concentration. "Excuse me, but did you say permission."

"Yes. I did," he replied flatly.

"And what gives you the right to dictate who I can and cannot touch?"

"As your mate, I have every right."

"My what?" she exclaimed as she shot to her feet, sending the lightweight chair tumbling backwards.

CJ was unsure what shocked her more, the fact he said what her heart secretly desired or the fact he seemed so damned certain when he said it. For heaven's sake, they had just met. They had never even kissed or been on a date for that matter.

"Dating is for strangers, Little Star. You and I are not strangers," he replied. "As for the other, that can be easily enough arranged." Mika leaned back in his seat, a devilish smile crossing his face.

"But...what the..." she stammered as she took a step backward, almost falling over the upturned chair. Quickly, Mika was at her side, keeping her steady. Instinctively CJ wrapped her arms around his neck bringing her face within a breath's distance of his. She could feel the warm strength of his body against hers as he held her tightly against the solid wall of his chest.

The tip of CJ's tongue darted nervously between her lips. Now was her chance to see if his lips were indeed as soft as she had imagined. But what if he kissed her and it was like kissing an old shoe?

"There is only one way to find out," Mika said, bringing his face closer to hers.

White hot anger shot through CJ. "Stay out of my head!" She pushed against him.

"Forgive my intrusion, but we have been connected for so many years. To hear your thoughts and sense your feelings is no different for me than breathing."

Mika's arms were folded languidly across his chest bringing her attention to his hands and the silver of his rings. Strong fingers curved across his upper arms. She followed that curve to the taut muscles she knew lie beneath. Images of Mika without his shirt flooded her mind and her breath quickened at the thought of him naked and close - lying above her.

Deliberately, Mika walked to her side, his intense stare never leaving hers. She wanted to run, but her body refused to back away. Cautiously, she watched as Mika leaned in closely, lightly stroking his cheek across hers. His touch was feather light, but that minute contact was enough to send her reeling. Her knees buckled and she grabbed tightly to Mika's arms to keep from falling.

CJ screwed her eyes shut while her mind spun wildly. He was wrong. He had to be wrong. There was no way she could be his mate. Yet, somehow, she knew he was telling the truth. She needed to be his. To be claimed by him. But this was Mika. The ever-vigilant voice inside her head for thirty years. Mika. Her protector. Her friend. Her imagination.

Where CJ was concerned, Mika found it hard to keep rational thoughts in his head. She felt exquisite in his arms. The soft curves of her body molded perfectly along the hard planes of his own, and her touch, innocent as it was, brought the wildness in him to life.

He struggled to leash the animalistic urges that threatened to overtake him. It took all his will power and concentration to keep from pulling CJ into the deep shadows of evening and claim her as his own. Mika let his mind wander, hoping it would take another, less intimate path. He needed something else to hold on to other than the feel of CJ's naked curves writhing beneath him.

From the den he had listened as CJ slammed drawers and cursed under her breath thinking no one could hear. She needed to get out her frustration and anger without being disturbed, and he was willing to allow her that.

But the hardest part was leaving her be while she cried. Her tears had always been his undoing. There were times he thought he knew exactly how many tears she had shed over the years since each one seemed to have left a permanent scar on his heart. To know she was in pain and be unable to do anything about it had almost been more than he could bear.

Mika breathed deeply, taking the scent of her into the depths of his being. How could she ever doubt he was real? Was the fact he was here, holding her in his arms, not enough for her? "I am real little one," he reassured her. "I am flesh and bone, no matter what your mother would have you believe."

"Mika," CJ whispered breathlessly, placing her forehead against his shoulder. "I want to believe, but..."

"Make no doubt of your place in this Universe, Wicahpi," he whispered into her soul. "In time your head will come to accept what your heart already knows. Your place is at my side and as my mate." Slowly, Mika tilted her face toward his. "There is no other for me."

CJ couldn't hold his gaze. She truly wanted to believe him. To accept his words as truth, but it was all too much. Maybe after they had spent some time together...

"Fergus calls," Mika said. "I must go in. There is much I am in need of telling him."

"Fergus," CJ mumbled absently. "Yes. Of course."

"Do you need me to send Ghost to sit with you?"

"Ghost?" CJ blinked up at him. "No. No. I'll be fine." But in actuality, CJ wasn't sure who she was trying to convince Mika or herself. How on Earth could she be fine?

"As you wish," Mika said, walking to the door. "Oh, and CJ," he added as he stopped at the door. "Before you ask, coyotes mate for life."

CJ stared at the spot left vacant by Mika. What was it he had said? Coyotes mate for life. The man was daft. That had to be the only logical explanation for what she had heard. There was no way she could be his mate. None. But was being his mate not what she wanted? God help her. Her heart had sung out with recognition. This is the one, it whispered. He has come for you.

A slow dull pain pulsed above CJ's right temple. Letting out a small groan, she rubbed the spot hoping to stop the pain. It had finally happened. Mika's last statement officially pushed her brain into overload.

She needed to think. She needed to decompress. She needed Bethany Rose and Arial and retail therapy.

CJ stifled a groan. She must be desperate if she was willing to spend time wandering aimlessly through stores. It was late into the evening and way too late to go shopping. But she could call the others and set up a time for tomorrow.

She needed to tell them both good-bye and explain the situation. Like there was a rational explanation. She could hear it now. "Hi guys. I needed to tell you bye. My imaginary friend from childhood popped in. I have agreed to move to the other side of the country with him and become the Guardian of a group of shape-shifters." Then, she would smile sweetly and Arial would call in the men with the little white coats.

Nope. Sane was not a word one could use to describe what she was about to do. Maybe, if she left out the shape-shifter part that would help.

Silently, CJ sent a small prayer of thanks to the "Powers That Be" for sending Mika and not someone like Fergus to her all those years ago. She couldn't imagine having been a little girl and Fergus, in any form, watching her as she played with her toys.

She watched Fergus as he spoke to both Ghost and Mika. There was nothing about him that said "warm and fuzzy" or that he would have the patience to deal with children. Let alone female children. He didn't seem the type. Then again, CJ rationalized, if she had to deal with Ghost for a hundred years, she might be a bit surly also.

Through the kitchen window she could see Mika. He stood near the window with his back to her as he talked. Over the years, she had known him as the vigilant voice inside her head. He was precise in what he said and never was there subterfuge in any of his statements.

Above everything else, there was a calmness. There was no extraneous flailing of his arms or hands. Only occasionally did he nod or shake his head. CJ cast her thoughts to Mika, trying to touch his mind. She wanted to read his thoughts as easily as he did hers. Instantly, a band of pressure settled about her head, making it hard to concentrate.

She shook her head trying to clear away the cobwebs. The sensation was not only strange, but painful as well. Was that how it would always be? It didn't seem fair that Mika could read her thoughts, but she couldn't read his. She would ask him about that when she felt better.

Where Mika and his kind were concerned, CJ knew there was much to learn. The weight of her new job fell onto her shoulders. She closed her eyes, rolling her head back and forth to release some of the tension that lay there.

Mika had told her she would not be alone. That she would not do this all by herself, but who else was there? After all, according to them, she was truly the last of her kind. Her only hope was that Mika was right. She had to trust him.

Again, she glanced in his direction. Slowly, as if sensing her stare, Mika sent her a reassuring smile. CJ's breath caught in her throat. In her eyes, Mika had to be the sexiest man to walk the face of the earth. His eyes had a way of penetrating straight into her soul, warming her to the core.

Now that she thought about it, he was probably the reason she never dated in college. Mika may not have been there physically all those years, but he had been spiritually. He loved her unconditionally, supporting her with words and thoughts. He even sang to her when she was ill or scared.

And now, he was here. Not only could she hear him, she could see him. Touch him. He was the other half of her soul, and although she knew that on the deepest of levels, it was still hard to accept someone like Mika, with his zero percent body fat and perfect cheekbones, could ever fall in love with a woman like her. She was too—too—

"Plain?"

CJ yelped at the sound of Ghost's voice behind her. She had not seen him leave the kitchen, but there he was. Wow. That was the only word she could think of when it came to Ghost. Just wow. *The fairest of them all,* the words rang through her mind.

Dressed in dark blue jeans and a gray T-shirt, he leaned casually against the railing of her deck, his arms braced on each side of his body for support. The right side of his face half hidden in shadows, yet his sky-blue eyes caught every bit of light making them sparkle.

"You know, you guys really have to stop popping in like that," she scolded, trying to ignore the fact he had been inside her thoughts. An ability she thought only Mika had. She rubbed the temple above her right eye as a tiny pinprick of pain started there. "I thought you were in the house with the others."

"I was, but I needed some fresh air, so I popped out here," he said with a graceful flick of his hand.

"Did you and Fergus get your differences worked out?"

An odd stillness fell over Ghost at the mention of Fergus' name. Slowly, he slid from the railing and stalked closer to her. "Fergus and I will always have our differences."

"I guess that comes from being the youngest, huh?"

Ghost lips tightened into a thin line. His eyes narrowed. "Fergus is getting a bit long in the tooth as they say. He cannot remain alpha forever." Malice danced in his tone.

"Wouldn't Fergus have to be pushed from the pack for that to happen?" CJ asked innocently. "I mean, I assume your pack works the same as a regular wolf pack."

"Or he could be killed in battle," he answered casually.

Protectively, CJ wrapped her arms about her as a cold chill ran through her body. This was her first chance to be alone with Ghost, yet something did not seem quite right. His eyes and tone were more vicious, less playful than the Ghost she spent time with earlier. Stepping more fully into the light, Ghost gave CJ a better view of his perfect features. She allowed her eyes to roam across Ghost face. Something was amiss, but she couldn't put her finger on it. His hair seemed a bit shorter. Maybe it was brushed differently. It could have been a trick of the light, but his skin seemed a bit paler. Other than that, he was Ghost, except—his scar was gone. How was that possible?

Did shifters could remove or cover scars? If so, then why wait and do it now? Why did he not do it when he shifted in front of her? There was so much she did not know about shape-shifters, so much she had to learn. Suddenly, CJ had the urge to run, but her legs refused to listen. Mika? She called out mentally. Searing, white hot pain shot like lightning through her temples, knocking her to her knees.

"Tsk. Tsk. Tsk," Ghost clucked, walking closer. His bare feet almost touching her finger tips. "You really shouldn't have done that."

Mika! She tried to call out again. Tiny pin points of lights danced behind her eyes as a wave of nausea flooded her body.

"What..." she gasped. "What's happening to me?" she could barely finish the sentence as another wave of pain shot through her.

"Ah, yes. Where you and the coyote are concerned, I had to use a bit of a cloaking spell," Ghost said, kneeling beside her.

"What are you talking about?" CJ asked, gasping from the pain.

"I can't have you talking to him on that little telepathic link of yours."

"Mi-" she tried to say his name aloud, only to have another, more intense pain rack her body.

"The pain is merely a side effect, but rather persuasive deterrent don't you think?"

"Let her go Ævar!" Ghost barked from the edge of the steps.

"Æger," Ævar sang out. "How nice of you to join us big brother, but I am afraid I will be unable to do as you ask," he said, grabbing CJ by her hair and pulling her to her feet."

"I said let her go." Ghost demanded, taking a step closer.

"Ghost, who..." CJ looked from the Ghost on the steps to the Ghost that had her by the nape of the neck. Stars danced behind her eyes, blurring her vision.

"Honestly, is that any way to greet me after all these years? No brotherly embrace?" Ævar smirked.

"You are no brother of mine."

"Our mother would tend to disagree with you," Ævar grunted.

Ghost's eyes opened wide at the mention of his mother.

"Oh yes, Kenna is alive and well. She doesn't speak of you much. Still trying to protect you after all these years, I suppose." Ævar felt CJ's body tense and he knew she tried to contact Mika again. "Will humans never learn?" he asked absently.

"What do you want?" Ghost asked.

"What do any of us want really?" Ævar met Ghost's burning gaze. "A nice woman, maybe a family. Those are a couple of things that come to mind."

"You and I both know you want neither of those."

"No, you're right. I don't. I have bigger wolves to skin, as it may be." Ævar brushed his cheek against CJ's face, causing her to jerk back.

"My brother and I have unfinished business," he explained to CJ. "And until that is cleared up I will never truly be ruler of the Wolf People. I guess you can say, I need Ghost to be, a ghost."

Ghost let a low growl of warning rise from the back of his throat.

Ævar laughed wickedly. "Please dear brother. Not here." He nodded toward the house where Mika and Fergus were. "That would be too easy, not to mention suicidal on my part. No. No. I have waited 120 years. I can wait another day."

"If it is me you want, then take me. CJ has nothing to do with any of this."

"But she does. She is a Guardian and she, like her father, must die."

"You?" Ghost whispered.

"Guilty," Ævar confessed casually, bowing his head slightly.

"Let-her-go!" Mika commanded from the open doorway.

"I know she's not a shifter, yet with decapitation the result is the same is it not?" Ævar asked. Instantly a dagger appeared in his hand, its blade pressed tightly against CJ's throat.

"You wouldn't," Ghost said.

"I would, and eventually, I will. But I really must take my leave."

CJ cried out with pain as Ævar jerked her head backwards, forcing her face upward.

"Human women are so soft. So, utterly delicious. Don't you agree?" Ævar asked, running the tip of his blade across her bottom lip. "You know Mika, I do find your sense of chivalry and restraint admirable. Still, you really should have kissed her when you had the chance." Forcing her face closer, Ævar kissed CJ firmly upon her lips. Weak from pain, she tried in vain to fight against his advances. Her body went completely limp the moment he released her.

"Be well my brother," Ævar called out to Ghost as his body began to fade. "I want you in perfect health for the day I kill you." His voice rang through the night as his form shimmered from view.

CHAPTER TWENTY-TWO

Mika lunged toward Ævar, only to capture CJ before her body completely crumpled to the ground. His heart clenched with fear as he felt her lifeless body in his arms and he lowered her to the solid surface of the deck.

His mind spun wildly. How was it possible two Ghosts had stood before him? Intense hate flooded Mika's body as he gaped up at Ghost who knelt beside him and CJ. Tears stung the back of his eyes as he fought to keep a grip on his sanity.

"Speak to me, Wicahpi" Mika pleaded. The words getting stuck in his throat. Pulling her into his lap, he cradled her body protectively against his. How could the Great Spirit be so cruel as to give CJ to him, only to take her back? Surely this was not right.

CJ's head rolled back. Her eyes wide open. She stared off into nothingness. Mika buried his face against her neck and brushed his cheek against the silky softness of her hair. Rocking her gently, he spoke into her ear. "Please, CJ. I beg of you. Do not leave me this night. As your mate, I cannot allow it."

"By the gods what has happened?" Fergus roared as he dashed onto the deck.

Mika stared up at him in confusion. He was unsure how to explain what he had seen.

"Is she alive?" Fergus dared ask the question.

The tiniest of breaths escaped CJ's lips, yet Mika felt it cross his skin. His heart leapt for joy. She was alive and his soul rejoiced for that small favor. Searching her face, Mika tried to push past the veil of mist that seemed to cloud her mind. The more he pushed at the barrier, the thicker it became.

"Yes. She is alive, but I am unable to touch her mind. What type of magic is this?" Mika directed his question to Ghost.

Ghost shook his head. "I have no idea what he is capable of," Ghost said, rising.

"What who is capable of?" Fergus asked.

"Ævar," Ghost stared into the woods as if saying his name would cause him to return.

"Ævar?" Fergus' tone was filled with suspicion. "You are sure?"

Ghost spun quickly. "No Fergus, I'm not sure seeing as how I haven't seen him in about 100 years," he snapped. "But how many other shape-shifters do you know that look like me and oh, by the way, want to kill me? There's only one I can think of. What about you?"

"Do not take that tone with me," Fergus demanded.

"Or what Fergus? What are you going to do to me?" In an act of aggression Ghost stepped forward, his face mere inches from Fergus.

Fergus could feel the anger and power as it built within Ghost's body charging the air about them. Anger charged by fear.

Fergus never wanted it to come to this. He knew it had been a futile wish, but he had hoped Ghost would never come face to face with his twin. Ævar's arrival would set in motion events that Fergus would be unable to stop.

Many times over, Fergus had promised that no matter the cost, he would always be there for Ghost. Watching him. Protecting him from those who would do him harm. It was a promise made to a scared child, but it was one that never left him.

By the Goddess, he would do what had to be done to fulfill that promise. Clinching his fist tightly, Fergus counted to ten. Now, more than ever, he would need control and restraint to do what must be done.

"Do not push me Ghost," Fergus growled through clenched teeth. " I am still pack leader."

"All hail, the infallible Fergus Wolfe. Unwavering. Uncaring Lord Protector of shape-shifters and humans alike. Maybe it is you who should be called Saint, not your brother."

With lightning speed, Fergus grabbed the smaller man by the collar, lifting him from the ground. "You petulant, self-serving little mongrel," Fergus spat. "I should have let you die when I had the chance. It would have saved us all a lot of time and trouble."

Time seemed to stand still as the air around them popped and crackled with energy. Slowly, Saint's image came into view as he walked out of the night.

"Cuir ceal-chasg air," he stated calling upon his native language. "I demand you stop this immediately."

"You have no authority over me, Aodhàn," Fergus spat.

If Fergus' comment ruffled Saint, he showed no signs. Patiently, Saint removed the worn brown satchel he had slung over his shoulder before stepping closer to Fergus and Ghost. Gently, he placed a calming hand on Fergus' shoulder. "Put him down brother. Ghost has done nothing to you."

Fergus cast a sidelong glance toward Saint. "Nothing except spend a century being an irritant to me."

"Now, Fergus," Saint stressed, refusing to back down.

With a mighty roar, Fergus pushed Ghost away from him and onto the hard-wooden decking. The young shifter stumbled before righting himself. Without a second to spare, he lunged at Fergus only to be caught about the waist and dragged back by Saint.

"I said enough!" Saint commanded with enough authority in his tone to stop Ghost's flailing. "There are more pressing matters at this moment than your two egos. When we are finished here and safely back at Haven, I shall allow the two of you to destroy each other, if that is what is necessary."

Saint released Ghost and picked up his satchel. As much as it pained him, Fergus and Ghost were at war, and there was little he could do for either of them. But CJ was a different story, and one in need of his attention. Deep concern settled in Saint's forest colored eyes. CJ's hapless body lay limp in Mika's arms. Saint was unsure if he would have the ability to help, but he had to try.

"I came as soon as possible, my friend," he said kneeling next to CJ. "Before I begin, I must ask your permission before I proceed."

"Do as you must, but bring her back to me."

"I will do my best, but I make no promises," Saint said, ignoring the two men behind him who continued to huff and pout like small boys.

Saint brushed CJ's wild curls from her face. Slowly he moved his hand across her eyes, to close her eyelids. Without warning Mika grasped Saint by the wrist, stilling his hand. "I know this is hard my brother, but she needs this to be done. Her brain must rest and as long as her eyes are open, I am not sure that is happening," he reassured his friend.

Reluctantly, Mika released his grip and nodded for Saint to continue in his ministrations.

Rummaging through his satchel, Saint produced a silver medallion intricately carved and set with a large quartz stone. He placed the medallion upon CJ's forehead and rested his palm above it. The other hand he held a scant inch above her body.

Saint methodically glided his right hand the length of CJ's body, stopping momentarily above her heart, then once again near her abdomen, before returning to his starting position above her throat.

"Well?" Fergus asked, stepping closer.

"This is powerful magic, the likes of which I do not understand," Saint directed his comments to Mika. "Physically, she is fine."

"But?" Fergus asked, taking yet another step closer.

"But," Saint began, rising and placing his satchel back over his shoulder. " Her brìgh does not fair as well."

"Brìgh?" Mika asked, confused by Saint's use of Gaelic.

"Her essence. Spirit. Whichever you wish to call it," he answered.

"But," Fergus tried to cut in again, and was quickly silenced by Saint. "Really Fergus, I do not have time for your buts, nor do I have time to referee you and Ghost." He shot a quick glance to the other man. "It is imperative the new guardian be removed from this place and taken back to the safety of Haven."

"Should I call for the plane?" Fergus asked.

"That won't be necessary. I can get her there faster through a wormhole. Mika will help me to steady it," Saint said, answering Fergus' question before he had a chance to ask.

Saint went to Mika's side.

"We are ready," Mika said, as he lifted CJ into his arms.

"Very well," Saint agreed and with a graceful wave of his hand, opened a spatial shift between himself and Haven.

He motioned for Mika to step in first, following close behind.

"As for you two," he directed his comment to Fergus and Ghost. "I trust you can make it home on your own. And without any bloodshed." He pointed his statement toward Ghost and waited for some sign of understanding.

"He started it," Ghost protested.

With a sigh of resignation, Saint again waved his hand, closing the wormhole and leaving Fergus and Ghost to fend for themselves.

*****

Luckily for her, no one noticed the woman hidden among the branches of the old moss covered oak. For a moment, she thought Saint had seen her. He glanced in her direction almost immediately after coming through the wormhole. The breath caught in her throat and it took all the power within her not to call out his name.

No doubt Saint was taking the Guardian back to Haven. He would try and find a way to break the spell Ævar had cast on her, but that would be impossible even for one such as Saint. Bridget should know. She watched her employer as he spoke words that wove a snare so deep and dark only he could allow it to be broken. Bridget snorted in derision as she leapt from the tree. She really did feel slightly sad for Ævar. He was as much a pawn of Loki or Lucas, whichever you wished to call him, as she was. Maybe even more so. At least she knew she was being used.

She went to the spot where Saint had knelt. Lovingly, she caressed the wood beneath gloved fingers. It was crazy to think psychometry would work. He had been there only a second, but maybe that was long enough to leave a trace of energy behind. A foolish action, but one she couldn't resist.

Sliding off her glove, she tried again. Ah, yes. She thought as her hand stilled. There it was. The smallest trace of residual energy. It was pure, beautiful and powerful like his soul.

Even after 80 years she still remembered the feel of Saint's energy. His was one of the strongest life forces she had ever encountered. Bridget knew no matter how reserved Saint Wolfe acted, he possessed more raw power than any shifter she had ever met.

It was that power she once sought to corrupt and for that she would pay until the end of time.

CHAPTER TWENTY-THREE

Helpless. That was the only word Mika Elkhart could use to describe the way he felt as he sat next to CJ's bed. He glanced up at the various wires and machines that beeped and whirred as they monitored her vital signs.

For hours he had sat by her side, holding her hand or touching her cheek. He sang to her lullabies in Lakota. The same ones he sung to her when she was a child and in need of soothing from her fears and worries, but none of those times seemed as important as this moment.

Mika stopped his song the moment Saint entered the room. Like clockwork, Delta Pack's resident medic came to check CJ's vitals for any signs of change. Mika studied Saint through weary eyes as he scrolled from one screen to another on the monitor. If there was any change, Saint did not let on.

Gently, Mika smoothed the dark curly hair from CJ's forehead. She rested peacefully upon the small rolling bed that sat in the middle of the examination room.

For all his gentleness and kindness, Saint would never lie to save someone's feelings. He had assured Mika that CJ's body showed no signs of pain or distress, and he believed him. But what worried Mika the most was not the present condition of CJ's body, but rather of her soul.

Could Ghost's twin have actually taken her soul? Was it even possible to do such a thing, and if so, how would one go about it? The bigger question was how would he go about retrieving it?

"You need not stop your song on account of me. I am sure CJ finds it most soothing." Saint said.

"That is my hope," Mika answered.

As meticulous in his movements as in his dress, Saint went about adjusting the drip valve on CJ's IV. When he was done, he removed his long black opera coat and placed it on a hook near the door. As always, his white shirt and black trousers were perfectly starched with a deep crease. Tugging on the bottom of his matching black vest, Saint walked back to CJ's bedside.

"That was a lullaby was it not?" Saint asked.

Mika looked up at Saint. He found something oddly comforting in his adoptive brother's inability to change his wardrobe. It was nice to know there was at least one constant when so much around him seemed to be changing.

"You remember your Lakota."

Saint merely smiled at Mika's statement, of course he remembered. With Saint's perfect memory, it would be stranger had he not remembered.

"I would sing it to her when she was..." Mika caught himself before he finished his statement. If the other shifter caught the slip, he did not let on.

It was still hard for Mika to admit he had a prior relationship with CJ. One the others had known nothing of. Facing Fergus had been one of the hardest things he had ever done. To do so meant admitting to years of lying to his friend and leader. Even though Ian Stone and his wife had been the ones to see to the day to day physical needs of Mika, it was Fergus who taught him discipline and honor. It was Fergus who taught Mika how to hunt and fish, it was Fergus who taught him when to fight and when to walk away.

Then again, Saint had also been a large part of his upbringing and the reason why Mika knew anything of his Lakota heritage.

On Mika's behalf, Saint befriended an Oglala medicine man named, Two Bears. The shaman agreed to teach Mika the ways of the Lakota. Every few weeks, Saint would take Mika to visit Two Bears and his people so Mika would have some sense of identity.

Two Bears taught him much. Including how special he was that the Great Spirit had seen fit to bless the young shape-shifter with not one but two white fathers. One a great warrior and the other a powerful shaman, and rarely, if ever, had Mika defied either of white fathers.

"It is all right brother," Saint said, walking way. "When you are ready."

Mika watched as Saint walked across the room to his makeshift desk. "You knew. Didn't you?" Mika asked.

Saint sat down at the long white counter strewn with books that sat against the wall nearest the door. He picked up a pair of rectangular framed glasses and placed them on his face before reaching for a yellow legal pad.

Slowly, he flipped through the notepad's well inked pages. Mika was unsure if Saint searched for anything in particular or merely pretended to do so in an attempt to ignore answering his question.

"Saint?" Mika queried.

"Yes, I knew," Saint answered in distraction, looking from his notepad to a book.

"How long?"

Mika sat silently and waited for Saint's answer. Even from across the room, he could see the wheels spinning in Saint's mind which meant his friend was trying to remember, which also meant his friend had known for quite some time.

"Approximately fourteen years," Saint said.

Maybe Mika should have been surprised, but he wasn't. Saint was, among many things, psychic, even if he did hate the term. Instead, he preferred to be thought of as connected.

"You never said anything," Mika said, rising from his station.

Saint studied Mika over the top of his glasses. "Would it have changed anything?"

"But, you seemed genuinely surprised that Charles had a daughter."

Saint went back to his notes. "Did I?"

Mika took this as his cue that this part of the conversation was over, and returned to his position at the bedside of his mate. Tears welled in his eyes as he looked down at her soft face. The rhythmic beep of Saint's monitors let Mika know that her body did indeed live. He could watch her breathing and hear the light beating of her heart.

He nuzzled at the gentle slope of her neck to place a bittersweet kiss against the faint pulse beating along her throat. Her skin was warm and smelled of night blooming jasmine. Mika inhaled the scent of her, storing it deep in his memory.

Again, he walked the mental pathway that linked him and CJ all these years. He journeyed the darkened path where once existed life and happiness and love. Slowly, he receded, bringing himself back to the present. She was gone. The thought ripped at the fabric of his soul. How could he continue without her?

Through all the fights and all the battles, Mika's one sustaining thought had been knowing that, one day, Charlie

Jean would take her rightful place both as Guardian and as his mate.

For years, he had stood by his brothers' sides. Together they fought whatever Theriontrope had set them against. It was they who protected the world, but in those instances, he had always known his enemy and the possible consequences of those battles.

But how was he to fight an enemy he didn't understand? One that none of them understood. An enemy that seemingly didn't play by the rules if, he indeed, had any. There had to be an answer.

"Saint?"

Saint removed his glasses and placed them on an opened book. "Yes, my brother?"

Mika lovingly stroked her cheek. "Do you believe you can heal her?"

Saint heaved a heavy sigh before answering. "In truth, I do not know."

"Do you believe there is a way to bring back her soul?"

"If an item can be taken, then it stands to reason it can be replaced. Tell me, what do you see when you touch her mind?"

"Nothing."

"Nothing? No memories or thoughts at all?"

"Only emptiness."

CHAPTER TWENTY-FOUR

Lucas Darkwater sat behind the desk in Ævar's office. Absently, he rummaged through the papers and folders that lay strewn across its top. He didn't seem to mind or even care that his invasion of Ævar's privacy bothered the shifter. He had no time for the creatures' feelings.

"I take it everything is in order then?" Ævar asked, not turning around.

"Yes. The guardian is safely in the void," Lucas answered.

"And you are sure that the others will come?"

"Positive."

"What if you are wrong? What if they leave her there?"

"Impossible," Lucas answered without looking up. "The coyote's feelings for her run too deep. He will come for her." Lucas picked up the remote control to the plasma screen that hung on the opposite wall. He scanned from channel to channel until reaching Headline News. He watched with intensity as the stock ticker sped across the bottom.

"Our stocks are up, Ævar. You should be happy.

"I will be happy the day my brother's body is nothing but ash," Ævar spat.

"All in due time, old friend. All in due time." Lucas continued to watch the news. He felt it was his duty to keep up with what was going on in the world of humans, and a television was much more fun and easier to use than a cistern of water. "By the way, how is your little Siberian friend?"

"She is ready to go whenever I say the word."

"Excellent," Lucas said, clicking off the television. "I have business that I must attend to."

"Dinner plans perhaps?" Ævar asked, as he continued to look out at the lights upon the water.

"Go for a run," Lucas said, ignoring Ævar's question. "It will help you loosen up. Clear your mind," he encouraged.

Ævar looked back at Lucas. "Maybe you are right," Ævar conceded. "I think I will."

"Very good. I will contact you later," Lucas said as he disappeared into a wormhole.

Ævar sighed. He had always known that the location for his operation had to meet two criterion. One, the location had to be far from prying eyes and two, that the building had to be near water. Fortunately for him, America had plenty of both.

Eventually, he wanted to return home to Iceland, and once this mess with Æger and Fergus was finished, he fully intended to do so.

Jealousy ate at him and it amazed him, that after 100 and some odd years, his feelings toward his brother were as strong as ever.

He had not always hated his brother. As children, he and Æger were inseparable. Being twins it was only natural for them to spend every waking hour together, knowing full well that one day they would depend upon each other for the survival of their people.

Then came the day their father, Balder, went to the hunt taking only Æger with him. Ævar had been left behind and he remembered thinking how cruel and unfair their father had been. Æger-the first born and heir to the thrown as leader of the Wolf People.

Æger began to spend more and more time with Balder and less and less with his brother. Soon there was no time for play or Ævar. Only the grooming of a new leader.

That was the spring of their tenth year, and the year Ævar was to meet Lucas Darkwater. He had stumbled upon Lucas while playing alone in a nearby stream. Lucas was about his age, yet seemed older. Smarter.

In a child's mind bent with sadness and jealousy there was no need to question where Lucas came from or who his people were. He was a friend who listened and that was all that mattered.

In their second year of friendship, Lucas told Ævar of a witch that spoke directly to the Gods. It was said she had the power to bend the future. She could make right that which was wrong and she was barely a day's travel from their village.

Mostly Lucas told Ævar that if he wished, the two would seek out the witch who would confirm what Lucas knew to be true. That Ævar, not Æger should be the leader of the Wolf People.

With trepidation, Ævar agreed and the two set out on their journey. It seemed to take less time than Lucas had said, but in the end the two stood at the tiny door built into the side of a cliff.

Ævar was unsure what to expect of a witch, and if Lucas knew, he said nothing. The door creaked open. Timidly the two boys entered through the small door into the darkened room illuminated only by candlelight. To this day, no matter how many women found their way into Ævar's bed, Ragnfiðr would remain the most beautiful woman he had ever or would ever meet.

It was she who told Ævar to rule the Wolf People was his destiny, and the only thing to stand in his way was Æger. "Your brother must die and you must take your place beside your father. Act soon, for your brother is ill and grows weak." Ævar could still hear her voice as if she stood beside him.

"But if he is ill, then he will die without my hand," Ævar rationalized.

"No," she said. "He will only be a weak king, and you will be chained to his side. The strongest of the two, subservient to the other. Would the sun become slave to the moon?"

Ævar was the sun. Strong. Bright. Ever burning. Æger the cold, lifeless moon. Hatred, fueled by the words of the witch, grew strong and dark in Ævar's heart until he thought it would burst.

He was stronger and faster and smarter than Æger. It should be him at Balder's side. But he was second born and, in his father's eyes, second best.

"The hatred of your brother shall be your downfall," the soft female voice drifted past Ævar's ears.

Silently, he cursed himself for being so lost in his thoughts that he hadn't heard her enter his office. "My hatred toward Æger or anyone else is none of you concern," he commented, trying to ignore her presence. He listened to the rustling of her velveteen gown as it shifted with her movements, scraping along the floor.

"You are always of my concern," she said, placing a gentle hand on his shoulder and sending a hint of heather wafting past his nostrils.

Ævar closed his eyes, clamping down on the unwanted emotion that seemed to rise in his throat. "What is it you want, Mother?"

Slowly Kenna withdrew her hand. "I came to speak with you," she said softly.

"You mean, you came to plead for Æger's life." Familiar white blue eyes stared up at him.

At his words, Kenna's hand flew to her throat. Dressed in deep claret velvet, she was a stunning beauty. Kenna Thorolfur was close to 200, yet she did not appear more than a woman in the prime of her life. looking at her made Ævar realize how grateful he was that shape shifters were blessed with not only a long life, but an extremely slow aging process.

"Yes mother, you are that transparent."

"Only because I grow tired of this. Lucas has fueled your hatred and..."

"Lucas is not to blame for this. If there is anyone you wish to blame, then blame yourself.

CHAPTER TWENTY-FIVE

CJ floated weightlessly in the empty space of nothingness. She felt neither cold nor hot. Neither pain nor pleasure. Opening her eyes, she beheld complete darkness. Not even a pin-prick of light was visible.

She tried to move, but the darkness was disorienting and she was unsure if her body moved or not. "What the hell?" CJ said aloud, only to have her voice fall silent into the darkness. "Hello?" she called again. Still, only silence fell from her lips.

Try as she might, she could make no sound. "Mika?" She tried to call out to him, fully expecting the pain she had felt earlier, but none came. *Mika!* She yelled along their telepathic link, but her thoughts too were dispersed into a million pieces making it no farther than inside her own head.

This is impossible, CJ thought and snapped her fingers. She needed to hear a sound other than the ringing silence in her ears. Again, there was nothing. Panic gripped CJ. She tried to right herself only to tumble head over heels.

Spinning wildly and flailing her arms, CJ searched for something to hold onto. She screamed into the darkness in frustration when she found only emptiness surrounded her. It was as if she hung in the middle of a great void.

Suddenly, a spot light landed directly on her and she stopped spinning. She squinted and placed her hand before her eyes to shield them from the brightness of the bluish light. Slowly, the silhouette of a man came into focus. "Nothing is impossible," he said. "Mostly, it is improbable."

She searched her memory trying to recognize the voice, but it was one she had never heard before. "Who are you? And where the hell am I?"

"Who I am is of no consequence. As for where you are, I will tell you that Hell is an appropriate word."

CJ stared at the figure trying to let her eyes adjust to see him clearly, but the figure wavered slightly then disappeared, reappearing behind her.

She spun quickly, disorienting herself more than she already was. "Where is Mika?" She demanded.

"How quaint. You have no idea how much danger awaits you, and your concern is for the coyote. How very touching that is," he said, feigning sincerity. "Then again as Guardian, it is your job to care. Is it not?"

Though she couldn't see his face, CJ could hear the contempt in his voice. "Bite me," she snapped.

The man's laughter caught CJ off guard. "Was it something I said?" she asked haughtily.

"You should be careful when offering yourself as a snack. Especially in the circles you keep. Someone might take you up on it," he answered.

"I demand you take me home immediately."

"Behold all that surrounds you," he said motioning to the all-consuming darkness. "Do you really think you are in any position to make demands?"

CJ did as he suggested. The room, if you could call it that, was cloaked in complete darkness. The only light visible was what lay behind the man, and seemed to change on a whim depending upon where he wanted to stand. Even his image seemed to waver and shift like heat rising off asphalt.

She had to admit he seemed to have the upper hand, but there was no way Mika could or would leave her here. Wherever here was.

"Very well, if there is nothing more," he said, his image fading even more.

"Wait!" CJ called out, trying to move forward. "Mika told me Guardians were to be revered and protected, not held captive."

"If I followed the rules of the Theriontrope Foundation, then he would be correct. However, I take orders from no one."

"Please," CJ softened her tone. "None of this makes sense to me. What is this place?"

"This place," the man paused in his explanation as if searching for the right word. "This is the Ginningagap. It is the great yawning abyss. Or what is left of it."

CJ felt her body still completely. "There is no such place as the yawning abyss," she said, trying not to sound as terrified as she felt. "There is always something."

"Maybe in your world, but not in mine," he seemed to sigh. "So please my dear. Scream and shout until your heart is content. No one will hear you, and my daughter will see to it that you are not disturbed."

"You're daughter?"

"Yes, my daughter, and she is nothing, if not obedient to her father."

The light faded and CJ found herself alone, surrounded once again by darkness and silence. The urge to cry flooded her, but try as she might she couldn't. Where there should be tears, there was nothing. Only...emptiness.

*****

Ísold pulled the top of her robe tightly to her throat as a chill swept across her body. She contemplated the splotches of color that littered the cold, gray walls of the library. Tilting her head slightly, she listened to the sounds of the old castle.

Had she not known better she would have sworn she heard a woman's voice. It must have been the wind, she thought. Placing her book on the chaise lounge, Ísold moved to stand near the giant hearth and the fire that burned brightly within.

A deep sense of hopelessness moved like a breeze across the room to settle deep in Ísold's soul. Without warning or provocation, tears flooded her eyes and spilled onto the stone hearth beneath her feet.

Dropping to her knees in anguish, she released the great sobs that welled within her breast. Her heart felt as if it would burst from the pain. She stared into the flames of the fire. Confused, she searched for an answer, any answer, to what had brought on such a fit of despair.

Wrapping her hands about her knees, Ísold lay upon the cold stone floor, rocking herself back and forth to alleviate the shear torture of her pain. Never before, not even when her own brother had locked her away from the world, had she felt so despondent and alone.

But, as quickly as the bombardment of emotions rocked Ísold, they were gone. She rubbed her tear drenched face with the back of her hands. She had no idea how long she had lain upon the hearth, but her body ached from the cold that seeped into her skin.

Gingerly, Ísold pulled herself into an upright position, using the chaise lounge to crawl her way off the floor. Staggering to the door, she pulled on the ornate strip of tapestry that hung nearby and would soon bring one of the servants to her aid. She needed tea or water. Something to help warm her and stop the trembling that seemed to overtake her body.

Ísold clinched her hands into tight fists, forcing herself to get her bearings. Her world seemed dimmer. Hazy. As if she had not quite awakened from a dream.

She whirled from corner to corner peering deep into the shadows. She saw no one, yet she couldn't escape the feeling she was not alone.

The sound of footsteps in the hall brought Ísold's thoughts back to the present. Over the years, she had learned the sound of each of the servants stride as they roamed the halls of the Fortress of White.

The short steps and light shuffle meant Greta was on her way. The main housekeeper had come to work for Ævar not long after Ísold had been imprisoned. At the time, Greta was a woman in her prime. That had been some thirty years ago and, while Ísold did not seem to age, Greta had become old. Her steps slowing as her body fought against the deep cold that seemed to linger in the damp castle walls.

Ísold braced her hands against the back of the chaise and waited for the woman to enter. Slowly the door opened and Greta stepped inside.

Ísold closed her eyes tightly then opened them again. The woman who stood before her was not the Greta. This woman was barely older than Ísold, with a wild mass of curly, dark hair and emerald green eyes. Even when she was younger, Greta was nothing like this woman.

"Where is Greta?" Ísold asked, fighting the urge to take a step back.

"I am right here Mistress," the woman answered in Greta's voice.

"What manner of trick is this?"

"Are you all right, M'lady?" Greta asked, taking a step closer and transforming back into the Greta Ísold knew.

216

Ísold's knees buckled slightly, causing her to tightly grip the cushioned back of the chair. No matter what tricks her half-brother would play on her, Ísold refused to allow him to take her sanity. She would never give him that satisfaction.

"M'lady, are you in need of a physician?" Greta asked taking another step.

"No," Ísold answered roughly. "I... I wish for dinner in my chamber this evening."

"Of course, Mistress. Do you wish for anything in particular?"

As if she would ever make a specific request for food. Ísold couldn't remember the last time she enjoyed a meal. Since being locked away food held little enticement for her. She vaguely remembered the spiced cookies her mother would make for her on her birthday, but that was a fleeting memory upon her tongue.

"Broth will be fine," Ísold said finally.

"As you wish, Miss. Will there be anything else?"

"No. That is all Greta. Thank you," Ísold said with a forced smile.

"It shall be brought to you within the hour," Greta said, leaving the room and Ísold alone in her thoughts.

CHAPTER TWENTY-SIX

Dirt flew from beneath the massive paws of the great white wolf as he raced through the foothills of Montana. He could smell the fresh, musty scent of the forest and hear the scampering of the smaller creatures as they ran for cover at the sight of the mighty predator.

Ghost wondered if he had spent too much time as a human. He had almost forgotten the liberation of being an animal. It was an experience unlike any other, and it made him feel alive.

Stopping abruptly, the wolf stared back in the direction of the large stone manor–house that was the focal point of Haven. It was the only home he had known since the day Fergus carried him up the grand staircase and placed him into a soft clean bed in the room that would become his. My room. My bed. My home.

Oh, how his heart ached at the memory. In so many ways he was still that scared little child that prayed so hard for death.

Thinking back, Ghost was amazed at the clarity with which he remembered the night Fergus came to rescue him. He had been so sick and his body shook uncontrollably from the fever and pain. Very few moments of consciousness existed for him, which, Ghost knew had been for the best.

He heard the deep rumbling of a man's voice tinged with an unfamiliar, lilting accent. He couldn't be sure if what he heard was real or imaginary. Yet, the voice crept through his fevered delirium soothing a small part of his fear.

Ghost remembered a sensation of floating. Of being lifted off the cot. That too could have been a dream, but he had known it wasn't. The stranger's voice was too close. To real.

Weak from blood loss and infection, Ghost was barely able to open his eyes. Yet he had to. He had to see who owned the voice and took such care with him.

Opening his eyes, Ghost stared into the face of the man that would soon become his mentor. Long shadows covered Fergus' face, making it almost impossible to see him clearly. But it was his eyes that caught the attention of a dying boy. Eyes that glowed with the brilliance of the sun.

Ghost tried with all his might to speak. To beg Fergus for a swift and less painful death, but the damage to his throat was too great and try as he might, the child was unable to voice his plea.

'I should have let you die when I had the chance.' Fergus' words cut to the very core of Ghost, spurring him onward in his race. How was it possible that the man, he considered his surrogate father, could say such a heartless thing?

Maybe Fergus was right. Maybe all of this was his fault. After all it was Ævar, Ghost's biological brother, who had brought the death of Charles Stone. It was his brother who had taken the life force of the new Guardian, and it was his brother who wanted him dead.

Ghost tried not to think about that last part. Instead, he focused on the sound of his paws as they crunched along the forest floor. As wolf, Ghost leapt over sticks and fallen logs. He reveled in the feel of the deep underbrush as it struck out at him, brushing through the thick top coat of his fur.

For some reason the feel made him think back to Arial and how wonderful it had felt to have her hands rub along the ridge of his spine. The way her fingers burrowed deep into the thick undercoat of his fur. Arial, with her deep auburn hair and lusciously curvy bottom. She seemed like a nice enough girl. Woman. Hot babe.

Ghost gave his head a quick shake to clear out the images he saw there. Arial was not what he needed to think about. As Saint would say there were other more pressing matters to attend to.

This isn't fair. This isn't freaking fair! He thought, pushing his body harder still. He had kept his end of the bargain and the promise he made to his mother.

"You must force out all thoughts of us," she said as she carried him through the snow. "Promise me you will never try and contact us; especially Ævar. Promise me my darling, you will never speak our names."

Often was the time that he heard the voice of his brother, calling to him. Beckoning to him to answer along a telepathic link, but no matter how great the urge to do so, Ghost had always found the strength to refuse.

Somewhere in the back of his mind, Ghost had always feared the consequences if such an action had ever taken place. Ævar's name carried with it the curse of death. None, not even Fergus, dared to speak it in Ghost's presence.

Fat lotta good that did, Ghost snarked. Ævar had found him, and already destruction lay in his wake. The pit of Ghost's stomach churned at the thought of his twin brother, and the hatred Ævar felt toward him. As long as Ævar was in the picture, no one was safe.

The white wolf broke through the clearing. In the dim moonlight, Ghost could make out the form of the large fallen oak. Barely more than the trunk remained as it lay partially in the water and partially on dry land.

Blood flooded his veins as he raced faster and faster toward his target. The tree was less than ten feet away when Ghost took to the air and landed solidly with all four paws upon the ancient tree. Throwing back his head, he howled in triumph. He needed this. He needed to clear his head and put things in perspective.

He lowered his head and pointed his body toward the manor house.

No matter how deeply Fergus' words cut, Ghost would always look up to him. *Damn him!* Ghost thought as he sat down upon the ancient, giant log and gazed at the shining sliver of the moon. Tears stung the back of his eyes and he cursed again.

It was obvious what the leader of his pack thought of him. Why the hell should Ghost care what Fergus Wolfe thought of him now or ever? Ghost questioned his sanity in how he could have allowed such an uncaring, self absorbed, bull-headed dictator to matter so much? Ghost asked the stars for answers.

Because. Because Fergus was all of those things and none of those things, and the one man who mattered most in his life. Most saw Fergus' demeanor as harsh and uncaring, but like the permafrost covering the volcanoes of Iceland, so did a stoic façade cover the warrior's heart and passion that beat beneath Fergus' breast. Therein was the enigma that was Fergus.

Over the years, Ghost had allowed Fergus to take the role of father. Maybe that had been a mistake on the young shifter's part, but he had needed a father and Fergus was there. Growing up Ghost longed to be more like Fergus. No one could best him in strength or ability. In Ghost's eyes, Fergus was bigger than Thor and that said a lot.

In the beginning, Ghost tried to be more like his adoptive brothers. He had seen how proud Fergus was of Mika when he learned to open the doors between the two worlds or how he always teased Saint about 'his oversized brain', but there was no way he could ever match Saint's intelligence or Mika's knowledge and ability to connect to the Great Spirit. It was impossible to live up to such greatness. Maybe that was why Ghost failed so many times.

It shamed Ghost to admit he had needed Fergus more than the others and, in many ways, he still did. All he had ever wanted from Fergus was to know that his surrogate father was proud of him. The Goddess knew no one else was, but if it had not happened in a century, it never would.

'Petulant.' 'Childish.' 'Mongrel.' All these words, all of Fergus' words, played over and over in Ghost's mind. He inhaled deeply enjoying the feel of the cool night air in his lungs and taking in the sights and sounds of Haven.

With his decision made, the great white wolf jumped to the ground and trotted back to Haven.

CHAPTER TWENTY-SEVEN

Mika hung between the borders of wake and sleep. His vision blurred from exhaustion. His body needed to rest. Yet he couldn't bring himself to leave CJ's side. What if she woke? What if she needed him in some way?

He couldn't allow her to lie alone, in a sterile room with only the beeps and whirs of machines to keep her company. It was possible he could leave. Even though Saint was gone, Mika knew he would be back within the hour to check on CJ.

If she needs you, you will wake. The familiar voice of the universe spoke to him. In a momentary fit of rage, Mika slammed the door on their conversation. There was nothing the Universe had to say that he was willing to hear.

For as long as Mika could remember, he had always been the ever-faithful servant. He listened to the Great Spirit and followed the direction it had always taken him in. But the Universe had lied to him. Cheated him out of the life it had promised. No. There would be no more conversations between them. Leave the connection to Saint. It was no longer Mika's concern.

When CJ was whole, Mika would take her far from here. Far from this life. They would start over and raise beautiful fat babies. Lovingly he stroked CJ's face and bent to place a chaste kiss upon her forehead.

Mika could sense Ghost slightly beyond the doorway. "What is it you want, Ghost?" Mika asked.

"I came to check on CJ and you," he answered, not daring to enter the room.

"You may come in," Mika said.

"Only if you are sure."

Mika merely nodded and stepped aside for Ghost to get a better view of CJ. Ghost walked to the bed where only a few days before, he had lain. Shutting his eyes, Ghost attempted to block out the images of his earlier stint in this room.

Ghost fought the overwhelming urge to cry. Rarely did Ghost allow the others to know the guilt he felt. Guilt from one hundred years of being the one that no one, not even his mother, wanted. Guilt from not protecting Charles or being able to save Charles' daughter.

He was far from a saint. Besides, that job already belonged to someone else.

He had listened to Fergus all those years ago when he said that maybe the Universe meant for him to be there. To be at Haven and be part of something greater, but what had that brought them? It had brought death and pain. He had brought death and pain. If he did not have a psycho for a brother, none of this would have happened.

Then again, Ghost's real family had chosen to protect and raise a liar and murderer, so what did that really say about him?

"You could not have predicted this," Mika said. "None of us could."

Ghost shoved his hands in his pockets. "You wanna go get some sleep? I can sit with her."

Mika started to refuse the offer, but there was something in Ghost's tone that told him the younger shifter needed to do this. He needed someone to trust and believe in him. Especially after the things Fergus had said.

Fergus' outburst still made no sense to Mika and when this was all said and done, he would speak to Fergus about that.

"Only if you are sure," Mika conceded.

"I am. Go and rest. You need to eat something too. You must keep your strength for what is to come." Ghost noticed the bemusement on Mika's face. "What?" he asked.

"For a moment, you sounded like Saint."

"Yeah," Ghost shrugged. "I guess after a century, he's starting to rub off on me."

"Maybe so," Mika said, stepping back to CJ's side. He leaned in closely. His mouth almost touching her ear. "Wicahpi, I must go rest, but you will be in good hands," he said, glancing up at Ghost who nodded his confirmation. "Ghost will watch over you." Mika pressed his forehead against hers.

"She'll be fine," Ghost said, laying a reassuring hand on Mika's shoulder. "I'll call if anything changes."

"I know you will," Mika said straightening. "I shall be in my room." With one last glance, Mika left the room, leaving CJ in the hands of Ghost.

Luckily, Saint would soon make his appointed rounds, so he did not feel quite so apprehensive about leaving CJ's care to Ghost. Mika groaned. Great. He was doing it. He too had started to question Ghost's ability as a pack member and that was not good.

Weary to the bone, Mika made his way up two flights of stairs and entered his bedroom. The large pine bed called out to him, but in truth he was too tired to sleep. He removed his shirt and boots and sat down in an overstuffed leather chair. His shoulders ached from exhaustion as he began removing the plaits from the long braids that hung down his back.

Once finished with the task, he ran his hands through his dark brown hair, combing the separated strands with his fingers. It was an action he had done many times before. The repetition was comforting, and with each pass of his hands, his mind eased slightly.

As much as he did not want to admit it, Mika knew Ghost was correct. He needed to keep up his strength. There was no telling what lay over the horizon, but he had to be prepared for whatever was to come.

Mika stretched his jean clad legs out before him, crossing them at the ankles. Scooting further down in the chair, he leaned back his head to close his eyes for only a moment. His heart clenched at the thought of CJ alone in an unknown land. How was he to live his life without her? The inability to touch her mind was almost more than he could bear.

Slowly, the world began to drift away as the comfort of sleep overtook him. Darkness surrounded him as he floated aimlessly through time and space. Floating ever higher and higher until coming to rest in a great forest not unlike that of Haven.

Soon Mika recognized the untamed land from his childhood. He had played there many times with the children of Two Bears village. Sure footed, he moved through the forest, in the direction of where Two Bears teepee should lay.

Stepping into the open field, Mika had to smile. At the edge of the clearing sat Two Bear's teepee. The old shaman walked out of his home and waved at Mika to join him.

"Coyote, you have returned," the old man said, motioning for him to sit near the fire.

Mika did as Two Bears asked. He sat upon the soft pelts laid upon the earthen floor. Out of respect for his teacher, he waited for Two Bears to join him.

"You come about the woman," Two Bears began as he pulled dried herbs from the medicine bag that hung about his neck. He rubbed the leaves over and over in his hands, sifting them into the center of the fire. "She means a great deal to you. She is chosen as your mate."

Mika did not try and stop the tears which fell upon his cheek at the thought of CJ and what she meant to him. There were no words. Only feelings.

"You need not answer." Two Bears watched the smoke rise from the fire.

Mika watched the smoke too, but unlike Two Bears he couldn't decipher anything within the rising gray puffs.

The shaman dropped more leaves into the fire. "You must not blame Wakatanka, coyote. All things are as they must be."

"How can that be? She has been taken from me."

"Ah, the white wolf that comes in the night."

"You know of him?"

Two Bears did not answer. Instead, he closed his eyes and tilted his face toward the sky. Mika knew Two Bears listened to the voice of the Universe. The voice that he had shut out.

"She is a Dream-Walker. Skill your woman has, as do the others."

"Others?" Mika questioned.

"Yes, but that is for another time," Two Bears said, rising with the grace and speed of a man half his age. "Your mate rests within the emptiness."

"How do I find her?" Mika asked rising.

"The way of a warrior is the way of knowledge and understanding. Listen with your heart spirit as well as your head spirit. This you know," he said.

Mika ran his fingers over a tender blade of grass. "Meaning?"

"Mother speaks. You do not listen."

Mika knew Two Bears spoke the truth. But there was little the Universe had to say that would be of any importance to him.

"Listen to Mother. She will guide your steps and that of the red wolf." Two Bears added as he squinted up into the sun.

"Fergus?" Mika asked confused.

"Hee ya," he answered in Lakota. "No. Only the Shaman father can take this journey with you."

"Shaman father," Mika repeated. "You mean Saint?"

"Huh. Powerful medicine he carries," Two Bears said, leveling his gaze on Mika. "Put aside your anger. Listen with both spirits. Is that not what you told your mate to do?"

Mika stared deep into the old man's eyes. "Yes," Mika sighed running his hands through his hair. "I did."

"Heed your own words, Elkhart. That is the only way to make your mate whole."

Mika started to speak, but was mesmerized by what he saw. He watched in awe as the irises in Two Bears eyes expanded from the center, covering his entire eye in blackness. The old man clapped his hands above his head, and instantly shifted from the form of a man into that of a great eagle.

Powerful wings lifted the bird easily from the ground and sent him soaring off into the sky. Out of the corner of his eye, Mika caught a flash of light. There amongst the tree line stood a woman.

Hair the color of midnight stood in stark contrast to her snowy skin and crimson colored gown. A necklace of silver lay about her throat. It caught the light of the sun as she moved to watch the eagle as it climbed higher and higher.

Mika watched her as she watched the eagle's flight. When the bird was completely out of sight, she noticed Mika. Startled by the sight of him, she darted into the trees.

Mika ran after her, using the unparalleled speed of his kind, but by the time he made it to the forest, she was gone.

Mika's body jerked violently as he woke from his dream. Rising, he walked to the bathroom and splashed cool water onto his face.

He replayed this dream in his mind. It was good to see his old friend, if only in a dream. As always, Two Bears words rang genuine. For CJ's sake, Mika must leave his anger behind.

He had no idea what part Saint would play in what was to come. But, as Two Bears reminded him, Saint carried powerful medicine. He must also convince Saint that he had a part to play in all this, which in the end, probably would not be all that hard.

Two Bears had also said there were others like CJ. How was that possible? Michael Grey had never mentioned such. Then again, Michael had not allowed Mika to tell the others about CJ. Could there be others Michael had hidden? If so, then how were they to find them? Surely, Haven needed all the Guardians there were.

He thought of the woman from his dream. He was meant to see her, for nothing in life was a matter of chance. And still the questions remained–Who was she and what answers did she hold?

CHAPTER TWENTY-EIGHT

Ísold woke as she had fallen asleep—in tears. But unlike the tears from the night before, these tears were of joy.

Closing her eyes tighter, Ísold snuggled more deeply beneath the cover. She needed to remember every morsel of information she could about the dream. Colors. Sounds. Feelings. Anything.

Ísold found herself walking through a lush forest. The deep greens and browns of the forest covered as far as the eye could see. The sun peeked through the canopy of leaves and branches to cast golden patches about the forest floor.

She wandered into a sunbeam. Lifting her face to the sky, Ísold smiled at the memory of the feeling of golden warmth upon her skin. It had been so long.

Eyes closed, she listened to the sounds of the forest taking in every nuance. Leaves laughed in the breeze as the birds serenaded overhead. The smell of sweet smoke wafted its way to her. It beckoned to her in a way she couldn't understand and she followed the scent. Ísold strolled through the forest, coming to a halt mere steps from the tree line. Across the way, she saw two men talking.

The taller of the men was dressed only in blue jeans. His dark hair fell down his back, touching the tops of his thighs. Never had she seen hair that long on a man. The other man wore decorated buckskin. He too had long hair, but he wore his in a single, long braid down his back.

The smaller of the men spoke while the other listened. She saw the buckskin clad man reach above his head and with a flash of light, transform into a massive eagle. She watched the eagle as it flew higher and higher, until it disappeared against the cloudless blue sky.

Turning back, Ísold found the other man staring at her. Their eyes met for a brief moment before fear overtook her. Startled, she ran as hard as she could into the forest. Not minding where she was going, Ísold caught her foot on a scraggly root and tripped. She fell forward and braced her body for the shock of the fall, but she kept falling and falling, until she woke in her own bed.

For the first time since having the torc of horse hair placed about her neck, she had dreamed. She had no idea what it meant or if it even meant anything. Either way it gave her hope.

*****

Mika bounded down the grand staircase, stopping in the foyer. He drew in a deep breath, drinking in the unmistakable scent of freshly baked bread.

In hungry protest, a loud growl rose from his stomach. He wanted nothing more than to make his way to the medical floor and check on CJ, but it was obvious his stomach had other plans.

Thinking back, he realized the last meal he had was sometime the day before. You must keep up your strength. Who would have guessed he would take a suggestion from Ghost? Without further coaxing, Mika made his way to the kitchen.

There he found Saint with an apron looped over his head and tied around his waist. The apron had been a gag gift from Fergus with the saying 'Bakers Have Hot Buns' emblazoned across the top. Fergus had been sure Saint would get flustered and throw it into the fire. Instead, Saint smiled graciously and put it on. From that day forward it had been the only apron he ever wore.

Not to be outdone, the next year Ghost gave Saint a set of oven mitts that read 'Don't Cross My Buns' in the shape of Hot Cross Buns. Again, Saint thanked him and used them. In fact, he was wearing them now. It was such a dichotomy from what one would expect, and Mika half-way figured Saint wore them as a way to irritate Fergus.

On the counter sat multiple loaves of dark, rich bread. Mika's mouth watered at the thought of such a treat. The recipe was one Saint had learned at the Monastery and, luckily for them, he had never forgotten.

"You know I do my best thinking in the kitchen," Saint defended his position, pulling the mitts from his hands.

"And my stomach thanks you," Mika said, trying to mask the anxiety he felt.

"Ghost is still with CJ and Fergus is in conference with the Foundation. He thought Michael Grey may be able to shed some light on the situation."

"And?" Mika asked, watching as Saint sliced one of the piping hot loaves and place two slices on a small plate.

"They are still talking," Saint answered and handed the plate to Mika along with a jar of currant jelly and a spoon. "There has been no change in CJ's condition, so that is somewhat of a good sign."

Mika grunted as he took a bite of the bread. A pang of guilt hit him. How could he be so cold to sit here and eat when CJ's soul was hidden away somewhere?

"Because you must keep up your strength if you are to save your mate," Saint said as he placed a glass of milk alongside Mika.

Mika stopped in mid-bite. "How did you..."

"Know she was your mate?" Saint asked, removing his apron and hanging it neatly near the stove.

"I never told you."

"No, you did not, but neither do you hide your feelings where she is concerned. Only one who is both blind and deaf would be none the wiser. That or your name is Fergus Wolfe," Saint commented. "Why do you insist on gawking at me as if I had sprouted horns?

"Forgive me brother. I am merely tired," Mika threw out. Obviously, Saint was still ill with Fergus' earlier actions toward Ghost, and who could blame him? There was no good reason for Fergus to act in such a manner.

Mika forced himself not to press Saint any further about the dig toward his older brother. Whatever there was would surely come out in time. His main concern was to finish his meal and return to CJ.

Placing his dishes in the sink, Mika headed from the room and down the second flight of stairs to the medical floor. He had fully intended to speak with Saint about his dream and what Two Bears had said, but there would be time for that. Soon Saint would be downstairs and they would talk then.

Through the observation window of CJ's room, Mika could see Ghost. His feet were propped up on Saint's make-shift desk and he leaned casually back in the chair. An oversized volume of Norse Mythology rested on his stomach as he alternated glancing at the book and then above the rim of Saint's glasses.

Saying nothing Mika walked to CJ's bedside and kissed her forehead. "I trust Ghost took great care of you," he whispered.

"Of course I did," Ghost said off-handedly. "Do you think these make me look smarter?"

"What?"

Ghost stared over the rim of Saint's glasses. "Glasses. Do you think I would look smarter if I wore glasses?"

"Do you really think now is the time for this?" Mika asked straightening.

Ghost grunted and pulled the glasses from his face. "I think that is the only reason Saint wears them. There's nothing in them but glass."

Mika wondered if Ghost worked to try his patience or if it came naturally. In the end, he figured it was natural.

"Anyway," Ghost continued, ignoring Mika's silence. "I've gone over Saint's notes, and I think I figured out a couple of things."

Saint stood in the doorway, his hands held loosely behind his back. "You were going through my notes?"

"Umm...yeah..." Ghost mumbled, placing his feet on the floor. "I was bored. No offense Mika."

"None taken," Mika said.

"And what have you figured out?" Saint said, walking to Ghost and holding out his hand for his glasses.

"Well, for one that you wear those things as a fashion statement, which in retrospect actually boggles the mind," Ghost said, handing the wire framed specs to Saint.

"And the second?" Saint asked.

"And the second is, I think CJ is with Hel."

"What do you mean CJ is in hell?" Mika moved dangerously close to Ghost.

"No," Ghost said. "Not in hell, with Hel."

"With Hel?" Saint asked. "You mean the Queen of the Underworld?"

"That's impossible," Mika insisted. Quickly he returned to CJ's side and took her hand in his. "She lives. Your machines tell us she lives." Mika clung tightly to CJ's hand for fear if he let it go, he would be letting her go.

Saint perused his notes and the page Ghost had left open in the book. Without pretense, he pushed the younger shifter out of his way so he could rummage for yet another book.

Books cascaded into the floor as Saint pulled one and then another, until he found the precise volume he needed. Furiously he flipped from page to page, skimming each quickly. With a groan, he let the book fall to his lap.

"Tell me," Mika said.

"The true meaning of Hell is a place of concealment," Saint conceded. "A place to hide souls."

"You want me to believe that CJ is being held by the God that watches over the underworld?"

"Goddess. Female, not God and yes, it is highly possible," Saint confirmed.

Mika bowed his head, allowing his long dark hair to cascade about him like a curtain. The Shaman Father must make this journey with you. The words of Two Bears echoed through Mika's mind.

"How do you get her back?" Ghost asked.

Take the journey. A voice, loud as thunder, reverberated through the room.

"What the heck was that?" Ghost spun about in a circle.

"You heard that?" Mika asked.

"Folks in Mexico heard that," Ghost quipped.

"Mother Universe is trying to tell us something," Saint answered, rising from his chair.

"Sounds like she's doing more than trying," Ghost said.

"Yes. I guess she is," Saint answered amidst the distraction of checking CJ's vitals and IV.

"So?" Ghost asked when Saint was not more forthcoming.

"So, it seems I am to take a bit of a trip."

"To the Underworld?" Ghost seemed shocked.

"If that is where the Guardian rests then we must go for her," Saint answered.

"But how? As far as I know, the Underworld is mythical place," Ghost said.

"By all accounts you are a mythological creature. Yet you exist do you not?" Saint countered as he rummaged through a cabinet of supplies.

"Well... yeah, but that's different," Ghost argued.

"No, it is not," Saint answered flatly.

That was the last thing Mika heard of Saint and Ghost's conversation. He tuned out the rest, knowing that the two could go on in a loop of endless questions and answers.

This was a time that Mika needed to still his mind. To listen, as Two Bears had said, to both his Heart and Mind Spirits. They would tell him what to do.

Closing his eyes, Mika blocked out the rest of the world and concentrated. He had walked the In-between many times, but this would be different. This would be a place of death and of uncertainty.

He did not fully believe in the Gods of the North, though folklore had said it was because of them that his kind was created. And if he truly believed that all peoples and cultures are connected, then he must allow himself to believe that so were the gods. *It is as one.* His inner voice said.

Mika did not comment. Two Bears had said nothing about answering the Great Spirit, merely listening. He knew it was a childish act, but at this very moment he couldn't help himself. He still blamed the Great Spirit for allowing this to happen.

Pushing his anger aside, Mika wondered how one was to journey into the Underworld. Mythology spoke of those who had gone before and, if memory served him correctly, none of them came out well. So, what would make his trip different?

Mika glanced up from his thoughts. Saint went about his duties, with Ghost hovering mere inches away. It reminded him of when they were children. Ghost would follow Fergus, asking his incessant questions.

"You still haven't answered my question." Mika heard Ghost say. "How are we going to get there?"

Mika waited for Saint's answer. He was sure he knew what Saint was going to say, but he wanted to know if Saint would actually say it.

"Ghost," Saint began. "There is no we in this trip. There is only I."

"But," Ghost tried to cut in.

Saint held up his hand for silence. "To do what must be done, is too dangerous. I cannot in good conscience allow you to go."

"You don't trust me."

"Do not think me the same as Fergus. I do trust you," Saint said, laying a reassuring hand on Ghost's shoulder. "I need you here, little brother. I need you on this side, to help bring me back."

"What do you mean, bring you back?" Ghost asked.

"There is only one way to journey to the land of the dead, and that is to die," Saint answered. Dropping his hand from Ghost's shoulder, Saint walked from the room.

I cannot ask this of you. Mika rebutted, using the common link between them. *I am coming with you.* Saint did not answer. Mika decided to use the logical approach. *CJ is my mate and as such is my responsibility.* Still Saint did not answer.

"Saint!" He yelled aloud.

Finally, Saint replied with three little words - *As you wish.*

CHAPTER TWENTY-NINE

Ísold stood high upon the stone wall of the old keep. She squinted her eyes against the sun's blinding reflection off the snow. Often, she would climb the wall to feel the breeze upon her face and clear her head. Today her thoughts were filled with questions about her sanity and whether or not she had imagined the shouts and cries that had found their way to her.

At first the sounds seemed little more than the soft wailing of wind against her window. Slowly they crescendo-ed, growing ever stronger and stronger until the sound became a deafening roar. She had to cover her ears with her hands to block out the sound as best she could.

Ísold stood upon the old stone wall, casting her glance in all directions. Searching for any signs that someone had been there. But, if there had been anyone other than the servants, there were no physical signs of them.

Hoping beyond all hope, she called out into the wind. "Hello?" She closed her eyes and concentrated. She was not crazy, there had been a woman's voice.

Stilling her body and mind, she listened more intently to the sounds that surrounded her. There were footsteps and muffled voices of the servants as they busied about, moving items from the storehouse into the castle, but nothing more.

A shadow covered Ísold's face, blocking the sunlight from her. Her eyes flew open. Circling above her head was a bird with golden red feathers. It was bigger than any she had seen near the keep before. The bird flew lazily, gliding upon the wind rather than flapping its huge wings.

The bird circled in the sky and made its way back toward her. With incredible grace, the bird landed upon the wall less than twenty feet from where she stood.

The two regarded each other. There was something familiar about the majestic bird. She knew him and he knew her. Ísold's heart leapt with recognition. Before her sat the eagle from her dream. Unable to stop herself she bounced up and down with excitement, but stopped quickly when the eagle ruffled his wings.

Birds always had a way of making her nervous. Especially ones the size of this, but Ísold was sure that buried within the great bird of prey was a man. She had no need to fear. This man was no different than her brothers.

The eagle tilted its head, watching her every move, his beak open slightly. Bravely, she took a step towards the bird. Her hand outstretched.

"I know who you are," Ísold whispered. "Well at least what you are."

The bird merely watched as she inched closer. "Please," she begged. "Please speak with me. Tell me what you want."

The bird fidgeted slightly. Stretching his large wings, he leapt from the wall and soared away.

"No!" Ísold cried as she ran to the edge of the wall. "Don't leave!" She watched as he flew higher and further away from her, until he was no more than a dark speck against the blue of the sky.

Heartbroken Ísold wanted to cry, but what good would it do? Maybe that wasn't the eagle from her dreams. Maybe it was merely a coincidence. But in Ísold's world there was no such thing as a coincidence. Only skeptics believed in coincidence as a way of denying the existence of the gods.

No, the eagle had meant something. It had to.

*****

Saint did his best to ignore Fergus who insisted on glowering at him from across the large examination room. There was very little time for him to get everything ready for his and Mika's departure, and his older brother was doing little to help.

Luckily, he was able to enlist the aid of Mika and Ghost. They had moved two other beds into the room, one on each side of CJ's. Intravenous fluid stands were then placed at the head of each bed and a bag of saline solution hung on each one.

Briefly, Saint looked up at Fergus, then took his attention back to his work. "Glare at me all you wish Fergus. I am still doing this," Saint said as he continued prepping the room.

"Like hell you are," Fergus demanded.

"I do find your choice of words interesting. Nevertheless, you are not going to change my mind."

Saint could hear the tiny sound of creaking leather as Fergus twisted his wrist in frustration. He also heard the not so tiny, "Hrmph" as Fergus crossed his arms over his chest.

"I know what you are doing Saint. Do not think me the fool," Fergus said.

"No one would ever accuse you of being a fool, my brother." Saint went over his mental checklist. "Everything is in place. Do you know when Michael will be getting here?" He directed his question to Fergus.

"No, I do not," Fergus groused, adjusting the snaps on his bracers.

Saint glanced to Mika and Ghost to gauge their reaction to Fergus' mood. Silently, Mika sat beside CJ's bed, still holding her hand, yet acutely aware of everything that was taking place around them.

Ghost sat in the chair nearest Fergus, still playing with Saint's glasses. Seeing the two of them so near and still at war tugged at Saint's heart. As far as he could tell, they had not spoken since their altercation. If anything went wrong... Saint stopped himself. He couldn't allow those types of thoughts to enter his head. He could only think of the good. The Goddess would protect him. She always had.

"Brother, I beseech you," Saint said as he walked to stand before Fergus. "Do not do this."

"What would you rather I do Aodhàn?" Fergus snapped. "Would you rather I be happy that my baby brother wishes to kill himself and take one of my best friends with him?"

Saint smiled at Fergus' words.

"Why are you smiling?" Fergus asked.

"Because after two hundred years you still think of me as a baby."

Fergus scraped the toe of his boot along the floor. "That's because you are acting like one."

Saint tilted his head at Fergus' statement. "Pouting does not become you, my brother," he said softly. "You must trust that I know what I am doing."

"It is not you I worry about," Fergus tempered his tone. "It is Grey. What if he makes a mistake? What if he gives you too much of that damned potion you've concocted. Has it even been tested?"

"Michael Grey will follow my instructions to the letter, and as a physician, he is perfectly capable of tending to our needs."

"What about testing it first," Fergus suggested.

"On who? There is no time nor means to test my potion, as you put it." Saint tugged on the hem of his vest.

"Look at him brother," Saint said, taking Fergus' attention toward CJ's bedside and Mika so diligently watching her every breath. "To be without her is tearing him apart. I cannot allow his suffering to continue. I would do no less for you and you know this."

"But why does it have to be you? I will go in your stead."

Shaking his head, Saint answered. "I do not know why it must be me, but it does." Saint lifted his face toward the ceiling. "Michael is here. We can begin." Saint moved to check that everything was in place.

"I forbid it," Fergus said to Saint's back. "Do you understand me Saint? I absolutely forbid you to do this."

Saint did not meet his brother's gaze. "Please understand that I say this with the utmost respect for you as both my brother and my pack leader, but...tough."

Both Mika and Ghost gawked at the Wolfe brothers. It was unclear what surprised them more. The fact that Saint defied Fergus or the fact that Saint said 'tough', which was equivalent to him cursing.

Never had he defied his brother. Always the assiduous servant, Saint stood in the background. Watching. Assessing. But the time for watching and assessing was over and Saint was concerned that with every passing moment, CJ slipped further and further from them.

"Dr. Grey," Saint said, breaking the deafening silence that filled the room. "Thank you for coming."

"I wish it were under better circumstances," Dr. Grey crossed the room. "Is everything in order?"

"I believe so," Saint answered, removing his black vest and laying it neatly across the back of a chair. Then rolling the sleeve of his white cotton shirt above his elbow, he sat upon the bed to the left of CJ.

"I take it you are ready to begin?" Michael asked.

Saint leaned forward, watching Mika for any signs of forfeit.

Mika leaned into CJ, speaking soft words in her ear. Reluctantly, he released her hand and moved to take his place upon the other bed. Like Saint, he too pushed the sleeve of his shirt far enough up his arm to expose the vein that lay inside the crook of his arm.

Laying back upon the bed, Saint extended his arm toward Dr. Grey. "I believe we are."

"Do you know what you are doing?" Michael asked as he placed the needle of the IV in Saint's arm.

"Not really," Saint admitted. "But life is merely a series of learning experiences, is it not?"

"I suppose it is," Michael said, as he taped the plastic IV tubing that led to Saint's arm. Without another word, he moved on to Mika.

Saint lay back in the bed trying to get comfortable, which seemed nearly impossible. He could feel the icy cold saline solution as it began to flow into his veins. Soon Michael would inject the cocktail that would send him and Mika near the brink of death.

Saint could see Fergus standing stock still in the center of the room, his arms crossed defiantly over his broad chest. There was nothing Saint could say that would change what Fergus was thinking or feeling, so there was no need to try. Saint remembered how hard it had been for him during those dark years when Fergus was gone.

It had been difficult to keep his own sanity, let alone hold Mika and Ghost together at the same time. Yet Saint never complained.

Both he and Theriontrope searched endlessly for any word of Fergus and never gave up. Saint could only hope Fergus would have the same faith in him.

Ghost sat eerily silent, and Saint wondered how much more the youngest of them would be able to take? Fergus had promised he would speak with Ghost. Saint vowed to hold him to that promise, as soon as he and Mika were back at Haven.

Laying his head back on the tiny pillow, Saint stared up at the plain white ceiling tiles. He listened to Michael Grey's footsteps as he walked back across the room to stand at his side. Needle in hand, Michael began pushing the small vial of liquid into the port on the IV tubing.

Soon Saint would know whether the sedative he had made worked. With any luck, it would take but a few moments for the solution to make its way through his system and into his brain. Closing his eyes, Saint waited.

So many thoughts flooded his mind. His thoughts of people and places seemed to come from other lifetimes. He thought of family he never knew and friends that had to be left behind. Of that stupid apron Fergus had bought him and of the Fleur-de-Lys.

He felt his body relax as the potion began to work its magic. Soon, very soon, his body would be forced into a feigned death.

Saint? The gruff voice of Fergus pushed past the already thickening haze inside his head.

Yes, my brother? Saint tried to answer, but it was too late. Like a loving mother, darkness wrapped her arms around Saint and rocked him gently to sleep.

CHAPTER THIRTY

Neither sound or light penetrated the void, and without solid ground beneath her feet, CJ was unable to tell whether she was upside down or right-side up.

She was exhausted from crying her non-existent tears and her silent railing into the darkness.

What had she gotten herself into? Okay. Some dark shadowy guy had told her she was in the yawning abyss. Just what the heck did that mean anyway? Her heart longed for Mika. She searched and searched her mind for him, but his presence was nowhere to be found.

Why was it she had never noticed how much of a part of her he had become? How much suffering had that man endured over the years because of her?

For as little as she knew about Mika the man, she knew a great deal about Mika, the imaginary friend. She knew that he was kind and understanding and the most patient man on the face of the earth. He had to be. That is the only way he could have survived listening to her for the past thirty years.

She had grown up with him inside her mind listening to all her childish dreams and fears. He had been there on her first date and her first kiss. The night she...oh my God! CJ froze at the realization Mika had been inside her mind the night she almost lost her virginity.

After truly meeting Mika, she was glad that night was an almost, and what a strange night it was.

It was CJ's sophomore year in college and his name was Clark Winston. Clark wasn't the most handsome of guys, but he wasn't a dog either. He was charming and easy to get along with.

They had dated on and off for a while. It was no secret there were no electric sparks between them, but there was a friendly comfort. The discussion of marriage had come up a time or two, and if truth be told, back then CJ was sure she would never do any better than Clark.

The couple had even gone so far as to schedule their first sexual encounter. On the chosen night, the couple went to a party, then back to his apartment. Nervous and shaky, CJ sat on the sofa. She had made her bargain with Clark and she was determined to go through with it.

From the moment he joined her on the sofa, the Gods conspired against them. First Clark's mother phoned. Then his roommate came home unexpectedly to get something he had forgotten. Someone knocked at the door, but when Clark went to check, he found no one there.

Then, the oddest thing happened. The building's fire alarm went off, closely followed by the sprinkler system. CJ took that as the ultimate sign she was not to have sex with Clark and after that night, she seemed to lose all interest in him.

Their whole relationship seemed more like a business arrangement than two people in love. Probably because it was. She would never, could never love Clark.

CJ covered her face with her hands. How could she ever face Mika again? He knew absolutely everything about her, and what did she know about him? Not a whole lot, other than he was right when he called her his mate.

The instant their eyes met, she felt the silver threads of her life joining to his, entwining them, heart to heart and soul to soul. For as much as she wished to deny her feelings for him, CJ found it impossible.

She was meant for him and him for her, and without knowing why, she loved him and that scared her. She had never loved anyone before. Not like this. But there was so much about the whole situation she did not know or understand.

Yet, floating there in the vast darkness, CJ realized that none of that mattered. The only thing that mattered was Mika. She may not know a great deal about him, but as soon as she got back home, she would spend every moment possible learning everything there was to know about him. Starting with if he was responsible for the fire alarm.

CJ closed her eyes. She was the Guardian. She had no choice except to survive so that Haven would survive. More importantly, she had to survive for Mika.

*****

Help me! A tiny but fervent voice cried. *Someone? Anyone? Help me!*

Ísold sat straight up in her chair, allowing the book she was reading to fall with a thud onto the stone floor. She stilled, listening to the sounds of the castle and the crackling of the fireplace.

Can anyone hear me? The voice rolled past Ísold. Quickly she grabbed a silver goblet from the nearby table and filled it with water. Taking three sips from the chalice, Ísold prayed to the Goddess to direct her thoughts and bring the answers she sought.

"Where are you?" Ísold whispered to herself and stared through the clear liquid to the silver beneath. A dark cloud formed at the bottom of the goblet, spreading upward turning the whole of the liquid black as pitch.

Still Ísold stared. Someone or something did not want her to see, but she would not give up. Slowly, the water began to clear, bringing into focus the image of a man. Long and lean he lay face down upon steep cliffs that plummeted into a river below. Peering from above, Ísold watched his body as it lay motionless upon the grass.

Though her only view was of the man's back, she found something all too familiar about him. His clothing seemed nothing special, merely black trousers and a white shirt. But it was his dark auburn hair that most intrigued her. A few strands had found their way loose from the silver clasp that lay against the nape of his neck. The errant strands obscured her view of his face.

Ísold's heart ached. The man's hair and build reminded her so much of her beloved Red Prince. So much so, that she found herself trying to will the man to move. She needed to know if he was indeed alive and who he was. "You must get up," she spoke to the image. Still he did not stir, and Ísold began to fear that whoever the man was, he was truly dead.

"Please, oh please get up," she pleaded into the chalice. "Show me who you are."

Seemingly from out of nowhere, a woman appeared. Both her clothing and her carriage spoke of wealth and nobility. Regally, the pale woman knelt beside him. Ísold watched as the woman studied him.

Jealousy stole into Ísold's heart as the woman lovingly stroked the man's hair with the caress of a lover. She knew it was foolish, but he seemed so much like Fergus, that Ísold couldn't help the feelings that pulsed through her. With a gentle stroke of slender fingers, the woman pushed back the hair from his face.

A wave of nausea washed over Ísold. She would recognize his profile no matter how many years it had been since she last saw him. Every detail of his face had been indelibly etched in her heart since she had wandered into his prison cell all those years ago.

Placing her head upon folded hands, Ísold prayed to the Goddess for the images to be untrue. She couldn't allow herself to believe that the man lying there, being so lovingly cared for by another, was her Red Prince.

By shear will, Ísold forced her attention back the goblet. Somehow the man had turned over, and lay upon his back. With eyes closed, he rested his head comfortably upon the woman's lap, wrapped within the folds of her dusk colored gown.

Was it possible that her Prince lay in the arms of another? Of course, it was possible. She had been locked away for more than thirty years. Maybe he had thought her to be dead, the way she had thought him to be. Or maybe he never cared for her in the first place, and had only used her blind love for him as a way to secure his own freedom.

Ísold was having a tough time coming to grips with what she had seen. Was he dead, or was he spent from an afternoon of making love with the woman who so loving caressed his face?

She swallowed back the fear that threatened to suffocate her. How much longer would she allow herself to dream of a man and a life that was impossible to possess? And how many more times could she allow her heart to break?

It was clear to her that no matter how much she longed for a life with Fergus, the Goddess would never allow it to be. Many times she had thought these things, but the time had finally come to relinquish her foolish dreams of what could be and accept what was.

Filled with resolve, she began her petition. "Dear Goddess, I understand and accept that in neither death nor life shall I be with the man I love. I only ask, my Goddess, that you allow me to see that the man before me is indeed alive. Do this, and I will willing accept whatever the Fates have laid out for me. Even if I am to live an eternity in solitude."

Ísold forced her attention back to the goblet. Still the man lay motionless, a sleeping child upon the woman's knees. She spoke to him, stroking his cheek lightly.

His eyes fluttered slightly as he jerked his head from the woman's touch. "Fergus," she whispered across the top of the water. He lived. Her Red Prince lived. Relief washed over Ísold.

As if she could hear Ísold, the woman looked skyward and straight into Ísold's eyes. With a wicked smile, she waved her hand through the air, clouding the image. Covered up in darkness, Ísold did not have a chance to see the man's forest green eyes as they opened.

CHAPTER THIRTY-ONE

Saint heard the soft voice of a woman through the dense haze in his mind. Melodiously it called to him, enticing him to wake from his slumber. Icy cold fingers drifted across his cheek forcing him to twist away from them.

Slowly he opened his eyes and found himself staring into a mass of shimmery blue fabric. The air smelled of fresh heather and dew of morning and he inhaled deeply, breathing in the scents of his home-land. Saint found himself staring into the face of a woman. As pale as the morning sky, she gazed down at him.

"The saint awakes," she said, smiling sweetly.

"Where...where am I?" he asked, tilting his head to get a better view of her face. There was a sadness in her violet blue eyes that he couldn't place, yet in truth, she was one of the most beautiful women he had ever seen.

With the help of his new companion, he sat upright and realized he had laid near the edge of a steep cliff. He could hear the rush of water below and had he rolled merely inches in the wrong direction, he would have plummeted over the edge and into the river below.

Running the palm of his hand across the soft thick grass beneath him, he gazed across the meadow of deep purple flowers. Easily Saint stood, taking in all that he could see and hear, locking it away in his eidetic memory.

Graciously, Saint took the hand the woman offered. The coldness of her touch permeated into his skin, causing his flesh to tingle. Still ever the gentleman, he did not release her hand until she stood fully beside him.

She seemed delicate, though she stood nearly as tall as he, with high cheekbones and a straight nose. A pale blue aura pulsed around her like a shield. It extended outward to encompass Saint within it before it retracted back to her.

Upon her head sat a diadem of silver incrusted with sapphires of midnight blue. Saint couldn't help the feeling of sadness that flooded him as he realized the precious stones were the only form of color on her.

"Walk with me," she said, looping her hand through his arm.

Again, Saint had to fight off the feeling of cold that filtered through his clothing at her touch. His brain was still a bit foggy, and he couldn't remember why he had come to this place. It was an odd feeling not be able to have total recall, and he was too curious about the sensation to be scared.

As he walked beside the woman, Saint allowed his mind to wander hoping his memory of the events leading up to this meeting would return.

"You have been a naughty little wolf," the woman teased through a thick Nordic accent.

"I beg your pardon?"

"I said you have been a naughty little wolf, coming into my kingdom without an invitation."

Saint never broke his slow, easy stride. Her kingdom? Where had he been going to have ended up here. The last thing he remembered was being in the medical wing at Haven and seeing the disapproving face of Fergus as he went to sleep. No, not sleep. A coma. Yes, that was it. He and Mika had been placed in a coma so they might go to the underworld in search of CJ.

The cogs in Saint's brain screeched to a halt at the realization of who walked beside him. "Hel?" he whispered.

"That is one of my names," she said. "It seems I have so many."

Saint was stunned. He truly had not expected his experiment to work. Yet, here he was, and with the Queen of the Underworld at his side. A rather beautiful queen, he surmised, even if her touch was ice.

"You seem surprised," she said.

"Only slightly," he confessed. "You are not what I expected."

"What is it you expect of Hel? Some grotesque monster mayhap?"

"To be honest, your majesty, I do not know what I expected."

"You have read all accounts of me, yes?"

"I have."

"Then you know that I have many faces."

"I do." Saint knew from legend that the Goddess of the Underworld had been known to appear to people at the time of their death. Depending upon how she judged that person, she would either come as a beautiful angel of death or a grotesque monster that would devour them.

"You are surprised that I chose this form for you?"

"No, your Majesty. Not surprised. Merely humbled and honored," Saint said with a slight bow of his head. He opened his mouth to speak again, but was caught off guard at the feel of stone beneath his feet. He stopped.

No longer was he in the meadow, but standing at the entrance to a grand hall. Arched ceilings peaked high overhead, with matching windows down the length of the room. Long tables lined each side of the wall for as far as the eye could see.

On the opposite end of the hall was a small raised platform. Upon it sat a grand wooden chair covered in fabrics the same silver and blue of Hel's crown. There was no question in Saint's mind that he stood in the Great Hall of the queen.

Saint walked the length of the long hall without saying a word. He listened to the rustling of Hel's gown and the click of his heels against the stone floor. His mind wandered to Mika and their reason for coming here. There was no telling where his friend had ended up. It had never crossed his mind that he and Mika would end up in separate places.

The fact was his experiment was that—an experiment mixed with a hearty leap of faith. He never truly expected it to work. Nor did he expect to find himself in the company of a Norse Goddess.

With each step, Saint drew closer to Hel's throne and deeper into his thoughts. He needed to find Mika and CJ and find a way back home. The question was how to do all that?

He knew from everything that he had read that Hel, although a gracious queen, was not one to readily give up her guests. What would she do with one such as he who came without her invitation? What kind of a deal had Ævar made with her for him to have been able to imprison CJ's soul here yet leave her body to live? Deals were not something Hel was known for.

Saint led the Queen to her throne and waited until she was seated. He studied the intricate carving of the wooden throne and marveled at its artistry. The image of a wolf was carved upon the front legs of the chair and across the back a serpent entwined itself within the gnarled wood.

Each culture had their own pantheon of deities. The creation myths of shape-shifters aligned themselves with the Gods and Goddesses of Northern lands. Because of this, Saint had spent the greater part of his life in service and devotion to the Goddess Freyja. She was the one for whom shape-shifters were created. She was their true mother.

During his studies, he had immersed himself in the folklore and legends of the Norse gods and knew all too well what could happen when allowing a god to know too much about you. But never had he expected to meet one of them face to face. Especially not Hel. Standing before the Queen, Saint had to wonder how much of the lore was fact and how much was fiction.

Fighting the urge to fidget, Saint placed his hands loosely behind his back and waited for her to speak. After all, this was her home and he was merely a visitor.

Her body had become completely still. A beautiful twinkling sculpture carved from ice rather than stone. Had he not known better, Saint would have thought her dead. Still he had an uncanny sense that within the blink of an eye she could alter her appearance from the frozen beauty that sat before him into the most fearsome of creatures.

Only Hel's eyes moved. Starting at his head, she lazily allowed her gaze to wander over every inch of his body. Saint had never liked being under the scrutiny of others and he had done well over the years to hide that fact.

Now, Hel did little to hide her enjoyment of him. "I can see why you are her favorite," Hel said in her sing-song voice. "You truly are beautiful. I suppose that is the curse of your species."

Saint was shocked that Hel had called him beautiful. Beautiful was not a word he would ever consider in conjunction with men, and especially not with him. It was a fact he could have argued, but considering the circumstances, he thought better of it.

"Thank you, your Majesty. I suppose one could say that it is a curse of your species as well," Saint said. Hel threw back her head and laughed. The warmth of her laughter surprised him.

"You would not be so quick to judgment if you met my brothers," she said with a wry smile. "Shall we discuss the reason you are here?"

"I traveled with a companion," Saint said. "Might I inquire to his whereabouts?"

"I know well of your companion and of his ties to the Guardian. She is why you have come, is she not?"

If she knew of Mika and CJ, then surely, she had knowledge of why he had journeyed to the Underworld. He also knew that if the stories were indeed based on fact, then Hel would not readily give up her visitors.

"You seem perplexed," she said. "Did I somehow confuse you?"

"No," Saint said, moving to stand more squarely before her throne. "I merely wonder how omniscient you truly are."

"I admire your honesty. That is a rare condition among humans."

"You forget, I am not fully human," Saint stated.

Hel again laughed at Saint's statement. Effortlessly she rose from her throne. "Come," she commanded and walked a few steps past him. "You and I have much to discuss and I fancy a stroll by the lake."

"Of course, Majesty," Saint agreed, offering Hel the top of his arm. "What is it you wish to discuss?"

A soft smile curved in the corners of her mouth as she inclined her head toward him. "The terms and conditions of the Guardian's release of course," she said, laying her hand and wrist upon his.

Saint fought the urge to shudder. Only this time he was unsure if his chill was due to Hel's ice cold touch or her last statement.

CHAPTER THIRTY-TWO

"How much longer is this going to take?" Fergus pressed Dr. Grey for an answer.

"As long as it takes," Grey said, checking Saint's heart monitor.

"What kind of an answer is that?"

Glancing up from the computer screen, Michael Grey sighed. "It is the only one I have."

Fergus raked his hands across his whiskered face. It had been well over an hour since Saint and Mika were placed into their coma and, as of yet, neither showed signs of waking. To say he was worried was an understatement.

Michael had followed Saint's instructions to the letter and within seconds, the two men had slipped quietly into their comas. But who would be the one to wake them? As far as Fergus could tell that set of instructions had not been given to anyone.

While Fergus had been busy learning the business of battle, Saint had pursued knowledge and spirituality. Where Fergus took life, Saint gave hope. Where Fergus was darkness, Saint was light.

In all the years and all the battles Fergus had never allowed Saint to take a life. Not once. Fergus had not wanted his younger brother to become like him: a soul-less mercenary with no hope of salvation.

Even as a child, Saint had always been sensitive and self-sacrificing. Fergus had known that leaving on missions for the

Theriontrope Foundation was difficult for Saint. Each time Fergus left, he could see the pain in his brother's eyes.

But no matter how often or how long Fergus would go away, Saint never complained. That is why he had given Saint their mother's hair tie the night he went on his first true mission for Theriontrope. Fergus knew Saint needed something to hold onto. Something to give him hope. That night Saint made Fergus promise that no matter what the cost, he would always return to Haven, and so, he did.

Fergus' thoughts wandered to Ghost. The youngest of them sat silently, still wearing Saint's glasses. A part of Fergus wanted to demand Ghost leave Saint's belongings as he had found them. But Fergus understood Ghost's preoccupation with the wire frames was a way of being close to Saint since there was no way for any of them to speak telepathically.

Fergus shook his head. For months, he had felt Ghost's turmoil. He too had heard Ævar's call. Many times, Fergus could block the telepathic messages, but not always. To Ghost's credit he had not given into that call, but Fergus knew Ævar would not give up.

He never imagined Ævar would go so far as to murder Charles, but Ghost's twin was capable of great evil. He had seen firsthand what Ævar was capable of the night he walked into that small cottage in Iceland to find the half-dead Ghost.

No matter the cost. The words seemed to haunt Fergus and sometimes he wondered if, in Ghost's case, the cost had been too great. If he had truly known the outcome of transferring his ancient blood into the body of a child, would he have still done it?

Fergus did not have an answer for that. He wasn't the same man he was then. Back then there seemed no price too great to save another of his kind. He knew the Goddess wasn't keeping score, but for Fergus, it was the best way to pay her back for the lives he took.

Pulling his attention from Ghost, Fergus glanced at Mika. It was hard to see the pain on the other man's face. It reminded Fergus of days long past when Mika was only an infant.

During the Battle of Rosebud in 1876, Fergus was a scout in the 2nd Calvary Regiment led by General George Crook. General Crook battled the great Oglala chief Crazy Horse. At one point, Fergus went ahead to gain information on Crazy Horse's position.

He came across a Brule Medicine Man named Wind Walker wandering through the woods toting an infant. Wind Walker told Fergus a young woman had placed the child in his arms. She explained to Wind Walker that soon a great red wolf would come to claim the infant.

At first Wind Walker thought the Great Spirit was out to play a trick on him. There was no way he would ever give a baby to a wolf, but Wind Walker saw the coyote that lived inside the infant. He knew the child was special and he must do as the Great Spirit had set forth.

Wind Walker called the infant Mika, the Lakota word for coyote and waited for the day the great red wolf to appear. Just as the Medicine Man could see the coyote beneath the skin of a child, he could also see the great wolf that lived within Fergus. Without question, Wind Walker handed the child to Fergus and like dust upon the wind, faded to nothingness.

Fergus stood there for the longest of times, struck dumb by what had happened. He stared down at the sleeping infant in his arms, then up to the clear blue sky above. There was no way he could go back to General Crook with a baby. He did the only thing he could do, he took the infant and fled.

Unfortunately, Fergus had not grown fully into his powers at the time, and was unable to bend space to create a wormhole which would have safely taken them home. Instead, much like he did when he brought Saint to safety, he traveled by foot for three days, back to Haven.

Fergus let out a heavy sigh. No. He was no longer the man who would put a child's safety above his own. That man was left to die along with the one girl he was unable to save, but who had saved him. No matter the cost.

CHAPTER THIRTY-THREE

Tap and scrape. Tap and scrape. Gradually the sounds filtered through the dense fog in Mika's brain and into his consciousness. He drifted somewhere, off in a dream and thoughts of CJ within his arms.

Using his acute senses, he listened to the approaching sounds. Tap. Scrape. Shuffle. The muted sounds drew closer and more distinct. He was disoriented. His head felt detached and his body heavy. Two things he did not expect. Then again, how could he have known what to expect? It wasn't every day he willing placed himself into a coma.

Mika went completely still when the sound ended abruptly. He could tell that whoever or whatever made the noise, stood mere inches from him. There was no way he would be able to defend himself in his present condition. However, if the person meant to do him harm, then the element of surprise might play into Mika's favor.

He felt a slight push against his side. Then another and again another. The attack was not painful, simply irritating.

"Get up," an aged voice said as its possessor poked again at Mika's side. "You don't belong in here," the old man groused and started to jab Mika's ribs once more.

With greater speed than Mika thought possible, he grabbed the tip of the gnarled walking cane before it had a chance to make contact with his side again. Opening his eyes, Mika saw the owner of the voice hovering above him.

Rather withered and frail, the old man gripped tightly to his staff, using it to hold himself upright. A mischievous pair of emerald green eyes stared down at him, giving the wizened face a much younger appearance.

The man smiled a gap-toothed smile. "I thought you were awake," he said, peering down at Mika. "Get up," he added and began to walk away.

Mika sat up slowly, watching the old man start to walk away. Shaking his head, Mika stood. Out of habit, he bent his body at the waist to the left and the right, trying to loosen the kinks from lying on the ground.

A flash of movement caught the corner of his eye. Quickly Mika spun about. He was poised for battle and ready to strike. He was still a bit groggy and it took a moment for him to realize he stared not the face of a stranger, but into a mirror.

Relaxing his stance, he stepped back. Over fourteen feet tall and at least six feet wide, the mirror stood on an ornate frame of tarnished silver. Two giant adders were intricately carved and interwoven with ornate scroll-work that completely circled the mirror. The heads of the serpents met at the top. Their fanged mouths opened and interlocked with only a tiny space to separate them.

Mika checked right, then left. The room was massive, stretching farther than the eye could see. Torch light danced and reflected off mirror after mirror making the ceiling appear like a star-studded heaven.

"What is this place?" he asked, still studying the expansive, shadowed chamber.

"That is not your concern," the old man answered. "Come. You mustn't be here," he said and walked toward a speck of light far down the corridor. His cane tapping rhythmically against the hard stone floor as he began to drag his weary body toward the light.

Only cotton candy tufts of hair remained on the old man's head and his tiny body was almost swallowed in the light gray robes that he wore. The man seemed as gnarled and knotted as the staff he carried and as old as time itself. And yet, Mika knew from the bruise left in his side, that to consider this man weak would be a false assumption.

"Where are we going?" Mika asked, catching up to his momentary companion.

"To the door. Your kind is not welcome here," he answered, continuing on.

"My kind?"

"It is not your time. You should not be here."

Mika grabbed the old man by the arm. "Wait," he demanded, as one mirror caught his attention. This one appeared to be made of bronze and gleamed brightly in the dimly lit room. Mika walked to the mirror, and without knowing why, caressed the intricately carved frame. It glided cold and smooth beneath his fingers. The darkness within the glass rolled and shifted like a cloud moving across the sky.

"Stop!" The old man yelled from behind him. "Do not touch that."

Mika refused to stop and he watched as the glass became clear. There, floating aimless was CJ. Despair and longing unlike anything he had ever felt before filled Mika. "Cikala Wicahpi," he whispered.

"What is this place?" Mika demanded. "Tell me, old man. Where am I?"

"The Hall of Lost Souls," the man snapped back.

"Lost souls?"

"The ones that do not know they are dead. My Queen places them here."

Mika studied the mirror, paying attention to the serpents. "How do I get her out?"

"You cannot. Once placed there, no one can be released unless the Queen allows it."

The serpents dared him to step closer. "There must be another way."

"I do not know." The old man shrieked as his feet left the floor. Mika held him by the front of his robes a good two foot off the ground.

"If you cherish your life in this place, you will tell me what I wish to know," Mika said in hushed tones.

"There—there is a key," the man stammered. "but—but I do not have it. Only the Queen has the key and she does not give it up easily."

"Then you will take me to the Queen," Mika said releasing the man and returning to the mirror. "CJ!" He yelled as he banged repeatedly on the glass.

"Sssh!" The man called to Mika in hushed tones. "You do not wish to wake the guardian."

Mika found the man's statement funny considering that was exactly what he was trying to do. "But I do wish to wake the Guardian," Mika said and pounded again on the opaque glass.

A blood curdling scream rushed toward Mika like a fast-moving train bowling him over and sending his body sliding along the floor. Rising slowly, he brushed the dust from his body. "What was that?"

"I told you not to wake the guardian," the old man said as he scurried quickly behind a large marble column. "You would do best to hide!"

Again, a scream broke through the silent corridor. Never had Mika heard anything so terrifying, and he clung tightly to the mirror as not to go tumbling backwards.

Peering off into the dimly lit hall, Mika detected slight movement along the floor. Firelight from the torches bounced off something shiny as it made its way along the great hall toward them.

"What is that thing?" Mika asked over his shoulder.

"The Lindorm," the man hissed from behind the column. "Be silent and still and maybe she will go away."

"Lindorm?" Mika asked as he stared at the play of light as it serpentined across the floor. What on earth was a Lindorm? Wherever Saint was, Mika was sure he would have the answer, and he cursed the fact he couldn't reach his brother when he needed him.

Once Mika figured out exactly what a Lindorm was and how to handle it, then he could figure out how to get CJ from behind the glass. His next move would be to find Saint and get the heck out of here, but first things first.

The Lindorm glided almost silently through the hall, but if Mika listened closely he could pick-up the unmistakable sounds of slithering. The closer the sound came, the faster it seemed to get until it came to a complete stop.

Mika stared in disbelief as the image of a giant snake came into view. Methodically, it moved its head from side to side as its tongue darted in and out of its mouth searching. The fangs of the Lindorm were at least a foot long. Even if the serpent was not poisonous, one bite could still prove fatal.

Mika searched the hall for anything to use for protection. There was no furniture of any kind except for the large mirrors and the torches that hung along the wall.

Great, he thought. How does one defeat a giant snake and where is Saint when you need him?

CHAPTER THIRTY-FOUR

Saint watched the swirling mist as it rose from the lake, spinning and dipping like dancers upon a floor of glass. He found it odd that he felt such peace and comfort here. He even found Hel's company quite interesting, or at least he had up until now.

"So, we have reached an accord?" Hel asked, a polite smile curving her lips.

His blood chilled at her words. "Yes, your Majesty. I believe we have," he answered.

"A wise choice if you wish to see the continuation of your species," she said taking his arm again and leading him away from the water's edge.

"You will take me to Mika and the Guardian then?" Saint asked.

"We go there now. It isn't much farther."

Saint held his left hand clenched into a tight fist at the back of his waist. His mind wandered and he wondered how long he had been here. The sun had not changed positions in the sky since he had awakened. For all he knew, he could have been gone two minutes or two days. There truly was no way to tell.

He thought of Fergus and Ghost and hoped the two had not gone into battle with each other in his absence. Fergus had been more irritable than normal, so it had been impossible for Saint to admit to finally entering Charles' old bedroom.

The room was completely remodeled. Gone was the antique flocked wall coverings and dark drapery. The heavy mahogany furniture had been replaced with light oak. The room was bright and airy and spoke of a woman. Only Charles' leather wing-back chairs remained.

Saint smiled at the thought of those chairs. They brought back fond memories of many nights where he and Charles would sit by the fire and play chess. Now who did he have to play with? Mika was a fair opponent, but he would be busy with his mate. Ghost never really got the hang of it, and Fergus...well, the best word for his chess playing ability was abysmal.

A pang of grief struck Saint's heart. He missed Charles, his one loyal friend and confidant. There was so much about him only Charles had known. Now who would he talk to? Maybe there was something to be said for being able to give confession.

"We are here," Hel said, bringing Saint back from his wanderings.

He admired the flamboyant arched doorways and Gothic Architecture of the gray stone building. It reminded him of the monastery where he once lived, and was not what he expected.

"Surprised?" Hel asked as she walked the wide steps to the entrance.

"Slightly."

"There is no need. If you took more time, you would see my world encompasses the best of what your world has to offer." Hel stopped short of crossing the threshold.

"Are you not coming?" He asked.

"No, dear wolf," she answered sweetly. "This is where I leave you. All that you presently seek is beyond these doors."

The Queen laid open her hand. In it was a large bronze skeleton key which she pressed into his hand. "Show the guardian this key and she will let you pass."

"And how do I find this guardian?"

"Your friend already has," she said with a playful smile.

Saint couldn't help but stare deep into the Queen's violet blue eyes. They shimmered and sparkled with the luster of stardust. Saint was once more struck by how beautiful the Queen of the Underworld truly was. So much beauty and grace, but a heart as cold as the stone beneath his feet. Still somehow Saint found it poetically sad.

He searched his memory for some poetic phrase that could fit her and the emotions she seemed to illicit in him. If only he were a poet, then he could write such an ode.

At Hel's urging, Saint entered the open doorway. Tightly he gripped the key in his hand, turning the ridge of his knuckles white.

"Having second thoughts?" Hel called from behind him.

"No, your Majesty. No second thoughts," he answered.

"Very well," she said.

Saint could still feel her there. Waiting for him to enter the building. Once he fully stepped inside there would be no going back. She had made that point clear.

Saint felt confused. Normally there were no questions where his actions were concerned, but with Hel, things were different. Stepping back to Hel's side, he searched for the right words. "I feel..." he began.

Hel became eerily silent again. Watching him. Waiting patiently for him to finish his thought. "I feel...I feel that there is something unfinished between us."

Saint felt her icy fingers as they caressed his cheek. Her thumb gently brushing the corner of his mouth.

"Go sweet wolf. Your family needs you."

He said nothing more. Stepping through the doorway, Saint entered into the Hall of Lost Souls.

"You know he lets you win," she called after him.

"Pardon?"

"Fergus. He lets you win," the Queen said, then with a broad sweep of her hand, the door swung shut.

Saint stood dumbstruck. "He lets me win? He lets me win? We'll see about that," he mumbled.

The sound of voices shouting in the distance made its way to Saint's ears, followed by a loud thud. Forgetting his irritation with Fergus, he raced into the expansive hall. It wasn't hard for him to find Mika, staff in hand, fending off the largest snake Saint had ever seen.

"It's about time you showed up," Mika grunted as he lunged at the serpent's head. The snake coiled its body tightly, watching Mika's every move through glassy eyes.

"I have been a bit busy, thank you," Saint said.

"Really?" Mika grunted as he dove out of the way of the serpent's barbed tail.

"Yes, really," Saint answered without a tinge of fear in his voice. "By the way. That is rather a large snake you seem to be battling."

"It's the Lindorm," came a meek voice from behind the column.

Saint saw a small man crouched behind the marble pillar. "Really? A Lindorm do you say? I thought them to be only a myth. Amazing."

"Saint? A little help here!" Mika called out, dodging the serpent's poisonous fangs. "You can be amazed later,"

"Of course," Saint agreed and walked to the man behind the column. "Are you the guardian?"

"No," the man answered, pointing a shaky finger toward the serpent. "She is." Quickly he ducked back into his hiding place.

"The Lindorm is the guardian?"

"Yes," the muffled voice answered.

"Excellent," Saint said. Without further hesitation, he walked toward the giant serpent, holding Hel's key out before him.

"What are you doing?" Mika panted.

"Getting the guardian's permission," Saint answered casually.

"The what? Permission?"

"Yes. Permission. All I have to do is show the guardian the key and she will let us pass. Hey oh," Saint yelled to the Lindorm. "Over here."

The serpent's attention flew from Mika to Saint. She pulled her head back ready to strike.

Saint held out the key for the serpent to see. Its reflection showed in the black slits of her eyes. "Is this what you seek?" He asked.

Methodically, the Lindorm moved its head from side to side in a type of hypnotic dance. Slowly it lowered its head to within inches of Saint's hand and the key. Her tongue darting quickly, sensing the object in his hand. Again, the serpent reared its head as if to strike, then without warning, it left, slithering back into the recesses of the great hall.

"Where...Where did you get that?" The little man asked as he scurried from his hiding place. "Only the Queen holds that key. You must have stolen it from her!" He accused, jumping at the key and trying to remove it from Saint's hand.

"I did no such thing," Saint defended. "She gave it to me."

"You lie," he said and jerked his cane from Mika's hands.

"I speak the truth. Ask her yourself."

"I...I... I would never be so bold." the man stuttered.

"We must find the Guardian and get her home," Saint said, ignoring the other man's accusations.

"She is here," Mika replied and trotted toward the mirror. Gently he touched the worn spots on the frame. The tarnished silver glass became opaque once again. There, still floating in the darkness, was CJ.

"Interesting," Saint whispered, rubbing the key between his hands. "So, where does it go?"

"I cannot let you pass," the man growled, his voice contorting with his form. Black fur sprouted along the length of the old man's body. His gnarled limbs straightened and lengthened as he fell to the floor.

Mika and Saint watched as his back bowed and flattened and his face stretched forward producing powerful jaws and fangs. Transformation completed, before them stood a massive black wolf. Red eyes stared unblinking at them. In a show of power, the massive wolf reared back his head and howled.

Mika placed his hands upon his hips. "So, how do you like the odds?"

"Two of us against one of him," Saint said. "Somehow that doesn't seem fair."

"I am the Keeper," the wolf huffed. "You shall not pass."

"Is this really..." Saint was unable to finish his sentence as the wolf leapt toward him, knocking him from his feet. The key flew from Saint's hand and skidded across the stone floor.

"We really don't have time for this," Mika said as light began to spin, radiating from the core of his abdomen. His body exploded into a thousand points of light, shifting and expanding. They danced about the head of the black wolf disorienting him. The wolf chomped at the air, trying to catch the lights within his powerful jaws.

Saint took advantage of his position to plant both feet firmly in the wolf's stomach, flipping him over his head and sending the wolf flying through the air and landing with a thud against a large marble column. The wolf rebounded quickly and landed solidly on all four paws.

For such a large beast, the black wolf was incredibly fast. There was no time to think, only react. Even fully shifted, Mika was only half the size of his opponent. Still he jumped on the back of the large beast, sinking his teeth deep into the beast's shoulder. The wolf shook his head back and forth violently in an attempt to throw Mika off.

Mika held on as tight as he could. If only he could speak with Saint, but there was something about the Underworld that made their telepathy impossible. He had no idea how much longer he could hold on. He could only hope that Saint would think of something and fast.

His answer came in the sound of howling. Out of the corner of his eye, Mika could see the red wolf as it circled around them. The two men had lived and fought as a pack for the entirety of Mika's life and, even without being able to communicate telepathically with Saint, Mika knew what to do.

Mika released his hold on the wolf's neck and was flung to the ground. Quickly he regained his composure and joined his friend as he stalked their enemy. The black wolf, his ears laid low, watched as the two members of Delta Pack circled one direction, then the other.

Saint bared his teeth and growled, sending a warning to the other wolf. The Keeper refused to back down. Moving forward towards Saint. Mika grabbed the black wolf's tail, pulling him backwards. At the same time, Saint lunged forward biting down on the wolf's ear, but the Keeper was stronger and faster.

With one massive paw, he knocked Saint to the ground. The larger wolf towered over Saint. Wrapping his massive jaws around Saint's throat. The Keeper began to apply pressure. It would take nothing for him to snap Saint's neck in half.

"Þessi er nógur!" The voice of Hel rang though the immense cavern. The wolf did not move. Hatred flashed in his bright red eye as he stood perfectly still, yet he did not release his victim.

"I said enough, Keeper!" Hel demanded and pushed against the shoulder of the larger wolf.

Reluctantly, the Keeper did as she asked and released Saint from his grasp.

"Leave us," she commanded and pointed toward the door. Begrudgingly, the black wolf did as she commanded. "You may return to your human forms," she told both Mika and Saint who stared up at her.

Saint trotted over to where his clothes lay in a pile on the floor and waited. The rest of his kind may not have a problem transforming in front of others, but he drew the line at being naked in front of a Goddess.

"Please forgive." Hel moved so her back was to Saint.

"Thank you, your Majesty," Saint said as he finished putting on his shoes. "But, how did you know?"

"I told you sweet wolf, nothing takes place in my kingdom that I do not know about," she answered as she walked toward the mirror that held CJ. With a wave of her hand, the glass became transparent and she watched the body of CJ as it floated in the abyss. Hel waved her hand before the mirror. Instantly, the glass disappeared and CJ tumbled, headlong, through the open space and into Mika's waiting arms.

Saint moved to Hel's side. "Your Majesty," he began. Hel faced him and again Saint was struck silent by her mystical beauty.

"There is nothing more to say," she said, walking away from him.

"But..."

"Leave me, dearest wolf, before I change my mind."

CHAPTER THIRTY-FIVE

With a gasp, CJ sat up in the hospital bed. She had no idea where she was or what had happened to her. Casting her gaze about, she found Mika laying next to her, his eyes closed. If he was breathing, she couldn't tell.

Fear bore into her at the sight of the tubes and wires attached to his body. "Mika," she called out to him, sliding from the bed, and almost falling to her knees. Strong arms caught her and held her upright. She realized Fergus was beside her, helping her to stand. "Please," she pleaded, reaching for Mika. "What's wrong with him?"

"He is merely sleeping," said Dr. Grey as he came near. "Why don't you sit back down so I can examine you."

CJ pushed away from both him and Fergus. "No! Let me see," she demanded, stumbling towards the bed. "Is he dead?" she whispered, brushing her hand along his whisker roughened jaw.

"I assure you, he is not," Dr. Grey added. "Now that you are back, he will wake at any moment."

"How can you be so sure?" CJ asked, fighting back tears.

"Because I can," Michael said, stepping back from her and taking Fergus with him.

Out of the corner of her eye, CJ could see a forlorn Ghost, sitting quietly across the room. She couldn't put her finger on it, but something about him had changed. He seemed older, not as carefree as the Ghost she had met a few days ago. At least, she thought it had only been a few days.

Realizing there was nothing she could do for him now, CJ went back to Mika. She had no real memory of what had happened to her. She was vaguely aware of Ghost, or a person she thought was Ghost, kissing her. After that, everything went black and she awoke here.

No one had to tell her where here was. She knew deep in her soul she was within the walls of Haven. In the place she would call home. She was excited about moving to Haven. There was much she needed to learn about her father and the family she never knew. Especially if it would help her make sense of her abilities, but none of that mattered if Mika was not at her side.

The thought of being Mika's mate was not unpleasant to say the least. In fact, the thought of waking up with his arms wrapped about her was very pleasant indeed. But shouldn't she have a little say so in the matter?

CJ had no idea why she was thinking about all of this. She had thought about all of this when she was in the void. She had accepted that she was his mate, but what did that mean exactly?

CJ laid her head against Mika's chest and listened to the rhythm of his heart beating strong and steady beneath her ear. Once he was awake, she would add that to the list of questions she had to ask him.

It means, I would do anything to have you at my side. She heard his voice inside her head.

"Mika!" she exclaimed, wrapping her arms tightly around his body, squeezing him with all her might. "Mika. Mika. Talk to me."

I am talking to you, Wicahpi.

"No. Out loud," she said clutching him tighter. "I need to hear your voice," she pleaded.

I can't, he gasped. *You are crushing the breath out of me.*

"Oh," she breathed as she pulled back. Slowly his eyes opened. They were the most incredible honeyed gold, and she burst into tears at the sight of them.

"Sssh," Mika cooed to her. "Do not cry Little Star. I am here and you are safe. That is all that matters."

She felt Mika's hand brush through her hair and cried all the harder. He was right. They were together and safe and that was all that mattered.

"It's about time you got up," Ghost teased from the end of Mika's bed. "I was afraid I would have to go after you."

"It is good to see you brother," Mika said, pulling himself into a seated position.

"What do you mean, you cannot wake him?" CJ heard Fergus from the other side of the room. "Come on Grey, there has to be a way. Saint would not have done this without a fail-safe."

"I have already given him the antidote," the smaller man answered.

"And?"

"And he should be coming out of it." Michael fiddled with the monitor.

"Try something else," Fergus demanded.

Though Fergus' words were not menacing, his body language was, and CJ wondered if the man called Grey was indeed as calm as he appeared to be.

"There is nothing else for me to try," Dr. Grey countered.

"Then send me after him," Fergus commanded and began to unfasten the bracer from his left arm.

"I can't do that."

"Can't or won't."

"Both," Michael said, pulling himself to his full height of five-eleven. "I cannot, will not, risk losing you."

"Yet you risked Saint!" Fergus argued.

"Give him time," Michael said, placing a hand on Fergus' shoulder. "He will return."

"Leave us," Fergus said with absolute resolve.

"But..." Michael protested.

"Go see to Mika and the Guardian. I will see to my brother."

Fergus could tell that Michael was reluctant, but obediently he did as he was asked.

"As you wish," Michael conceded. "I will be near if need be."

Fergus did not respond. Grabbing a chair, he pulled it closer to his brother's bedside. He watched for any signs of change in Saint's vitals, but none came.

"Damn you, Saint Wolfe. I knew you would do this," he spoke in hushed, but stern tones. "I knew you would go after that she-wolf, Bridget, but you cannot bring her back. Nothing can." Feeling a bit self-conscious, Fergus stopped. Once he was sure no one paid him any attention, he continued. "I am sorry I wasn't there when you needed me to be. I would have given my own life if..." Fergus sucked in a deep breath and tried to calm the slamming of his heart against his chest. "Come on little brother, do not do this to me. Do not make me drink that swill Ghost tries to pass off as tea. I know I am part animal, but please show me mercy," he whispered to Saint.

Fergus hung his head toward the floor. What could he do? Right before his eyes, his worst fear was coming to pass.

"Finally," Saint's voice carried softly to Fergus' ears. Quickly, he jerked his head up. Saint lay peacefully upon the hospital bed his eyes closed and arms folded serenely across his chest.

For the briefest of moments Fergus thought he had imagined hearing his brother's voice. "Saint?" Fergus urged.

"Finally, you admit you like my tea" Saint said without opening his eyes. "And all it took was for me to die."

CHAPTER THIRTY-SIX

CJ stared out across the great lake nestled in the forest of Haven. She had asked Mika to take her to her father's grave and this is where he had brought her. She needed to see. She needed to feel a connection. To know that there were once others like her.

She stared out upon the calm still waters that were the resting place of her ancestors. A place that one day, she too, would be brought to join them.

Sadness filled her and her heart ached at the thought of aging and leaving Mika. He was already older than her by more than a hundred years, yet he did not seem to age and she would never stop. It wasn't fair.

CJ felt the slight shift in the atmosphere and knew her mate was near. He had left her alone with her thoughts as he ran through the woods. It still seemed strange to her that she could love a man like him. The past few days had been incredible getting to know him and the others. It had been frantic and scary and wonderful.

There was so much she had to learn. So many questions still weighed on her mind. Not the least of which was, what did the future hold for them? Not only was her life changing, but so were the lives of all the residents of Haven.

Mika told her and the others of his experiences in the Underworld and Saint filled in the missing bits. Even though CJ felt there was something missing from Saint's story, she did not feel comfortable enough with him to ask.

She smiled when she felt the warmth of Mika's body press against hers. His strong arms snaked around her, pulling her close as he nuzzled the tender spot beneath her ear.

"You seem worried, Wicahpi," he said, placing a tender kiss against her hair.

"No. Not worried," she said. "Maybe a bit sad."

Mika became motionless at her words. "Do you regret the choice you made?" he asked.

CJ heard the apprehension in his voice, no matter how hard he fought to hide it. "No," she answered relaxing her body into his, hoping to relieve some of his tension. "I will never regret my decision. I was just thinking about my father. I wish I had known him."

"He was a great man. A true friend."

CJ closed her eyes and tilted her head back against Mika's shoulder. A bittersweet smile crossing her face. She could sense the love and admiration he held for her father. She had noticed it with all the shifters when they spoke of him.

"You will tell me about him, won't you?" She asked.

"I will tell you anything you wish to know."

"Anything?"

"Anything," he answered, squeezing her tightly around the waist.

"All right then," CJ said, turning in his arms.

Her heart skipped a beat at the sight of him. He was so perfect. CJ fidgeted in place, worried that she would disappoint him with her unruly hair and plain green eyes.

"Do you know why I call you my Cikala Wicahpi, my Little Star?"

"No," she whispered, slightly afraid of his answer.

"You must understand. I was born in a time of great turmoil. In a time where my people, the Lakota, were being herded like cattle and pushed from their lands. I have seen war after war and battle after battle. Both humans and shifter alike. A heart can be filled with much darkness, and I began to wonder if darkness was all there was. But during that darkness came one, bright shining point of light. It gave me direction and hope. You are that light and my love. Never doubt my feelings for you, or your beauty. You are the star that breaks through darkness that surrounds my world."

CJ fought back the lump that rose in her throat. "I just—no one ever—"

Mika smiled down at her, warming her heart and melting away all her doubts and fear. He was hers. Her mate and nothing or no one would ever separate them again.

"You wanted to ask me a question," he said dipping his head to tease her ear with the warmth of his breath.

CJ was unable to concentrate, let alone speak.

"Yes?" he coaxed, languidly kissing the corner of her mouth.

"I was just wondering," she began as she pulled away from him and gathered her senses. "What do you know about fire alarms?"

ABOUT THE AUTHOR

Joan Hazel has found success at virtually everything she has ever put her mind to doing.

A native of Corinth, Miss., she is an accomplished actress and vocalist who has performed with theater and opera companies across the eastern United States. She has also dabbled successfully in theater as a director and vocal director for numerous award-winning productions.

She completed a double major in music and business from Delta State University and went on from there to earn a Master's Degree from East Carolina University with another double major, in music performance and pedagogy.

She has spent time as a vocal and piano teacher at both Troy University and Enterprise State Community College. As a teacher, she is much sought after for her skills and often works privately with students in her home. In 2010, she was a guest instructor at the International Music Theater Festival held in Venice, Fla.

In addition to her work on stage and with performers, she is also a skilled box office manager who has served as the Athletics Ticket Manager at Troy University for five years.

In her spare time, she spends time with a cast of characters who live in her head. She has written three novels that range from historical fiction and fantasy to reality-based crime fiction. She is currently working on the follow-up to her soon-to-be released novel The Last Guardian.

Hazel is passionate about the protection of animals and supports a variety of animal conservation efforts.

She currently resides in Troy, Alabama, with her husband, Ricky, and their two dogs.

BOOK TWO
of the
GUARDIAN of HAVEN SERIES

Available Now

Burdens of a Saint

Chapter 1

Saint Wolfe stared out across the ornate Italian gardens of his home known as Haven. When he was barely two weeks old he was brought to Haven by his older brother, Fergus. Except in those days, Haven had been located in Scotland, not in Montana as it was now.

Saint had no idea how long he had sat there, his gaze transfixed on the sunlight dancing across the reflecting pool. He felt comfort here, surrounded by nature and hidden from view of the main house. Here he found peace.

Sadness filled Saint's heart as he thought of how much his life had changed in the past two hundred plus years. Mostly, he thought of all the people who had come and gone from his life. Having an extended life span was, in Saint's estimation, a drawback to being a shifter. Friends he held dear would always come and go, yet he would remain.

He wondered if maybe he should be more like his older brother, Fergus, and never allow anyone to get close. Saint chose a life devoted to the greater good, a life of service to those in need, but two centuries of caring for the needs of others was beginning to wear on him.

He only wished... Saint stilled his thoughts. What was it he wished? He dare not voice his true feelings. What need was there to speak of things he knew would never come to fruition? He could curse the Fates, but to what avail. They knew what was best in not allowing him to have a true mate and children of his own. It was not his place to question the Sister's choices.

Saint pushed those thoughts from his mind and allowed the soothing sounds of falling water to wash over him, calming his frazzled nerves.

Water poured from the beneath the feet of the massive stone griffin sitting at the end of the large reflecting pool. The statue's unblinking gaze stared unwaveringly toward the main house of Haven, its great wings tucked neatly against a broad body. With one clawed foot resting on the world, the beast watched silently over the gardens, waiting for the moment he was needed.

At least, that was the story Saint told himself. As a child, Saint thought of the griffin as Haven's private sentinel, going so far as to name the statue Liam. Often he mused, if ever he truly needed a protector, Liam would spring to life to save him. The statue's massive wings would unfold and flex before launching itself into the air.

Saint smiled inwardly at the memory. It was a childish fantasy. Yet, it was one he still hoped would one day come true. Not that Saint needed a protector. He simply thought it was a smashing idea.

Rarely given into flights of fancy, Saint fought the urge to walk up to the statue and speak with it. Maybe, with everything Liam had seen and heard over the centuries, he could shed some wisdom on Saint's situation. Goddess knew there was no one at home he could speak with. Certainly not Mika Elkhart, who was busy adjusting to life with his true mate, and getting her acclimated to life as the new Guardian.

Saint could speak to the youngest member of his pack, Ghost Thorolfur, but Ghost also has his own problems. Saint was positive it couldn't be easy to find out that after one hundred and thirty years your twin brother wanted you dead and would stop at nothing to see that mission accomplished.

Not to mention, Ghost's take on most situations was a bit skewed. Mika was right; Fergus really should have taken Ghost's remote control away years ago.

Saint thought of his older brother and sighed. He could speak with Fergus, but the thought made him shudder. Fergus could be, for lack of a better word, obstinate.

All Saint had to do was merely mention the name Bridget LeCouer and Fergus would go into a tail spin, and in Fergus' defense, Saint really couldn't blame him. Bridget had been Saint's one true love, or at least, he thought she had been.

Throughout the world of shifters certain packs existed with the core belief all other life forms, including humans, were to be used as food. Some of the worst Saint had heard of were the ones that actually raised humans as cattle. These shifters were more animal than human and went against everything Saint believed in.

Never had he expected to fall in love with someone like that. Actually, he had never expected to fall in love at all. The fact she happened to be the daughter of the Alpha of such a group was an unfortunate coincidence.

"How could I have been such a fool?" Saint whispered as he languidly ran a hand through his dark auburn hair.

Absently, he let his hand fall to rest just above his heart. Like a vice grip, tightness lingered there and had since his return from the Underworld where he and Mika had rescued the new Guardian from captivity.

At times, the pressure was so great, the simple act of breathing seemed nearly impossible. Saint would have suspected a heart attack, had he been human. However, the continual changing and regeneration of cells during the process of shifting from human to animal made any illness virtually impossible.

When the pains first began, Saint shifted. Changing into wolf form, he and Fergus raced the outer perimeter of Haven. He was sure once he shifted back into human form, the tightness would disappear, but it had not.

That is when he realized the sensation had nothing to do with any physical ailment and everything to do with the emotional turmoil that lay beneath his calm exterior.

Saint never expected himself to want to be more like his adoptive brother Ghost. But at the moment, he envied Ghost's innate ability to completely disregard certain things. The irritations of life slid easily off Ghost's thick hide, a quality that both annoyed and amazed Saint.

Taking another sip of tea, Saint allowed the warm liquid flow over his tongue, tasting each individual flavor. This was one of his special blends meant to soothe and calm the nerves. He had designed it for Fergus many years ago. However, in Saint's mind there was no amount of tea or mediation that could cool the anxiety that boiled in the pit of his stomach.

Over the centuries, like many of his kind, Saint learned to fear very little. Lack of fear seemed to be a character trait in most shape-shifters, especially the ones who had been alive as long as he and Fergus. It was a side-effect born from the knowledge you are practically immortal. Unless a shifter sustained a mortal wound such as having their head severed or their heart ripped from their body, little could kill them. As long as a shifter could alter their form, they would survive.

Saint tried to look toward the positives. Many times his life had been blessed by the Goddess, and it was his firm belief that when the time came for him to transition from one world to the next, she would continue to watch over and protect him. He had been Freyja's servant for too long for her to abandon him.

Which is why, in his mind, there had been little doubt as to who should make the journey to the Underworld and bring back the new Guardian's hame or soul.

CJ Carson may have been Mika's true mate, but Saint had studied the old text. He knew it would take his knowledge of the Underworld or Hell, call it what you wish, to help rescue CJ.

He had not known what to expect. How could he? He definitely did not expect to come to face to face with the Goddess Hel, nor for her to be so beautiful and gracious. He also did not expect her to so willingly negotiate for CJ's return, as that was not normally her way. The mere fact she did so perplexed him still.

He swallowed hard at the thought of what he had done. I will always protect you, the familiar voice of the Universe whispered to him, and he lifted his face to allow the cool morning breeze to caress his skin.

How he wanted to believe those words. He had always entrusted his life to the Fire Goddess, and for centuries, she had watched over and protected him. However, this was one time he was not sure her protection was possible. But no matter the cost, the continuation of his species was worth it. Fergus had taught him that much.

Saint closed his eyes and leaned his head back against the cool stone wall of the grotto. Looking upward through the leaves, he searched the clouds for an answer. The problem was he didn't know the question. He only knew something called to him, pulling him back to the one place he did not want to return.

"Saint!" CJ Carson's voice splintered the silence of the morning. CJ was now the Guardian of Haven, having taken over after the death, or rather murder, of her father. She was also the true mate to a member of Saint's pack. For her to call on him instead of her mate, meant something was terribly wrong.

"Saint!" she yelled again with more urgency. He could hear the thud of her footsteps as she ran down the stone steps toward the grotto. "Saint, you've got to stop them before they kill each other!"

"Who?" Saint asked as he appeared beside her.

CJ yelped. "I will never get used to you guys doing that!" she fussed. "Never mind. It's Fergus and Ghost. You've got to stop them."

"What this time?" Saint sighed.

"I don't know. I was downstairs in the exam room doing inventory, and the next thing I know, there's a loud crash. I ran up the stairs, and I found the two of them at each other's throats. Literally."

"And Mika? Where is he?" Saint asked as he took the steps quickly, his black opera coat swirling about his legs.

CJ followed close on his heels. "He went into town."

"Human or wolf?"

"Wha...what?" she stammered.

"Fergus and Ghost, are they human or wolf?"

"Human the last time I saw them. Why?"

"Then there is chance Ghost will survive," he answered flatly. Without waiting for CJ, Saint charged into the main house, and bounded down the hallway, stopping just outside the media room to assess the situation.

CD's and DVD's littered the floor where someone had turned over freestanding shelves. The artwork along the walls hung askew and very little of the furniture was left intact.

At the moment, Fergus and Ghost stood in the center of the room near an upturned sofa. Both men were bloodied and banged up, yet neither was ready to surrender.

A low, rumbling growl emanated from Ghost as he lunged forward, catching Fergus about the waist, driving the bigger man backwards. Fergus' body thudded hard against the wall, and he roared in frustration.

Without taking a breath, Fergus picked up Ghost, and pushed him above his head. Walking steadily toward a window, Fergus paused in contemplation.

"Don't just stand there!" CJ yelled to Saint. "Do something!"

Saint hated to admit it, but he was torn. The storm between Fergus and Ghost had been brewing for quite a while, and frankly he was tired of playing the peacemaker between the two of them.

His logical side said to stop them. It was the right and proper thing for him to do. Yet his illogical side told him to let the pair fight it out. Whatever bothered them needed to be brought out in the open, even if it meant they tore each other limb from limb. After all, they were shape-shifters and would heal. However, the furniture had taken enough punishment.

With more calm than he actually felt, Saint crossed the battle torn room. "Let him go, Brother," Saint spoke in even tones.

"Not until this dirty little fice learns his place," Fergus grunted.

"Are you ever going to come into the Twenty-first Century? Really who says fice anymore?" Ghost asked nonchalantly, which seemed rather odd considering his present predicament.

"I say fice because that is what you are. No other word fits quite as well," Fergus answered.

"Your words mean nothing to me," Ghost spat. "I'm tired of standing in the shadow of the big bad ass Fergus Wolfe. Ass being the important word in that sentence."

Fergus lifted Ghost higher above his head. "Bastard!"

"Basta!" Saint commanded in Italian. *Ghost only thinks Fergus uses antiquated words, he has no idea the words I want to use,* Saint thought. Even though the battle between his brothers had pushed Saint beyond his breaking point, he remained the epitome of composure.

He placed a calming hand on Fergus' arm. "You know you do not want to do this."

"The hell I don't. I want nothing more," Fergus said.

Saint noted that neither Fergus' voice nor his body showed the strain of holding a fully grown man above his head. After nearly three hundred years, Saint was still amazed by his brother's strength and control.

"Then do it!" Ghost barked. "Throw me out like the trash you think I am."

Ghost's last statement struck an odd cord in Saint, and by the look on Fergus' face, it did him as well.

Did Ghost truly believe Fergus thought so little of him? Had the years caused Ghost to forget the sacrifices Fergus had made solely for him to live? Did he not remember the countless hours Fergus spent teaching him to hunt or fish or read?

When Ghost was only ten, his twin brother Ævar tried to kill him by slitting his throat and leaving his body buried beneath the snow. Ghost's mother, Kenna, found him there half-dead from blood loss and hypothermia.

Walking through the night, Kenna carried her son to a nearby village. There she left him until someone from the Theriontrope Foundation, the governing force behind Haven, could retrieve the boy and bring him to the safety of Haven.

That someone was Fergus.

At the request of the Foundation, Fergus traveled to Iceland to retrieve the dying child. But when he got there, Fergus found Ghost's body ravaged by infection and fever. There was no way the child could withstand traveling by spatial shift in his condition.

At Saint's suggestion, Fergus transfused his own blood into Ghost. Already well past one hundred, the older shifter's powerful blood made the child well enough to be moved. As far as anyone could tell, there had been no other way.

Ghost was so frail in those days. He held little or no memory of his rescue, nor did he know the toll it had taken on Fergus, and he never would. Fergus swore both Saint and Mika to silence where Ghost's rescue was concerned. He thought the truth would be too hard for the child to handle.

Maybe it was the blood bond the two men shared, but over the years Fergus had become more of a father to Ghost than a brother or mentor.

He watched over Ghost and indulged him the way only a father would his son. That is why Fergus' present treatment of Ghost seemed out of place. There was more going on than either man wanted to admit, and if Saint could ever get Fergus to release Ghost, he would find the time to get to the bottom of things.

Without warning, Fergus whirled and threw Ghost across the room, slamming him into the photo covered wall nearest the door and CJ. Ghost's body fell to the floor, showered in broken glass.

Quickly, CJ rushed to his side, but Ghost pushed her away. "Is that all you have old man?" Ghost asked, rising and brushing the shards of glass from his hair and shoulders.

The pressure around Saint's heart increased and he felt as if at any moment it might burst. Taking in a deep breath, he tried to expand his chest as much as possible to relieve the tight band constricting his rib cage, but nothing seemed to help.

Saint stepped between the two men. He had seen and heard enough. No longer could he stand by and watch his family tear itself apart.

"I have had enough," Saint said, voicing his thoughts aloud.

"You? This one has been a constant pain in my arse for the past hundred and fifty years, not yours," Fergus groused and waived his hand toward Ghost.

Saint turned slowly toward his older brother. "You are right brother; Ghost has not been a constant my pain in my arse for the past one and a half centuries. That job has been equally shared between the both of you."

"Don't put me in the same category with him!" Ghost interjected.

"You." Saint spun on the younger man. "You have no idea what this man has done for you." He pointed to Fergus. "If it weren't for him…" Saint heard a low growl of censure issue from Fergus. Saint fought back his own words. "You," he pointed to Ghost, "you would be well served to hold your tongue upon occasion."

"Exactly," Fergus added.

"Do not think Ghost is the only one culpable in this," Saint snapped as he turned back to Fergus. "The two of you either do not speak or are at each other's throats and I, for one, am tired of playing referee."

He had more to say to his older brother, so much more, but why bother? Saint could tell by the way Fergus adjusted the leather bracers about his wrist, nothing he said would change anything.

"If the two of you wish to rip each other apart, then so be it. But I, for one, refuse to stand by and watch. I do not care how you get this settled. I simply want it done by the time I return."

"Return? Where are you going?" Ghost asked.

Saint clamped his lips together tightly. He did not want to tell his family where he was going. They would only try and stop him, but in reality there was no way he could keep his destination secret. Fergus could and would eventually track him down.

"Do not act as if you are going to leave," Fergus grumbled. "This is your home. Everything you need is here."

"Not everything," Saint said, tugging on hem of his immaculately pressed vest.

"Seriously," Ghost asked. "You're not leaving, are you?"

"Actually, I am."

"And just where do you think you are going?" Fergus asked.

Saint paused, staring past his brother's head to the swaying tree tops just beyond the gardens.

There really was only one place that he wanted to go. Only one place he had thought of since returning from the Underworld. "It is time I return to New Orleans," he stated and left the room.

www.ingramcontent.com/pod-product-compliance
Lightning Source LLC
Chambersburg PA
CBHW020437270626
47155CB00022B/613